INTRO

01.28.2010, Rome (Italy) 3:00 a.m.

The door of the apartment slammed close with a threatening creaking sound on its hinges. With a muffled growl, Claudio froze for a moment, hoping his son didn't wake up.

The soft snoring coming from his son's bedroom relieved him. Keeping the light switched off, guided by the feeble illumination coming from the streets, filtering through the curtains, he prowled across the living room.

He slipped off the jacket and carelessly threw it to the couch when the ringing of his mobile phone echoed in the room. A whispered curse escaped him, already imagining himself under the sheets of his bed relaxing after a long day and night.

"Hello," he whispered, trying to open the door of the apartment, not to wake up anyone who was sleeping.

A female voice answered him, but due to the missing ID caller, he couldn't recognize the caller. "Mr. Calvani, this is the Venus Caprice club. I'm sorry to disturb you, but someone found a credit card bearing your name, and since you're one of our VIP members, we considered it appropriate to call you. Would you be able to come by and get it? We'll be closing within three hours, and we'd prefer not to store anything belonging to our customers." Claudio tried to clear his mind, thinking about his credit card. Indeed, that would have been an annoying inconvenience as he'd have to wait until the opening hour the following day.

Grimacing at his distraction for not having checked whether he forgot anything in the club, he started to walk to the elevator. "Thank you; I'll be there in about half an hour. Will you give the card to the bouncer, so I can retrieve it and leave right away?"

"Of course, thank you very much." Abruptly the woman ended the conversation as Claudio rushed to his car. In his mind, there was nothing else but returning to his apartment as soon as possible and getting some sleep. The morning after, he had an important meeting scheduled at half past eleven, and he couldn't afford to look sleepy or unsharp.

From this moment on, I swear to God, I will never leave the club without having a complete inventory of what I have in my pocket and what I might have left behind.

CHAPTER 1

01.28.2010, Rome (Italy) 6:00 a.m.

A relieved exhale released the stress Giulia accumulated during the night as she stepped out of the wagon. It was six o'clock in the morning, and the ride on the night train drained her of all the energies. Regardless of the traveling class, there was always something that didn't work the way she'd hoped. Her feet were swollen, and she was sure her hair stuck out of her head like those of an old crone. With a subtle movement, she adjusted her blazer and ran her hands down her hair. She paced to the next exit, suitcase in hand, looking for a taxi.

That wasn't supposed to be something hard to find. If there was something easy to get at the Termini station, that was a taxi.

"Good morning," greeted the taxi driver, gently taking the suitcase and placing it on the trunk of his black Mercedes.

"Good morning. I need to reach *via Colfiorito 8*," she exhaled with the last remnants of strength.

Without replying, the driver opened the door of the car for her, and as they were ready, he started to drive. She knew the ride would have been almost smooth at that time of the morning and hoped to be at home within 20 minutes. Glancing outside the roads of Rome caused her to produce a smile; the kind of smile a person gives returning to what is familiar and meant home.

Reaching the apartment, she closed the door behind her and slipped off her shoes. Considered the long journey, she wouldn't have gone to the office until the following day. Routinely she prepared herself a coffee and turned on the TV to listen to the news.

She was still massaging her feet when the telephone started to ring.

Generally, she wouldn't receive any calls before eight or nine o'clock in the morning, and at half past seven, that ring seemed to be off time, mainly because it came from the mobile phone of her son, Luciano.

"Lucio, I thought you were still sleeping. What happened?"

"Mom, I... I have to tell you ..." his labored breath choked his voice as his heart started to race in his chest.

5

"Luciano, darling, is everything okay? What's going on? Did you have an accident with the car? Are you hurt?" She tried to go through all the possible hypotheses coming to her mind to justify his frightened, broken voice.

"Mom, something terrible..." he said, taking long pauses between one word and the other. "It's not about me; it's about Dad."

"Oh!" her voice toughened, not clearly interested in listening to what happened to that asshole, as she addressed him.

"Mom, please, this is serious!" he reproached, yet understanding her bitterness would have never disappeared for how Claudio behaved toward her when he repeatedly cheated on her with that stripper. "Dad... oh, my God! I found him dead in his car. Someone killed him last night, and I don't know what to do." His voice trembled as he started to sob, unable to control his emotions anymore. It was as if uttering the words opened a faucet from where his tears could finally flow from the bottom of his soul.

There was a moment of silence when Luciano thought his mother dropped the conversation, assuming she didn't give a damn.

The pause caught her in reflection. She'd divorced her husband, Claudio, a few years before, but their son, who was eighteen years old at the time, decided to remain and live with the father.

"Luciano, where are you, dear? Have you called the Police?" Her tone rushed as she was running to get to the car to drive to his place.

"I'm out here, in the garage. I hoped someone would have come and helped me, but nobody's going anywhere today," he kept sobbing.

"Now, listen to me very carefully," she said as she started the engine of the car. "I'm coming to you. Then, when I'm there, we'll call the Police. They will take care of everything but try not to touch anything. Do you understand?"

Considering that would have been the best solution, he glanced around, and leaving the door of the car the way he found it, he faltered toward the exit to wait for Giulia.

"Okay, I'll be waiting for you outside— please, hurry. I don't want to be alone," he begged, turning to view the shiny black Lamborghini. Claudio was very proud of that car and for Luciano, having it even for one day meant being able to wake up before him and *borrow* it.

Looking at it, it was nothing but a coffin, and as his father's soul left the pain of this mortal life, too many questions started to swirl in his mind; most of those seemed to be complete nonsense.

One question started to repeat insistently; *was this the day he had to die?* – he thought. Things could have gone differently if he'd never known that goddamned strip club he used to frequent.

"I'll be there immediately," Giulia replied, ending the conversation. Her mind blurred with the fear of Luciano's state of mind. She knew he loved Claudio, and regardless of his mistakes, Luciano still felt the attachment rightfully belonging to a son for his father.

Having spent the night on a train from Reggio Calabria, where she had a meeting the previous day, slowed her reactions at the steering wheel of the car. She kept praying to have at least the necessary interval of sharpness to reach Luciano and call the Police. After that, she could have collapsed, *but not now*.

She approached the building where her ex-husband had his apartment and noticed Luciano on the street. Parking the car at the side of the road, she got outside and ran to hold him.

He was in a strange trance and oddly held her back, despite the desperate need to feel the familiar warmth of a mother's hug.

"Let's go inside the apartment, dear," she glanced at him, caressing his face, and combing his hair with her fingers. Locking her eyes on him, she held Luciano tightly to herself, unable to find the right words to be said in such a moment.

Claudio's death didn't come as a surprise; she knew that frequenting a corrupted environment such as a strip club could result in some nasty consequences. Cheating on her with a cheap prostitute wasn't something she would have forgiven—ever. Nevertheless, the consequences that incident brought to her son changed everything, and the most important thing was to have the Police make light to the mystery.

Ensuring that Luciano was comfortably seated on the couch, she grabbed her mobile phone and dialed the 113, the emergency number at the Police Department.

Keeping a steady voice, she could explain what had happened, or at least what she got from the phone call with Luciano.

Although the Members of the Police Department didn't know Claudio personally, he was quite famous. He belonged to the elite group of skilled entrepreneurs who inherited the family firm, transforming it from a profitable business to unimaginable success.

Immediately, Forensic Police rushed to enclose the crime scene and collect all sorts of evidence. In the meantime, Detective Maurizio Scala, who was designated to follow the case, reached the apartment to collect testimony from those closely related to the victim.

Scala remained standing up, not to contaminate any areas with his own traces. Giulia and Luciano sat down in the living room, on the couch where Claudio's jacket was still lying.

"Who is living in this apartment?" Detective Scala asked, taking out a notebook from his pocket and began to scribble something.

"I live here with my father," the shaky voice of Luciano came out as a feeble response to the question. His hand tightly held in his mother's.

"What about you, Ma'am?"

Averting her gaze from her son, she turned to the Detective. "I don't live here anymore. I divorced Claudio three years ago, but my apartment is not far. I divorced my husband, not my son."

With a nod, Detective Scala kept writing his notes. "And you were the one who found Mr. Calvani's body? Do you know anything that could help us?"

Luciano hesitated for a moment, trying to recollect his thoughts. "Yesterday, after dinner, Dad left. I know he used to go to a particular nightclub, but I don't know if yesterday evening he went there or if he met his new girlfriend. He left home at about nine in the evening. I hadn't heard any noise, as generally, I sleep with my earplugs. My father snored quite loudly."

A disappointed grunt escaped Giulia; the words 'new girlfriend' still burned, for she was the reason why the marriage, she thought was destined to last forever, smashed in a thousand pieces. There wasn't a time when she wondered what her husband could have found in a prostitute that was better than all the years they'd spent together.

Just giving her a fast glimpse, Luciano continued his story. "I remained at home, as today I was supposed to go to lectures at the university. Obviously, this is not going to happen, and I believe I'll be away from my studies for some time."

"So, the victim left, and you remained home," repeated Detective Scala continuing to write in his notebook. "Do you know the name of the club he used to go to?"

A moment of silence filled the room. Luciano felt almost ashamed to admit he had no idea where his father spent his evenings.

Claudio didn't need a guardian, being old enough to go wherever he pleased without telling anyone his plans. Yet, Luciano wondered whether knowing that detail could have somehow helped in that situation and perhaps could have also prevented the tragedy. He shook his head at that thought. Obviously, something similar couldn't have been predicted or avoided.

If there were someone after him, it would be a question of time before he would have succeeded. "No, I have no idea about his whereabouts, but perhaps his girlfriend can provide some information. Her number can be found on his mobile phone's directory," Luciano suggested.

"Does it belong to the victim?" Detective Scala asked, glancing curtly at the jacket on the couch.

"Yes, when I woke up this morning, I thought he was still sleeping. Generally, he gives me a ride to the university if our schedules coincide. Today, I thought I could get his Lamborghini for myself; that's why I didn't think to go and wake him up." Luciano recalled, feeling his desire to have the car foolish and meaningless. "I checked the jacket to find the key, but it wasn't there, so I thought it was in the pocket of his jeans. This meant I couldn't get the car unless I would have gotten the spare keys he keeps in the drawer of the desk in his studio. When I reached the garage..."

His voice trembled and couldn't talk anymore. Telling how he found his father dead in a pool of blood wasn't something easy to speak out loud. Probably he would never be able to talk about that sight when he reached the car.

Giulia held Luciano tightly in her arms, trying to console him, wondering whether the

Detective could continue the questioning later or another day.

With a nod, raising his eyes at Luciano, Detective Scala pursued. "Have you ever met his new girlfriend?" He understood it wasn't easy going through the facts, which could have led to his father's death, but there wasn't any other way to get a clear idea of all the players in Mr. Calvani's life and those who could have a reason to have him killed.

"No, I haven't. We tried to avoid talking about her, although I decided to live with my father, this didn't mean I approved of his lifestyle."

"Hmmm," muttered Detective Scala. "And where were you last night?" he turned his glance to the one who could have had a good reason to get rid of Claudio Calvani, his ex-wife Giulia.

"I hope you don't think I could have killed my ex-husband!" Her green eyes opened wide at what appeared to be an outrageous comment. "However, to satisfy your curiosity, I have been traveling by train from Reggio Calabria, where I had a job meeting. I arrived this morning at the Termini Station at about six o'clock and got a taxi to reach home, just in time to receive the call of Luciano." She averted the look from the detective and searched for something in her purse. "Here, this is the train ticket validated yesterday evening and checked by the ticket inspector. And this is the receipt of the taxi driver. I hope you're satisfied." She slammed the receipts on the sofa table in front of them.

"Mrs. Calvani, it wasn't my intention to doubt your words; I'm trying to understand what happened to your ex-husband," he tried to justify himself. Yet grabbing the travel documents as proof to be inserted on the list of pieces of evidence.

"My surname is no longer Calvani. My name is Giulia Martini," she pointed out, hissing, yet trying to remain calm.

Detective Scala observed the spaces of the apartment. "I'm afraid I'll need to look around, and for a few days, we'll need to close up this place for investigations. Do you have a place to go in the meantime?" he asked Luciano.

"Yes, I can go to live with Mum, but I will also need to get my personal items..." his voice trembled, thinking about the chance of not being able to return there for a long time.

"Sweetheart, this won't take long, you can get new clothes. Grab your books and laptop for now," Giulia reasoned.

"We can let you take your laptop with you, but the home should remain the way it is. If you can bring your computer to the Police Precinct, they'll make a copy of the hard disk, and you can leave right away."

CHAPTER 2

Remaining alone in the apartment, after Luciano and Giulia left, Maurizio walked toward the couch, waiting for the forensic team to reach the apartment from the garage to continue their search.

He started to analyze some details of the crime, beginning with the discussion he had with the two closest people to the victim. *The ex-wife, although she was the one to have a good motive, has a bulletproof alibi, the son didn't have any apparent reason to kill his father,* he ruminated. *He remained to live with him after the divorce; if there was resentment or desire to revenge for the offense to his mother, he would have also decided to stay with her. Yet, we need to confirm his alibi being close to the crime scene.*

He shuffled on his feet, as he finished writing in his notebook his first impressions. The door opening forced him to return from his thoughts, and Forensic Inspector Leonardo Romizi, leading the forensic team that reached the place, entered the apartment, glancing around. "You haven't touched anything, have you?" he asked, noticing Maurizio's hands not wearing the mandatory latex gloves.

"I was here writing in my notebook; I think I've done my work long enough to remember that detail."

Forensic Investigator Romizi shrugged, "Just checking."

"What are your first impressions? Is there anything interesting about the way Mr. Calvani was murdered?" Maurizio strolled toward Leonardo, placing the notebook in his pocket.

"Yes, and everything seems to point at a case that won't be easy to solve. He was killed with a single shot to the head from a very close range. We found only one shell, meaning that the gun wasn't a revolver," he said, raising the clear-sealed bag which contained it. "We will have to perform the ballistic models to see from which position he was shot, whether the assassin was waiting for him in the car or outside of it. There are so many points on the dynamic that need to be clarified, and hopefully, the surveillance camera installed will for once be helpful to get more information about the killer."

The rest of the team started to collect samples and items from the apartment, particularly from the studio, where Claudio was running part of his business life.

Suddenly an elderly woman in her sixties arrived, peeking from the door, hesitatingly looking around. "Ma'am!" Maurizio exclaimed, pacing toward her to avoid having an intruder. "This place is restricted now. You can't come inside."

"I'm sorry, but I live here on this same floor. You can't pretend people won't get interested in what's going on here," she protested, exiting the apartment. "What happened? Did you find the man dealing with drugs?"

Narrowing his eyes, trying to understand whether there was something to extract from her question, he walked her to a corner of the stairs. "Mr. Calvani was found dead this morning. Have you heard anything that can help us?"

The woman gasped, bringing a hand to her mouth. She could have guessed everything except something serious like a murder. "Detective, do you think there's a murderer who can threaten all of us?"

"No, I'm certain this was connected directly to Mr. Calvani. You can be sure nobody is after any of the other residents in this building. But if you heard any noise, something strange, please don't keep it for yourself, every piece of information can be vital, even the smallest," he insisted, knowing she could have been the right person who keeps track of every move the people living on the same floor make, if not in the whole block.

"I am a person who minds her own business. I don't put my nose in issues that don't concern me," she said proudly, inflating her chest. "Nevertheless, this morning, I heard Mr. Calvani returning later than usual. When he comes back in the night, the slightest noise echoes like a peal of thunder, and I got awakened by the slamming of the door."

"Hmm… how did you know it was Mr. Calvani and not his son or someone else?" He knew the answer, but he always loved to tease a bit with those *I-mind-my-own-business* people who always know everything about everybody. In many cases, they were intrusive presences, but when a crime is committed, they could be a blessing for the Police. They are sometimes better than a surveillance camera because they hold information nobody else knows.

"Look," she said, pointing at the door on the other side. "Here is Bruna's apartment. She's a friend of mine and lives alone. She's not used to going out for clubs," Her finger moved to another door. "There, lives the Magliani's family. They go to work early, and they have two toddlers, so if they were going somewhere at that time of the night, they would have been together for some sort of emergency."

Maurizio's face lightened, amused, "Yes, but it could have been Luciano, the son of Mr. Calvani…"

"No-no-no. No, sir!" She shook her head, closing her eyes. "The boy is going to university

19

and goes to sleep early. He was listening to music and then switched on the TV, so he wasn't the one who returned at three o'clock in the morning." She got closer to Maurizio as to avoid being heard by indiscreet ears. "He came home at three o'clock, but after a few minutes, he got out once again, after receiving a phone call. I thought he was going to the apartment of the new girlfriend because he didn't come back, but now that you tell me he'd been murdered..." She signed herself, pursing her lips. "Shall God have mercy on his soul."

Maurizio remained silent for a moment, and things started to make some sort of sense.

If he received a call, it might be possible it was the assassin. Immersed in his thoughts, he drifted back in the apartment, leaving the woman waiting on the corridor. *He came in, took off his jacket as the telephone rang...* He walked once again outside the door.

Whoever called him asked him out with a whatever excuse, yet this implied his intention was to be back within a few minutes, without going anywhere specific; otherwise, he would have brought the jacket with him. I need the telephone and the call log of the last few months, but particularly last night.

He glanced at the woman who remained to observe the coming and goings of the detective from the apartment.

"Mrs...." Maurizio hesitated.

"Moretti, Berenice Moretti," she replied, almost standing at attention.

"Mrs. Moretti, I wish to have you available for any questions I might have about what you remember of the previous night," he commenced, hoping not to be too intrusive into the life of a bystander.

"If you fear I might forget any detail, I wish to inform you that I have a perfectly functioning memory, and I won't forget anything, but if you prefer to question me right away, I'm more than available when it comes to serving justice."

"I need to take care of some other details, but I might come back this afternoon if you don't mind," he proposed.

"Well, I'm a bit busy today, but if you come after four in the afternoon, you will certainly find me here. I will brew coffee," she winked.

"How can I refuse to have a cup of coffee?" He chuckled sarcastically.

He returned to the apartment and looked around, searching for Forensic Investigator Romizi, "Leonardo!" he called.

"Found anything interesting?" Leonardo arrived from the bedroom.

"Maybe, one of the neighbors has heard Mr. Calvani returning this morning. According to her testimony, he had a call that forced him to return to the car. I'm going now to the precinct trying to make sense out of those preliminary information bits and brainstorm," he replied, starting to create a sort of list of things to do in his mind before returning there to question Mrs. Moretti. "This afternoon, I'll come here again to ask some questions, but particularly I want to know something from the person who holds all the information about the entire neighborhood."

"Perfect, we're almost finished here. We might return tomorrow after having analyzed the data we've obtained. Do you have the keys to this apartment?" he asked.

A grimace contorted his face. "I'll have to ask the son."

Leonardo grinned from ear to ear, "Or maybe we can use these ones," he said, swinging the keys in the air. "These were in Mr. Calvani's pocket."

There had always been a sort of mocking relationship between Maurizio and Leonardo, that started since the day they met. Their friendship was founded on a solid basis, but they always felt the need to remind each other of their flaws; like in a marriage, that was the way to keep the relationship alive and interesting.

"Well, good to know you won't be left outside. I'm going to my office anyway, and I'll be waiting for your report this evening."

He turned on his heels and left the apartment without waiting for a reply. As he was outside, he scanned the road. Parioli was one of the wealthiest neighborhoods in Rome, and he believed its residents would be shocked by a murder.

Of course, this could have happened anywhere, but in this case the victim is a person with high visibility in the community. Moreover, the brutality of the crime is rather to be expected in poorer zones of the capital, where people can't afford the costs of private security.

The victim wasn't a saint and depending on who you ask, you might get different answers. According to his ex-wife, and supposedly those around her, Claudio Calvani was a perfect jerk, who cheated on his wife. Others might have described him as a sympathetic, funny, and easy-going person – nevertheless, not a criminal or a violent man. He lit a cigarette, still glancing around, searching for some other clues to be investigated so to reconstruct the last day of Mr. Calvani's life, as well as the happenings in the last three to four years.

Something told him the divorce from his wife might have some sort of connection with the murder. *The first hypothesis could be jealousy, but his wife wasn't in the city at the time he got killed, and she would have been the most accredited person to have a jealous reason to kill. Another can be the girlfriend, perhaps she thought he was still in love with the wife, but in this case, I suppose she would have killed Mrs. Martini. Why kill him? Maybe she found out he was also seeing other women, and the only way to have him for herself was to kill him?*

He threw the cigarette away and walked to the car; he needed a plan to follow, and from the details he would have gotten time by time, he hoped to reach the solution of the mystery.

As he arrived at the office, he closed the door behind him and hoped nobody would disturb him. That was a mere hope because he already knew that having the door closed was a clear invitation for the entire precinct to come in and ask him questions.

He sat down at his desk, and for a couple of minutes, his eyes stared at the door, holding his breath, waiting for the first officer knocking or rushing in, with the most impossible issue.

Nothing happened, and with a surprised grin, he switched on his computer, as the most surreal feeling of something not going the way it should, grabbed his mind. Despite this detail, he started to write a plan. That was the way he worked. Without a starting list, he was completely stuck into the vortex of the thousand questions swirling in his mind. A list of priorities was a way to put his thoughts into a precise order.

A couple of hours went by and raising his glance to the clock on the other side of the room, he had the confirmation that the world had finally stopped, and some sort of catastrophic event was on its way.

"Two hours..." he muttered, surprised. "The door has been closed for two hours, and nobody knocked! Either everybody is dead, or they've learned the meaning of a closed door."

He stood up and keeping the most religious silence, he tried to focus on the noises coming from the corridor and the other offices. Indeed, it sounded like work was going on regularly, but nobody had anything to ask.

"Then, there's nothing else to do but to acknowledge that my colleagues understood, after 9 years that when my door is closed, they need to keep themselves out of my sight."

An amused smile relaxed his face, smoothing the creases on his forehead, and returned to sit at his desk. Glancing at the list he wrote and the comments at the side of each point, he considered himself satisfied, and after having the sheet printed, he went to pay a visit to his old friend Leonardo. The first point on his list was to obtain the data to be extracted from Claudio's mobile phone. He knew before he would have been granted access to it, a full scan of the fingerprints, organic material, and any sort of residue that could have given an idea of the places the phone has visited, was required.

Coming outside the room felt like being immersed once again in the world, after endless confinement in solitude. With a grin, he peered around with the same expression of a man who returned to a place he hadn't visited since his childhood.

"I was expecting you to arrive earlier," Leonardo observed, seeing Maurizio appearing from the laboratory door.

"Something happened since I returned this morning. I could finally work without being disturbed. I'm not used to this, and a couple of hours were spent going through the preliminary data," Maurizio explained, still failing to believe that sort of miracle that happened. "This means I have my list, and I'm going through the points on it. So, you found the telephone in Mr. Calvani's pocket? When will I have the chance to go through it?"

"You won't need that," Leonardo grabbed a folder from the desk. "Here's the call log and the preliminary results of the general analysis performed on its surface. For a more detailed one, or to have my permission to hold the mobile phone with your grubby hands, you'll need a couple of days."

Maurizio grimaced at him, and grabbed the folder, snapping it from Leonardo's hands. "I guess this can be enough for the moment. Do we have any other details?"

"Not yet, the coroner is working to establish the time of death, trying to extract as much information as possible on the body of the victim. We're working on the possible weapon, analyzing the shell we've found, and on every trace, we can find on the car. I will send you the preliminary report this afternoon before leaving. I can't go any faster. These things require time and patience if you want to have something that is even closely reliable."

Maurizio lowered his gaze eyeing the folder he got. For every murder case he predicted the onslaught of a lot of headaches and sleepless nights. *Story of my life...*

Glancing back at Leonardo, he sighed. "There's still much to do, so better to get started at least from something. I'm going to check those call-logs and try to find who the girlfriend is and have her interrogated."

The girlfriend was probably the last person to see him alive, and her testimony could give information about the last hours of his life. The mysterious call was also of crucial importance because that was coming from the killer.

Maurizio sat down at his desk, hoping to still enjoy the blessings of being left alone for the rest of the day.

"So, let's see what number called him last," he muttered, opening the folder. He was surprised to see that whoever compiled the log, also cared to make a search of the most important numbers, and the last one was completely inconclusive as it belonged to a Russian prepaid sim card. He took note of that number and continued checking the log.

"This is a number I might call, it belongs to a Madlen Fazekas," he said, getting on his feet. "Here, there's also her address, so rather than give her a call, I might want first to see whether she's home at the moment. I bet she's the girlfriend."

Grabbing his jacket, he paced out of the precinct, determined to reach her home, and perhaps also gathering some information about her from her neighbors. The apartment was located in a prestigious location. Maurizio remained open-mouthed as he parked the car outside the building. *I've chosen the wrong profession.* He walked to the entrance and searched on the video intercom her name.

"Hello," a seductive female voice answered.

For a moment, he found himself surprised by her deep and warm tone; one he wasn't expecting to answer the interphone.

"Good afternoon, this is detective Scala. Am I speaking with Ms. Madlen Fazekas?" His voice was a bit shaky as he hesitated to ask, still caught off-guard by her tone. A short pause of silence fell between them as if she were expecting a call from the Police or had too many reasons to be afraid.

"Y... yes, that's me..." she finally answered in a lower tone of voice.

"Ms. Fazekas, would you please open the door? I need to have a chat with you about Mr. Claudio Calvani."

A familiar buzz and the clicking of the lock of the main door informed him she agreed to meet him. "I live on the fifth floor," she replied with an apprehensive shade in her voice. He walked inside the hall of the building and reached the elevator. He wasn't sure whether it was normal for a stripper to be able to afford to live in such a building; he had no certain idea of the price to buy or rent one apartment there, but he knew for sure it was out of his reach.

CHAPTER 3

As Scala reached the fifth floor, a woman was waiting for him at the door of her apartment. Her long dark hair was secured in a high ponytail. She didn't wear any makeup but considering the smoothness of her skin and the shine of her hair, Maurizio assumed it was a sign of one who took pride in their looks. For him, it was more than clear the reason why Mr. Calvani lost his mind and destroyed what he'd built with his wife to chase this alluring creature. Despite the elegant beauty of Mrs. Martini, there was a light in the back of Madlen's eyes capable of enchanting and bringing a man to damnation. Particularly if the man in question was extremely sensitive to the female charm, like Claudio Calvani was, she could have engaged a deadly attraction.

And deadly indeed, he thought as he strolled toward the door.

The jeans and t-shirt she wore were an indicator of her desire to keep up appearances even if she was staying at home. Apparently, she wasn't waiting for any visitors.

"Good afternoon Ms. Fazekas, I'm sorry to turn up at your apartment unexpectedly without a previous call, but I have extremely urgent matters to discuss with you," he commenced feeling almost certain she couldn't be aware of the murder of her boyfriend. The press wasn't yet allowed to broadcast the fact, but he was sure this would have been a detail, which would have been fixed.

"Generally, the Police came to my apartment, to question me about my work at the club." She spoke calmly with a flirtatious tone in her voice. The foreign background was immediately clear by her accent, but she spoke a perfect Italian, actually better than some native speakers, as Maurizio could notice.

He nodded thoughtfully, closing the door behind him. "Ms. Fazekas, I'm afraid I am the bearer of bad news today, not only for you, but for many people. I would suggest you have a seat." His eyes avoided looking into hers, yet felt her stare wrapping his whole being.

"Honestly, I can't figure out a reason for your visit..." Despite the self-confidence and determination in her voice, a slight flicker, hardly detectable, and the imperceptible twitch of her lip, betrayed an internal turmoil.

"Early this morning, Mr. Calvani was found dead in his car. He has been murdered."

Her eyes opened wide, and her face turned pale. It was just for his prompt reflexes, and because he was expecting a similar reaction, that he could avoid her falling on the floor. Feeling her irregular breath on his cheek, he helped her onto a sofa, before she broke down in tears.

"It can't be true! Claudio can't be dead! Who would have wanted to do something like that?" Her voice lost all self-control and trembling like a puppy in the darkness, she sobbed, holding herself onto Maurizio, careless about the rules or any etiquette. The detective, at that precise moment, was her only hope.

He waited for some moments, before parting from her. Her behavior was understandable in her state of mind, and there wasn't a good reason to lose every sense of humanity in such a case.

"We'd just spent a beautiful evening together, and we were planning to have a small holiday this weekend." Searching her pockets, she found a tissue to wipe her tears, trying her best to gather some strength. "Only yesterday he came to pick me up and we went out for the evening."

"You might have been the last person to see him alive, Ms. Fazekas. We will need your full cooperation to reconstruct what has happened to him. Where were you yesterday?" He pulled out a notebook from his jacket and prepared to write down all the details she could have remembered of the last hour of Claudio's life.

She raised a hand to her mouth, sighing with a vacant expression on her face to cope with the turmoil caused by the unexpected news.

A few minutes passed in silence, as Maurizio patiently waited for her to react to the first shock and being able to tell something about what happened in the evening.

With a light shake of her head she turned her gaze at him. "As usual, he came to pick me up, and we had a drink before leaving here." She tried to recall.

"Can you tell me where you spent the evening? Did you go to a particular restaurant? To the cinema?" he asked, peering at her from time to time.

"Yes, we went to a restaurant close to the Colosseum. I can't remember the name of the place; we just chose it at the moment. We didn't book a place there. After a walk, we took the car once again and drove to the Venus Caprice. That's the place where I used to work as a dancer."

"You're not working there anymore?" Admittedly he considered it strange, but on the other hand, if it were a question about his girlfriend, he would have preferred to have her dance only for himself instead of having her almost naked body in front of several other men.

"No. Claudio wanted me to quit my job. That was the reason why he bought me this apartment and offered me an allowance." Her voice lowered in tone, almost as she realized what it could have meant having a boyfriend who doesn't live with her but pays her expenses. She didn't like the way people jumped to easy conclusions, considering her nothing more than a prostitute.

"What was the nature of the relationship between you and the victim?" Maurizio needed to go deeper into their strange romance because he was sure the more he would dig, the more he would find out valuable information. Unfortunately, he was also convinced this meant bringing a lot of side stories to the surface.

"I met Claudio four years ago. I was working at the club for one year already, and I thought this would have been the place where I would spend most of my working career." A short pause allowed her to swallow back the tears, which were impossible to hold back.

Recalling the preliminary chat, he had with Mrs. Martini and her son in the early morning, a detail jumped immediately in his mind. "Did you know he was married at that time?"

"Yes, I did. We started to frequent each other as friends, simply going for a walk every now and then, chatting about our lives and backgrounds. He was interested in my homeland, and we often spent our time together talking about the place where I was born and grew up. I was hoping one day we could have visited those places together." With a bitter smile she recalled her hopes, and dreams. "Then we understood something was growing between the two of us, and I fell in love with him. He told me he was married, but he wasn't happy. According to his words, his marriage deteriorated many years before, and with me, he felt alive once again."

Maurizio rolled his eyes. He'd heard the same story so many times. It was the typical bullshit many men tell women to bring them to their bed. He wasn't free from that sin, but since he met his wife, his life felt complete, and he didn't need to go looking for anything or anybody else. Certainly, Madlen was beautiful and much younger than Claudio, and therefore younger than his ex-wife.

Perhaps he was attracted by her exotic beauty, the particular job she was doing, or the fact that she might have fewer inhibitions in bed. Whatever the reason, it was a lousy line. So much exploited to become obsolete and vulgar. If I had a son, I would certainly teach him never to use this type of rationality with a woman or to disrespect her. A disgusted grin darkened his face as he kept writing.

"Did he ever mention the idea of marriage to you?"

"No, or better, he would have, but he was living with his son, and he was afraid if he remarried, with a former sexy dancer, he would have never accepted it." Her gaze lowered to her fingers twisting each other on her lap.

Interesting, he thought. "Have you ever met his son?"

"No, I haven't," she replied and continued to explain the story between Claudio and herself. "I didn't want to leave my job, as that was the only source of income for me. I needed to provide for myself. So, on our anniversary, he brought me here and asked me if I liked the place. I thought he wanted to move in here so we could have been free to live together even if not married. When I told him I liked it very much, he showed me the purchase agreement and that the apartment was registered in my name. He gave me an apartment all for myself, and he promised to pay for all my expenses. When he told me he wanted me to quit the job, I never would have guessed he came up with this plan, so I thought it could have been a good compromise until we wouldn't have the chance to get married or to live together like a family."

Turning his eyes at her, he started to put all the pieces together, "I'm sorry if I sound indiscreet, but unfortunately, this is my job. Exactly how did he pay your expenses?"

"He gave me a monthly allowance of 2000 Euros," she admitted, blushing as she explained the sum, she received from her boyfriend. "With my former job as a dancer, I couldn't dream of earning so much. For me, it was a good deal because I could quit my job and keep seeing Claudio in my own apartment. This was going to be the place where we could have our privacy."

Well, this at least puts a shade of doubt on her involvement. What kind of interest would she have had in killing the source of her income? Without him, she would have to find another job or return to work as a stripper.

"What are you going to do now?" His concerned tone warmed her heart, as there was someone who wasn't judging her as a prostitute who stole the husband from another woman and the family life from their son.

"I guess I'll have to find a job, perhaps I'll be back at the Venus Caprice, although I wish not to..." She shook her head, that wasn't indeed her first priority at the moment, she still had savings before she would have needed to find a job.

Maurizio stood from the sofa, placing the notebook back in his pocket. He thought he had enough information for the moment and planned to come back to her once he put all the information that he gathered today as well as the preliminary work he'd done.

He peered at the clock and realized he had another appointment with the neighbor of Mr. Calvani, but also, had to skip lunch.

"Just one last question. At what time did he leave?"

"It was about 02:15 am. I don't remember the exact time, but that's as close as it gets."

Grabbing back the notebook and fixing that detail, he turned to her. "For the moment, I don't have any other questions, but I would be grateful if you wouldn't leave the city until the case is solved," he concluded as he parted from the sofa.

"I understand, and I also wish to be kept informed on the advancement of the investigation. Of course, I understand I'm not his ex-wife, but I think I have the right to know who killed the man I fell in love with." She tried to keep her voice calm, but her attempts failed, as she tried to stand to guide Maurizio to the door.

"Before I forget about it," Maurizio said, retracing his steps. "Do you know this telephone number?" He took a leaflet where he wrote the Russian number that called the victim.

She took the paper in her hands and after having observed for a while, she replied. "No, I'm sorry."

"No problem, thank you very much, Ms. Fazekas," he greeted.

Once Maurizio left the apartment, Madlen stood in front of the closed door, thinking about what had just happened and what would have come up next.

The problems created by Claudio's death didn't have an easy fix. They would have required some fast action. The first thought that popped in her mind was the probability of the detective considering her a possible suspect for the murder, and if she wanted to continue her life in peace, she needed to find a bulletproof alibi, which at the moment, she didn't have.

Glancing around her, as if to find an idea, her telephone started to ring.

It took a couple of rings to bring her from the depth of her considerations and pacing to the table. She grabbed it and although she couldn't recognize the caller from the ID, she answered. "Hello."

"Hi Mom, it's me, Irina," a young female voice replied.

"My goodness, you called at the best moment," she commenced explaining. "But have you changed your telephone number?"

"No, I've lost my phone, and I've asked for another SIM card from my provider. I went to visit a friend of mine, so although they will send the new SIM card, it might take some time before I receive it," she tried to explain. "You sound shaken, is everything okay?"

With a long exhale, Madlen went to sit on the sofa, where a few moments before she received the news of the death of her boyfriend. "No, nothing is right. Claudio is dead! Someone killed him last night, and a detective just left my apartment. I don't know what to think, there's such confusion in my thoughts, and I can't find a way to organize or control them."

A long pause of silence fell between them, and the distances became endless, the loneliness unbearable, and the fear crawling from the innermost part of Madlen soul chocked her breath.

"I'm so sorry to hear this! I'm speechless. I'll get the first flight and reach you..."

"No, Irina. Please, this is not a good time. I need to focus on what to do next, and I need to find an alibi because I was the last person to see him alive yesterday evening." All Madlen was thinking was not to have any of the people she loved involved in that story. If Irina had come to spend some time with her, then unavoidably, she would have been involved in the murder case.

"I hope you know what you're doing, but please remember I'm here for you, and whatever you might need, you can count on me. You're the only person I have dear to my heart, and you know that." Irina couldn't hide her concern; she knew that dating one of the customers of the club wouldn't bring any good news. She was almost waiting for something similar to happen, and as Madlen informed her about the death of Claudio, she understood she was right.

However, Irina couldn't say she was sorry about his death. She was convinced he was simply using her. *She was like a luxury car, for him, something to show up to the friends. Probably it's better it happened like this; it would have been terrible to be dumped once her beauty would have started to fade with the passing of time. Now she can rebuild her life, and hopefully, with someone who's worthy of her trust and love,* Irina thought as she waited for Madlen to reply.

"Yes, darling. I appreciate your efforts to help me, but in this situation, you should stay there and far from here. I can't solve my problems if I need to worry about your safety. When everything is over, we will spend one entire month together; we will go for a holiday where nobody can find us." That was a promise she wasn't sure she'd ever been able to honor, but it wasn't the matter of going somewhere together, it was the need of spending some time in each other's company. That was something she'd been missing.

A frown creased her forehead. "How are you doing, by the way?"

Irina tensed her shoulders, "I'm fine. I'm planning to move away from Auntie's place. I got a part-time job, and I decided to rent a place and share the expenses with a friend. This also means that if you have problems in sending money, you can save them for yourself."

"I don't know for how long I can do so, but I believe I can still help you out until you're not completely independent financially. The fact that I sent you away doesn't mean I don't care about you. Here, I could afford what back home would have been impossible."

Her heart sank, fearing that from that day on, she had to decide who to help, her daughter or herself. Until she had a job at the club, this wasn't an issue, and when she accepted the deal offered by Claudio, she thought her problems were finally solved. Strolling to the window, she moved the white curtains aside to look out at the streets. From the living room, she had a good view of the cars coming and going from the gates of the property.

It was a sunny day, and although it was still winter, the chances of fair days like that weren't ruled out. In other situations, this would have been enough to bring her out of her apartment for a walk in the city or to join her friends to one of their favorite cafeterias. That day, she simply wanted to be alone and think about what to do next. The silence between them was worth more than a thousand words.

Irina sighed, "whenever you need to talk, remember I'm here. Don't let me out of your problems only because you don't want to create trouble for me. We're together, do you remember? We're still family."

"I know, it's just a bad day. I'll keep you informed about the development, and if I need help, I won't hesitate to call you." Madlen ended the conversation with a thousand thoughts chasing each other in her mind, and opened the door to the balcony, where she went to get some well-needed fresh air.

For the first time in her life, she felt like she would have been safer at home and didn't have any intention of leaving the apartment. The paranoia of being observed, followed, and judged possessed her soul, to the point of causing her to return inside and avoid being seen out on her balcony.

CHAPTER 4

Noting the time on his wristwatch, Scala still had one hour to the time when Mrs. Moretti, said she would be home. That meant he had the chance to grab a quick bite before reaching her apartment.

He entered the car and started to drive. His capability of miscalculating distances was once again spot on, and he didn't consider the traffic jam that always managed to freeze the central area of the city. Between his curses and prayers to be able to control his anger welling from his guts, he finally parked the car in front of the building.

A thundering noise grabbed his attention, forcing him to instinctively inspect the horizon, expecting to spot dark clouds approaching. The perfect blue sky didn't conform with the rumbling he started to hear, making him reconsider the fact that he probably needed a holiday when, finally, he realized the storm wasn't coming from the sky, but from his empty belly.

The journey through the city took longer than he'd expected—forty minutes more, to be exact. He didn't have a second to waste. Placing a hand at the height of his stomach a grimace twisted his expression, "If you can give me one hour to get my information, I promise you a Porchetta sandwich, the one you like so much," he begged, talking to his belly, as if it had a mind of its own.

As the storm quieted, he rushed to the floor where the apartment of Mr. Calvani was, and taking note of the name on the plate, he rang at the door of Berenice Moretti.

"Detective Scala, what a pleasure, please come in," she said, greeting him with a broad smile on her face. "I was almost certain you wouldn't show up."

Guiding him to the living room, she opened the blinds to allow the last bit of daylight to illuminate the room. "You see, I just returned from my errands. Please have a seat as I prepare the coffee."

Maurizio couldn't reply, as she was already headed toward the kitchen; he scanned around to have an idea of the type of person he was dealing with. The top of the antique desk beside the display cabinet was the first thing that caught his attention. He wondered whether it was something coming with age, to have the desire to furnish the home with darker furniture and keep an insane number of pictures in the display case.

Thinking about his apartment, where his wife insisted on furnishing with a more modern look and keeping the photographs stored in albums or on the computer, he wondered whether this would be the way his home would look like once he would become a grandpa.

He smirked at that thought – *There's still some time for it, at least I hope so.* His eyes continued to browse the old photographs of children, grandchildren, and relatives. Entire generations had a place in what resembled more a museum than a home.

There were war heroes, proudly standing to pose in their uniforms, the medals collected were displayed at the sides, and the family gatherings were duly reported through pictures.

"At my age, all you have left are the memories of those who are no longer with us and of those who come only for special occasions." The melancholic, yet energetic voice of Berenice shook his senses, and with a light jolt, he turned to look at her.

"I didn't mean to be nosey," Maurizio tried to justify himself, like a child being caught doing a bit of mischief.

Her eyes twinkled, "Detective, you don't need to apologize. I put the pictures on display, not only for myself, but to show them to those who come to visit. It doesn't matter whether you are here for work or for pleasure, those pictures certainly provide a good discussion starter. But let's not wait till the coffee gets cold. It won't be a pleasure anymore, after all."

With a nod, Maurizio turned on his heels and stared at the table where Berenice brought not just the coffee, but a large assortment of cookies and sweets. He recalled the days when he was a child, and a guest was expected to arrive home. Those were the times when, for once, there was the chance of having his belly filled with all sorts of delicacies bought by his mother for the guests and by the guests to greet the hostess of the house.

A chuckle relaxed his tensed expression, but immediately he recalled the reason for his visit and the fact that he wasn't supposed to accept anything besides, perhaps, the coffee.

"I'm on duty..." he mumbled in an attempt to refuse the hospitality of Berenice. He sat on the couch, and a loud rumble echoed in the room as a protest from his belly to his words.

A giggle escaped Berenice's mouth, "You are on duty, but your belly isn't, so I don't offer anything to the detective, but to the empty stomach, which is already suffering enough."

"I guess I have to accept, then." His hand reached the tray with the cookies and grabbed one. "So, Mrs. Moretti, let's go through the facts relating to what happened last night in the apartment of Mr. Calvani. What do you recall?"

"As I told you this morning, at three o'clock or so, I couldn't sleep anymore, and I heard Mr. Calvani slamming the door as he returned home." She snorted, disappointed for his irresponsible behavior. "This kind of thing should happen with his son, Luciano. He is at that age when you want to stay out at night with your friends or with girls. As an adult, Mr. Calvani, instead..." she shook her head disapprovingly.

Maurizio took out his notebook and started to scribble some notes. There were important bits of information also on her gossiping, as for example, Luciano wasn't probably the kind of guy who was spending his time having fun with his friends, and considering the economic availabilities, this was to be regarded with a certain suspicion or with an extremely responsible and mature youth.

"Anything else?" he asked as he raised his glance from the paper.

"Of course... right after he came inside, his telephone started to ring. You know these walls are not thick, and we can hear quite well what happens in the other apartments, particularly during the night, when all the other noises are eliminated. Anyway, he rushed out of his apartment, and I hadn't heard him returning home. I wasn't waiting for him, but at least until half past four in the morning, I couldn't fall asleep, and I'm sure if he had returned, I would have heard him." She sipped the coffee and placed the cup on the table. "Do you want more coffee?"

"No, thank you, I'm fine as I am, but I am taking another cookie," he grinned cunningly. "That must have been the call of the assassin."

"It was the girl if you want my opinion," she toughened her expression.

Twisting his mouth, Maurizio wondered whether she might have some information about the girlfriend too. "Why would she do something like that? What could have been her reason to kill the man who loved her? If she weren't interested in him anymore, she could have dumped him."

"Hah!" she exclaimed, swatting her hand on the arm of the couch. "That woman is no fool, Claudio, on the other hand, was. I bet all I have that he included her in his testament, so if he had died, she wouldn't have been left without any money."

"Have you ever met her?" Maurizio wondered at the ease with which she accused another person he wasn't sure she'd ever met.

"I don't need to. I know those girls who are working in these night clubs, are not looking for love. They are looking for the first fool to get money from and to have an easy life. Certainly, you have heard about those people, too!" Her eyes widened as he was still hesitating in believing that possibility.

Indeed, Maurizio wasn't excluding it, but it wouldn't make any sense. "Mrs. Moretti, it's not about this, or about what I believe, but Mr. Calvani has a son. From what I know at the moment, he's the only heir, and it's probable that he preferred to leave everything to him, figuring out a different solution for the girl. On the other hand, he was still young and it's also likely that he never thought about a testament."

Maurizio tried to reason, but he had to admit that Claudio's wealth could have been a good reason for killing him. Nevertheless, there wasn't any evidence to sustain her hypothesis, so he needed to be very cautious with his allegations and also with the way he was going to move the investigation forward.

"Ah, Detective, I know you need to follow certain procedures, but perhaps you should listen to what the people around Mr. Calvani have to say. You certainly will ask around about what his life was like, and by doing so, you will find interesting information about him, this girlfriend of his and about the rest of the family," she concluded with a smirk that revealed she knew more than she was willing to say.

"Tell me one thing, did you ever partake in a chat with any of the members of the family?"

"Before they divorced, I used to chat every now and then with the wife. Though she has always been a very reserved person, and our chats were mostly about general things happening in this building, she never let herself go into any sort of gossip," she recalled. Her voice turned into a melancholic shade, betraying the fact that somehow, she missed her presence. "Mrs. Calvani was perhaps too good for a person like her husband. I was devastated when I discovered he cheated on her, and despite the fact that I couldn't possibly know all the details of their relationship, I know she never gave him a valid reason to search for anything more. I cannot say whether it was the fault of the stripper who enticed him to the point that he couldn't refuse her any longer, or because he was indeed looking for something completely different than the fine woman he'd married." She took a short pause and looked down to her entwined fingers resting on her lap.

"What about their son?" Maurizio continued scribbling in his notebook.

She raised her shoulders. "What can I say? His sole purpose in life was to be noticed by his father. He loved him and would have done whatever, even remain living with him after the divorce just to have his attention..."

"But?" He raised his glance at her, sensing there was more to be said about their relationship.

"But since he met the girl, Mr. Calvani had time only for her. At most they spent the evenings together. He lost his mind completely for her, and there wasn't anything to bring him back to his senses to take care of his son, who desperately was trying to get his attention."

"Interesting," he mumbled. "Do you recall any occasion when they argued?"

"Who, father and son?" She wondered with wide-opened eyes. "That was rare, but not impossible to hear. When Luciano reached the level of exasperation, the whole building could hear his screams against his father, who generally tried to avoid yelling back at him, promising more time to spend together during the weekend just to calm him down."

"Did this ever happen? I mean, did they spend the weekends together, or did Mr. Calvani spend the time with the girlfriend?" Apparently, the victim behaved more like a teenager, rather than a responsible adult, but Maurizio was still a skeptic about what he heard from Mrs. Moretti. She was virtually living with them, but he had to gather his information from other sources to get a confirmation and a more complete picture of the relationship with his family, friends, cooperators, and girlfriend.

"Rarely, but it did. I suppose Mr. Calvani understood he also had duties toward his son. I think he did indeed love Luciano, but he was too caught up with this girl and probably didn't realize he was neglecting their relationship." She exhaled deeply, thinking about the son who was first suffering from the lack of attention from his father, and then he had to discover him dead.

There was a pause of silence when Maurizio took his time to recollect his thoughts and consider other questions to ask. Nevertheless, at that moment, he probably needed to have some confirmation about what Berenice said. He had to understand whether he just wasted his time listening to her gossip, or there was indeed something helpful in what she said.

He stood up, grabbing the last cookie. "I need to go now. I don't have any other questions for you, but I might return in case I come up with new ones. I need some time to process what I have right now."

"It has been a pleasure for me, Detective, and I hope you will find the person who killed Mr. Calvani, but keep in mind what I told you because the girl might have had a great reason to kill him," she warned. "I will be at your availability and will keep some cookies in case you will have more questions." She winked as she guided him to the door.

"Thank you very much for your help and for your hospitality. I will inform you if I have the need to return, and if you happen to recall anything, you can call this number," he handed her a business card and stepped out of the door.

He reached the car, and his stomach started to growl to remind him of the promise he made about having that Porchetta sandwich as he got out of the apartment.

"Yes, I know, and we're going to have it. I'm literally starving," he chuckled as he started up the engine of the car.

***

Since he returned from the Police precinct to allow the forensics to obtain a copy of the hard drive of his computer, Luciano closed himself to his bedroom and looked around. That was just a spare room and had none of the things he liked to surround himself with. He realized he'd been spending too much time in vain trying to get his father's attention and neglecting the relationship with his mother.

"I behaved toward her in the same way he behaved with me. I guess this is a sort of Karma striking back. Perhaps had I been more considerate toward her feelings, I would have also obtained more attention from him." He sat on the bed and wondered when he would be able to either return to the apartment or to get at least some of his belongings. In the hurry of the moment, he could get only his mobile phone, the laptop, and the books to study.

He never spent more than a few hours in his mother's apartment, and nothing was familiar to him. It was only the place where he was going to meet his mother every now and then. His heart didn't recognize it as home.

The ringing of his mobile phone broke the silence in the room, and Luciano rushed, searching for it.

"Hello," he replied without checking the caller ID.

"Luciano, I heard on the radio the news about your father. How are you?" Stefano's voice arrived like a storm through the receiver.

It didn't take much for the news to circulate around, Luciano considered. He hoped the press would have been informed later, and perhaps the news would have reached his circle of friends and acquaintances with some delay.

"I'm confused. I... I still can't believe it," he replied, trying to get a grip of his emotions. "I think that it was less than a day ago when I greeted him as he was going to meet his girlfriend... To think that only this morning, I was whistling for the chance of getting his car to reach the university... Everything is so unreal, and I feel like such a fool for my stupid desire of showing off with his Lamborghini."

Finally, he started to realize his father wasn't coming back anymore and whatever he had in mind to tell him had to wait for eternity.

"I still can't believe it. If there's anything I can do for you, don't hesitate to ask. Even if it's just to have someone listening to what you need to say, or you need to get distracted. Really, whatever." Stefano and Luciano had been friends since the beginning of the university. It was a new friendship, but they connected immediately and became very close. With his old utility car, borrowed from his mother, he couldn't compete with Luciano's wealth. Still, their friendship was not about being at the same social class, but about being on the same wavelength.

A smile appeared on Luciano's face as he heard the concern in his friend's voice. He suddenly felt less lonely, and probably talking with someone who wasn't directly affected by his fate was a good idea to avoid the feeling of emptiness taking space in his soul.

"I appreciate this. I know I can count on you. I'm sorry, I should have called you explaining why I wasn't at the lecture this morning. Everything happened so suddenly, and I didn't have the time to fully understand it."

"Are you crazy? You didn't need to do anything else but to take care of yourself and of your mother. I know she divorced him, but I believe it was a shock for her to realize her ex-husband had been killed. Don't feel guilty for not having called me!" Stefano assured as he continued driving home. "By the way, do you want to meet?"

Luciano wasn't sure whether he needed to stay home and think about what had happened, or it was better to escape for a few hours. He took a short pause to consider everything and shook his head. "Perhaps I should remain here and spend some time with my mother. We also need to arrange the funeral, the bureaucratic matters, not to mention the fact that from this moment on, we all need to be available for the investigation. I don't know what's going to happen next. One thing, though, I would be grateful for. Could you send me by email the notes you've taken and will take at the university? I'm afraid that, at least for the next two weeks, I won't be able to attend any lectures."

"Of course, as I arrive home, I'll send you a copy of today's lectures and any future ones. I will keep taking notes for you," Stefano replied, concerned about his friend. He knew how attached he was to his father and how frustrated he was about his careless behavior. Shaking his head, he continued driving to his home, looking forward to the time he could have checked his notes to be sent.

For Luciano, life was getting more complicated than he could have expected. The concern of being at the murder scene was surely bothering him. He certainly was there together with all the people who lived in the building and had access to the underground parking lot. Nevertheless, among all those people, he was the one who had a reason to kill Claudio.

His heart started to race in his chest, and pacing to the window, he peeked outside as if he was expecting the Police car to appear any time soon to bring him to jail for the murder of his father.

The door opened suddenly, and Giulia came in without bothering to knock. She wasn't used to that type of behavior in her home; neither was she used to do so when they lived together.

Luciano turned to the door, expecting to find a Police officer in front of him, ready to arrest him. A scream released the tension that built in his soul.

"I didn't mean to scare you," Giulia apologized.

Holding his hand to his heart as if to keep it in place, he collapsed on a chair beside the window. "No, it's not your fault, I was so caught up in my thoughts and I didn't even acknowledge your steps coming closer to the room."

She beamed and walked to him, "I'm so sorry, sweetheart, that it had to be you to discover him dead. It must have been terrible!" Her hands holding him tight to herself and stroking his hair lovingly.

At the feeling of his mother's touch, he once again released the stress and sobbed without any intention of keeping those tears any longer. "He never cared about me, but I loved him."

She wasn't sure what she was supposed to say to make him feel better. The only feelings she had for her ex-husband since the day of the divorce, were intense moments of bitterness followed by stretches of indifference. Nevertheless, they still had something important in common: the young man who sobbed desperately clinging to her waist, like his last hope.

"Everybody has a different way to show affection. Perhaps he was caught with his new girlfriend and with his job? Maybe he needed some time to get things settled, but I know he loved you," she whispered, unsure whether she believed what she was saying.

What was true and what wasn't didn't have any meaning at that moment. What counted was that his father was dead, and there wouldn't have been any chance to fix their relationship. Luciano pretended he didn't hear what she said. He knew she was trying her best to console him, and it was probably what he needed the most.

CHAPTER 5

The following day Maurizio didn't leave his office; he received the first results from the coroner about the murder weapon, the time of death, and the unfortunate details that the only DNA traces and fingerprints found in the car belonged to the victim and his son. Those weren't enough proof as they were located on the steering wheel, the door, and places where whoever used to drive the Lamborghini would have touched. The killer was probably waiting for him, hiding behind the vehicle, and jumped from there as Claudio opened the door.

"The dynamic is still something I fail to understand," he said, looking to Leonardo, who was brainstorming with him in the room. He stood from the chair and paced around the room, reaching the center and stopping there.

He grabbed a couple of chairs and aligned them one behind the other. "Mr. Calvani reached his car," he said, walking to the front chair. "He opened the door, when someone jumped from behind, pointing the gun at him." He pretended to open the door of the vehicle. "If someone is threatened by an assassin before coming inside the car, the first reaction wouldn't be that of running away?"

Leonardo stood and walked toward him, "Maybe he thought that getting in the Lamborghini would have protected him from the bullets, or that he could have driven as fast as possible to safety."

"Or the assassin waited for him to be in the car, blocked one hand with the door... No, he couldn't have done it," Maurizio reconsidered his thoughts. "Or... the victim knew the assassin. Think if you are Mr. Calvani and are going somewhere, you open the door and I, one of your friends, relatives, acquaintances arrive and ask you to stop for a moment. What would you do?"

Leonardo thought about it for a moment, and pretended he opened the door of the car, "I would have said that I'm a bit in a hurry. So, I'm sitting inside ready to go, but also waiting to listen to what this person has to say."

"Exactly!" Detective Scala exclaimed, pointing his finger at him, "This person, perhaps explained to him that it wouldn't take long, so he or she approached the Lamborghini, extracts the gun and shoots the deadly shot right at the victim's head," he concluded pointing an imaginary gun at Leonardo's head.

"And Mr. Calvani wasn't expecting him or her to extract a gun, because they were probably friends and he trusted this person, so he couldn't react. Most likely, he didn't have the time to realize he was holding a gun and fired at him," Leonardo reasoned, standing up.

"Do we have any results from the surveillance cameras?" Maurizio wondered. That evidence could have solved a big deal of headaches because it would have revealed, at least, the dynamic as it happened.

"Are you going to guess, or do I have to tell you?" Leonardo grimaced.

"Fuck! What was the problem this time? A short circuit, locusts, plague?" It wasn't the first time technology failed when it was needed most. "Come on! They installed the cameras for this precise reason, so if a crime occurred in the garage, it would be easier to identify the suspect." His voice trembled in frustration, as he raised his hands to his head.

"The cameras were under maintenance, and a guard was supposed to be there to compensate for that lack. Now, the problem is that not everyone knew this detail, and not everyone knew where those cameras are located. Therefore, we have two important clues: Number one, the killer is not an idiot, and didn't act impulsively. He or she studied the place accurately under every single detail. Number two, the assassin is either one of the people living in the building or a person who comes regularly there to visit a family member or..." Leonardo counted on the fingers hesitating on the last sentence.

"Or is in a relationship with one of the residents," Maurizio continued.

"Precisely!"

Rubbing his chin with his hand, Detective Scala lowered his gaze and walked to his desk. Fully immersed in his thoughts, he slowly sat down as if not make any noise to disturb his train of thoughts.

He then raised his eyes to Leonardo, "This means that it's either the son, the girlfriend or one of the people living in the building. Although, I do believe only a handful of them knew Mr. Calvani close enough to have any reason for killing him."

"What could have pushed his son to even conceive anything like a murder?" Leonardo's forehead creased at the unexpected suggestion.

Certainly, for a young man in his university years, having a Lamborghini, a fat bank account, and a beautiful apartment in the most expensive part of the city would have been a reason good enough to kill. Not to mention that he would have also inherited at least half of his father's business if Mr. Calvani decided to include his ex-wife in his will.

"What about the other heirs? Was Luciano his only son?" Leonardo tried to consider the whole scenario and all those who would have a reason to have Claudio six feet underground.

"Yes," mumbled Maurizio. "One thing for sure is that without recordings, things are going to be difficult. The murderer could be literally whoever, except the wife, who has a bulletproof alibi. At the time of the murder, she was on the night train from Reggio Calabria to Rome. His son was asleep in his room. What if he wasn't sleeping and he appeared by the car? Mr. Calvani certainly wouldn't have expected to have him shooting."

"I seriously doubt he was expecting anyone to shoot him. He wasn't a politician, a drug dealer, or a magistrate involved in an organized crime case." Leonardo shook his head, crossing his arms to his chest. "We are talking about a successful businessman, who never received any threats, with, apparently, no enemies, but with a soft spot for women. If this puts him into the position of being a target, then we should include half of the Italian entrepreneurs. This doesn't make any sense, and I don't believe his son would ever do anything like that. We are too early into the investigation to start reaching these types of conclusions."

Pursing his lips, Maurizio lazily browsed through the items on his desk. Grabbing a pen, he started tapping on the table with its tip.

Tick...tick...tick... a measured rhythm marked the time, together with his own thoughts.

At the fourth ticking sound, Leonardo grabbed the pen from Maurizio's hand, "Would you stop it, alright!" he hissed, slamming it on the desk.

"Cool down, brother," Maurizio replied, annoyed, holding the pen once again.

He grabbed his head between his hands, and a long exhale came from his mouth as he raised his stare once again at Leonardo. "According to Mrs. Moretti, the neighbor, we should look for the girlfriend, but she also admitted the relationship between father and son wasn't the most harmonic. She mentioned hearing, Luciano, yelling at his father. The reason was probably jealousy; he wanted to spend time with him, but this one was completely caught in the relationship with his new girlfriend."

"So, you think he thought that killing his father would have been the best solution? Something like *If I can't have you, then no one else will?* I would have considered instead to kill the girl," Leonardo observed, excluding completely the involvement of the young man.

Leaning on the chair, Maurizio's eyes met the clock on the wall. "I'm going to consider this day gone. I'll ask the rest of my team to gather more information as to whether there's a testament, a life insurance, anything that could lead someone to think killing a person would be a brilliant idea.

"Yeah, I think we start to turn the case around without getting anything done. After a good night sleep, we will all feel better with hopefully clearer ideas in our minds." Leonardo stood from the chair and waited for Maurizio to leave together.

"It's indeed quite late," observed Romizi, glancing at his wristwatch, "How come your wife didn't call you yet?"

"Hmm," Maurizio growled, considering he had a point. Generally, if he was late and forgot to inform his wife about it, she would have called him to question whether he was going to join them for dinner or they had to go on without him.

He slipped the mobile phone from his jeans, and with a cringe, he noticed he'd forgot the telephone was muted. There were indeed three calls and ten messages. The last one was a clear "Get yourself a sandwich, asshole."

Peeking from a side, Leonardo grinned, "Someone's in trouble! Is she going to make you sleep on the couch?"

"I don't think this is what she meant, but it's perhaps safer if I do so, after having apologized."

"That's why I'm not married," Leonardo chuckled.

"No, the reason why you're not married is nobody wanted you," was the clarification offered by Maurizio.

"But I'm not going to sleep on the couch either, so everything considered, I think I am on the winning side," he replied as they reached the parking lot.

As Maurizio was inside the car, he thought about what happened during the day and what was waiting for him from the moment he'd arrive at the apartment. Anna, his wife, was right, after all. It wouldn't have taken too much for him to inform her about his delay, nor that it would have been too much to unmute the mobile.

That wasn't the first time he forgot, and he'd hoped that being that a trait of his own personality, it would have been easier for her to understand and perhaps have a bit of patience.

With a sigh, he grabbed his mobile phone and, setting up the handsfree option, called her, hoping to obtain her mercy, so to, at least being able to be admitted in the bedroom with his queen.

***

It was about midnight, and since Luciano decided to take a break from the University for a couple of weeks, he didn't have to go to sleep early. Nevertheless, he didn't have a reason to remain awake. The television wasn't offering anything interesting, and for the moment, he preferred to be alone rather than going out with his friends.

Everything resembled a bad dream, and he wasn't sure he was awake. The sudden ringing of his mobile phone returned him to reality, the one he was still trying to understand from the confusion of his thoughts. He grabbed it and checked the caller ID. Irina was calling him, and although he wasn't convinced it was a good idea to call each other, she could have been the only connection with that new reality. He decided to answer her.

"Hello..." he couldn't formulate anything else and hoped she had clearer ideas to start the communication.

"Hi. I have been thinking about you the whole day. How do you feel?" Her voice was calm like nothing serious happened.

"I feel confused. I still cannot believe it... It's not right. How about you?" He wondered, hoping she would have given him a way to overcome the terrible guilt.

"I understand your feelings, believe me, and I know even if he wasn't caring about you, he was still your father, and you loved him, but..." She didn't have any good words to say to make him feel better.

"But he deserved to die?" He almost whispered that phrase, as if someone could have heard, and arrest him for the murder of his own father.

"We shouldn't talk about this; it's not going to help the way you feel, nor the reality of the facts. We need to meet somewhere. Can you reach me?"

Luciano looked around; if he were in his father's apartment, he could have invited her in. Like every time Claudio was away, she could have come and spent some time together without any restriction.

It wasn't the fact of having to ask permission; at his age, the only thing required was to inform his mother he was going out, but he knew it would have perhaps sounded suspicious if he would have gone out to spend some time with his girlfriend or with whoever else. In his way of seeing things, the best decision was to stay away from each other at least until the investigation would be closed. He knew he was one of the possible suspects for the murder of his father, due to the broken relationship between them, because of the money he would have inherited, or for whatever reason the Detective could have figured out.

"No, I'd prefer to meet you tomorrow at the University," he mumbled.

She wasn't frequenting the University. Being older than him, she completed the course work and discarded the idea to go further with her studies, but he hoped if there was someone listening to their conversation, this appointment would have sounded more like a normal behavior to be expected from him. She remained silent for a moment, and once she understood what he meant, she played along. "Sure, I will be at the faculty by nine. I'll see you there at the entrance. I love you."

The last sentence reached Luciano with the same effect of a punch on his face. His heart felt warmed by the tenderness of her voice, but his senses sharpened as the presence of a girlfriend could have messed up everything. He wasn't sure why he felt this way. *That's not the way I planned this whole situation between us.*

"I love you too," he replied curtly before interrupting the conversation. The mobile phone felt like a fire burning in his hand, and he flung it on the bed.

He stared at his mobile for some time as if he expected something to happen, but it remained there, lying on the blue blanket, the one he still remembered from the times he spent the holidays in his grandmother's apartment in Turin. She died a few years ago, and he was surprised to recall that detail.

It's probably good that I'm going to meet Irina tomorrow, although her presence is complicating everything. We need to figure out a way to get out clean from this situation, so our lives can move forward from this point on. A loud yawn filled the silent emptiness of the room, and lazily undressing, Luciano slipped through the fresh linen scent of the sheets. The fragrance carried the memories of his childhood and all the past years when he still had a family and life was made of only good news. "I'll get back to that feeling one way or another," he whispered, closing his eyes, tired and confused.

***

The morning after, he woke up before the ringing of the alarm clock. A ticking rain created a soothing sound, almost inviting him to turn around and continue to sleep.

Indeed, he could have done it if it weren't for the appointment he had with Irina. Groaning, he sat on the bed, peering around, trying to understand where he was.

He froze for a moment to recollect his thoughts. That wasn't a nightmare. His father was dead, the apartment where he lived for most of his life was seized by the police until further notice, and he found himself with fragments of his life to be put back together.

Walking to the kitchen after the shower, he found something else he thought he'd lost in a far past. On the table breakfast was ready and a message written on a post-it.

The yellow leaflet shone under a shy sun filtering through the clouds after the rain. And like in a dream, it glowed, inviting him to read.

I hope you could sleep at least a bit. I prepared you breakfast, just like the times when we lived together. Take your time; I will call you later to check on you.

Love you,

Mom.

The corners of his lips arched downwards to the bitter feeling of not having appreciated those moments when they were still a family. With tears blurring the sight, he sat down, eyeing the thermic pot with milk, coffee, the jar of jam, and bread.

His memories tasted exactly like that, but with the apartment already empty and his mother out to work, a bitter aftertaste corrupted the sweetness of the jam, along with the memories. The guilt feeling of having abandoned his mother to follow his dad overwhelmed him together with the certainty of having given his love to the person who didn't requite his feelings.

Silently he finished his breakfast and cleaned the kitchen. Living with his father was at least useful in developing a sense of housekeeping. He was sure his mother would have appreciated finding the kitchen in order when she returned from her work.

His gaze focused on the window, and noticing the clearing sky, he clenched his teeth and fists. His lips trembling with rage pursed as a dark thought emerged from his soul. *He just deserved to die...*

CHAPTER 6

Maurizio stormed into the precinct, minus any good feelings about the day to come. The argument with his wife, Anna, lasted well into the night. As a result, he got up late that morning and got stuck in the traffic, which made him, if possible, even more nervous. He arrived inside the premises, where he'd hoped to find a way to get a grip on himself, but that hope turned out to be vain.

"You're late..." Leonardo observed walking with his cup of coffee and noticing the way Maurizio stormed in. With his roughed-up hair and pouty growls, he acted like a hungry bear unable to find food.

Clenching his fists, Maurizio glared at Leonardo. "Mind your fucking business and disappear from my sight! You should be at the Forensic Department doing your job!"

Without waiting for a reply, he reached his office and slammed the door behind him. There, although everybody could still hear him, he released his frustration screaming curses to the whole world and throwing away the first item he found at the reach of his hands; in that case, being a chair.

Leonardo calmly walked toward the office; although a call to an exorcist may be necessary, he knew they had a long unfinished business, and a bad mood was not a good excuse to delay the investigation.

Lorenza Sabbatini, one of the officers who witnessed the scene, watched him walking in the direction of Maurizio's office and rushed to stop him. "Are you crazy? He'll kill you!" She warned; grabbing the crucifix on the wall, she handed it to him. "Take this with you. It's the most common weapon in cases of possession."

With a chuckle, he grabbed the crucifix she handed him and walked to the office, amongst the curious stares of the other officers.

He opened the door, keeping the crucifix as a shield. "Satan, leave the body of this innocent man!" Leonardo yelled.

Maurizio was seated at his desk, trying to calm down his boiling temper. As he saw Leonardo coming in with the crucifix in his hand, he couldn't contain his laughter any longer, and his stress had released, resulting in a long hysterical laugh.

Grinning from ear to ear, Leonardo closed the door behind him and gathered the chair lying on the floor. "Better?" He placed the crucifix on the table, planning to bring it back to its place.

"I don't know, but I needed to release; I've been up until one o'clock arguing with Anna. She's right, and I should have informed her of the delay, but what was done couldn't be undone, and perhaps we should have let the incident slip away and spent the evening in peace. This morning, I woke up later than usual and got caught in the deadly traffic on the Tiburtine..." Maurizio grabbed his head between his hands.

"Come on, shit happens, now let's focus on more pleasant issues and put together some clues on this murder, shall we?" Leonardo sat down in front of the desk and started sipping his coffee.

"That would be the best solution, at least for this morning."

Maurizio's thoughts immediately switched to the case but promised to call Anna as soon as something would have given him the hint of a long day at work. *I should call her right away, then. This is starting up like one of those cases that will require most of my free time, together with the last fragments of my sanity.*

He grabbed the notebook where he scribbled all the notes from the previous day. There was already a lot of information, but nothing was producing any clear image in his mind of what had happened that night.

"We need to know more about the habits and the life of this man. Mr. Calvani probably had a complicated lifestyle, and I'm going to find out every detail of it." He stood from the chair.

"I'm finishing my coffee, and I suggest you do the same. Nevertheless, I'm going back to the lab and try to put together all the details. I'll make a list of missing information and probably, be back at the crime scene in the early afternoon to collect the data needed. I want to scan every single corner of the apartment and garage. It might take quite some time," Leonardo stood and grabbed the crucifix. "I believe we won't need this any longer— you seem back to your normal self."

With a cold stare at Leonardo's cup, Maurizio remembered he didn't have time to have breakfast. He ran to his car, rushing from his bed to the bathroom for a shower. He knew his belly would have complained far too noisily about any abuse on its rights, and with a smile, he walked in the direction of the common room to get his morning coffee. That would have given him time to straighten up his thoughts and make a clear plan as to where he should have started from.

***

When Luciano arrived in front of the faculty, Irina was waiting for him at the statue of Minerva, and as she spotted him, she paced toward him. The awkward feeling of something that had changed between them with the death of his father forced her to hesitate, before saying anything or kiss him as they used to do.

"Hi," he whispered, lowering his gaze to hold her hand.

"You look tired. Haven't you sleep last night?" she asked, entwining her fingers to his.

Luciano took some time to answer. That simple question seemed the most difficult at that moment. "It's not the fact of not having slept... I...I still can't figure out what happened. It's like living in a nightmare, with the knowledge that soon I'll wake up. Nevertheless, this is something that takes far too long to happen. I don't know how to explain the way I feel, but I'm glad to be with you now."

Her presence represented the only fragment of lucidity in his life. If he could rewind his life there would have been many things he would have undone, except falling in love with her.

They started to walk the *via dell'Università* to a cafeteria, where most of the students liked to gather for breakfast and lunch. Around the University many cafeterias were to be chosen, but that one was their favorite, maybe because it was the place where they met for the first time, and where they shared their most tender memories.

Yet, the recent happenings shook the feelings Luciano held in his heart. As they walked inside, he was grabbed by an unspeakable need to leave and never to return. Hesitating on the entrance, he turned to her, as for approval to choose another place or for an explanation to that sudden sensation rising straight from his guts.

"What's wrong?" Irina wondered noticing his confusion and hesitation. Her hand reached his shoulder with a gentle touch, as if to offer consolation to the grief for the loss of his father.

He shook his head, "I don't know, but I don't want to be here. I can't explain the reason why, but it's like something is fighting my decision to come into this place; like a warning of some sort of danger." His lips twitched into a frown.

She'd never seen him as confused as he was at that moment and wondered whether it had to do with her presence, the sudden turn their lives would have taken or anything else mixed with the recent events. Whatever the reason, she understood she needed to be with him, and as close as possible.

"Let's go somewhere else, then. We don't need to be in this particular bar," she whispered softly, guiding him outside.

"Do you think I'm crazy?" He wondered, walking the street in the direction of the next cafeteria. "I know it's completely irrational. There's nothing to be afraid of. The Police will keep searching for the assassin, and after a maximum time of one year this story will be set on the backburner until new clues will show up. Yet, I don't feel completely reassured, something keeps telling me things can get quite nasty and we're going into very difficult times."

Holding her hand tighter into his own he realized the repercussions that murder could bring to their relationship.

Whether it would have been strong enough to withstand the storm or it would have come out torn by it, they knew it was important to stick together for the sake of their mental health.

They were in that situation together and would have come out together, either as lovers or friends. A long pause of silence fell between them, as they reached the bar on Tiburtine Road.

Although the rain offered a break to the city, they preferred to have a seat in the room inside the cafeteria. The scent of coffee and fresh pastry filled the room and pleased their senses as they came inside. The place had a few patrons seated at the tables, and they chose one that was on the far end of the room, where they could hope for some privacy and chat.

Nevertheless, they remained in silence for a while before one of them could find a way to express what was on their minds.

Willing to break the freezing silence between them, he turned his eyes at her. "Waking up in the room my mother prepared for me, gave me a strange feeling of what I'm also guilty for," he said, keeping her hands in his own, collecting all the thoughts swirling in his brain since the previous day. "For all my life I considered my father an example to follow. I have been looking up to him as a role model. Not even the fact that he cheated on my mother and got divorced by her to date your mother helped me to see his true colors. His behavior toward my mother didn't influence my opinion of him and the need to be not simply accepted but being appreciated became a priority. I needed him to be proud of me. I failed to understand he was mostly absorbed with his own life, which not necessarily included me."

Irina remained silent allowing him to take out the bitterness and the feelings he kept inside himself for perhaps too long of a time.

Since she met Luciano, she could sense his frustration toward an absent father, who could find something better than spend his time with his son.

"I'm not blaming your mother for dating my father; she fell in love with him, and it wasn't her duty to care about his relationship with me. I mostly blame myself for having been so blind and having decided to go and live with him, rather than moving away with my mother."

There wasn't a steady thought he could grab onto, the most important thing he considered was getting rid of the Police from his apartment and his life. His hands grabbed his head as if to avoid it from exploding.

"I do!" her voices filled with bitterness and resentment, toughened as she clenched her fist, squeezing Luciano's fingers. "She said she loved him, but I know she was aiming to have an easy life and get out of that club."

"What if they start suspecting me of his assassination?" He suddenly raised his head to look Irina in her eyes. "How am I going to defend myself from such an accusation?"

"Don't think about it. They couldn't possibly accuse you! Everybody knows how much you loved your father, everybody who knew anything about the relationship between you two..."

"...Could have said we were often arguing!" Luciano interrupted, bringing the family relationship into a more realistic perspective. "I'm almost certain our neighbor heard the times we were raising our voices against each other when he promised to spend the weekends with me, only to break his promises regularly. Everybody could testify my frustrations of being the last of his thoughts!"

"There isn't any proof against you; there isn't any proof against any of us. Did you have the chance to talk to the detective who's taking care of the investigation?" She lowered her voice, glancing at the two girls who came to have a seat at the table close to theirs.

She turned to face him. "We need a proper place where to talk; a place where nobody can hear us." Her whisper came as a breeze to his skin.

With a nod, and without having had the time to get a coffee, he stood from the chair, gently pulling her to follow him, and without saying another word to each other, they left the cafeteria.

"It's not easy to find a good place where we can talk in private. I believe the best one is my mother's apartment. I'm now living with her, and she'll be at work until five. There, we won't have anyone who can possibly hear us." He wondered why he didn't think about inviting her there before. That could have saved some time and the awkward feeling of being watched at every step.

They walked hand in hand to the parking lot of the University where Luciano parked his car. A giggle escaped Irina as she noticed the utilitarian car he used.

For the first time his face brightened, "I would have loved taking the Lamborghini, but I predict we'll have it back after a few months. The investigation of the forensic team might take some time to analyze all the traces. I hope they'll return it in one piece." He started up the engine and immersed himself in his thoughts.

"When was the last time you talked to your mother?" That sudden question interrupting the background noise of the engine reached her ears like the boom of thunder on a clear blue sky.

Almost wondering what he asked, she took a pause, "it was yesterday. The Police had already come to ask her questions about their relationship, and she was quite shaken. For now, they considered her the main suspect, except a random thief, or someone in his working environment who considered him an obstacle to his plans to be in charge of the firm." She paused for a second, thinking about the possible suspects. "She doesn't know I'm back in Italy; I simply called her yesterday with an excuse. I'm not going to come even close to her, as she begged me not to return here until things would be cleared. She is scared that my presence would make things difficult to explain."

"This is going to get more complicated than I thought," he mumbled to himself. His father didn't have any other siblings, and being the only son himself, the ownership of the firm he built was going to be given to him and perhaps to his former wife. *What am I going to do?*

He wasn't a complete stranger to the firm, and he chose the faculty of Business and Accountancy at the university because this would have helped him when he would have taken over his father's business. This was supposed to happen gradually, as Claudio decided to retire, and it would have required more time to get familiar with all the aspects of the business.

"Luciano, remember the plan and stick with it. None of us will be accused of murder. The Police will certainly investigate my mother's life, and there, my father will appear with his abuses and his criminal life. It won't take long before another suspect populates the list."

Nodding, he lowered his head. "I do remember the plan. I feel like the Police will think about me before going to investigate the past life of your mother."

"Everything will be fine; you'll see unless there's something else bothering you besides the investigation" Irina tried to guess his thoughts by the way he tightly gripped the steering wheel. She pursed her lips, almost regretting having asked an apparently stupid question. *Obviously, there are more implications to his father's death than just the need to stay away from any suspect.*

Luciano continued to drive as if he didn't hear what she said, but as the car stopped in front of the building where he was living, he leaned his head on the headrest.

"I guess I'll have to solve one problem at a time," he said after a long pause. His voice sounded calm, but the light tremors of his hands revealed a storm going on in his soul. He turned his head rolling on the headrest, and as his eyes met hers, he simpered. "This has nothing to do with us."

His hand reached for her thigh in an encouraging caress as his voice was but a whisper like the wind through the trees on a summer evening. He wasn't sure whether he was trying to encourage himself or reassure her about their relationship.

"I won't go away; I'll be by your side, whatever the situation will turn into," she tried to smile. "We need to plan our actions from now on, and we need to be careful. I'm not sure whether this might mean for us to stay away from each other for a while or not..." A frown creased her forehead.

"Let's talk about it inside, please. I can't be alone today." his voice trembled, overwhelmed by the thunderstorm building up in his soul.

"Sure," she opened the door of the car and got out, hurrying to get inside as avoiding being seen. Although nobody in the neighborhood knew her, she felt like her presence should never be connected with Luciano.

With rushed steps, they hurried to the building, scoping out the area, hoping there were no Police cars coming for more questioning. Although Luciano was expecting them to inform him about their arrival or to get some sort of appointment to ask some questions, there was always the chance to have them around unexpectedly.

Holding their breaths until they reached the apartment, a relieved exhale escaped Luciano as he closed the door behind him. He felt his knees suddenly weak and held himself to the door, trying to keep from falling to the floor.

A subtle hysterical laughter broke the spell, freeing the tension between them. His mind got clearer and his thoughts sharper.

Luciano knew what he needed to do, and perhaps it was better going on with his life. That was at least what was expected of him and with the time, things would have returned to a new normality. Glancing around, he wasn't alone, he had his mother, who would have never turned her back on him, and then there was Irina, the woman who shared with him more than any other human being during his first 21 years of life in the world.

"We shouldn't allow our fears and feelings overwhelm us. We need to be sharp and keep calm," he breathed, walking away from the door as his legs could carry him.

With a nod, she gleamed at him and scanned the surroundings to get familiar with the new environment. "This is a nice place."

"Thank you, would you like a coffee?" he asked, guiding her to have a seat on the sofa in the living room. He felt the whole situation surreal, in other circumstances, when they were alone in the home of his father, having a coffee would have been the last thing he thought about.

However, in that situation, he wasn't sure sex was even on the list of the things he could consider, especially in his mother's apartment. It was an environment, which was still alien to him.

After his mother moved away due to the divorce, their lives seemed to divide and although he loved her, the fact of not living like a family anymore created a deep rupture in their relationship.

Thinking of bringing Irina to his bedroom, felt like abusing the hospitality of a friend.

With a grin, Irina walked slowly toward him and wrapped her arms around his neck. "How about you show me the rest of the house, starting with your bedroom?" Her voice whispering in his ear.

The feeling of her body close to his and the scent of her skin, melding with her perfume, was enough to make him forget about everything; a new sensation arose, allowing his instincts to kick in. Driven by the growing passion and the need to feel the touch of her skin, he lifted her from the floor as their lips fused together into a passionate kiss.

CHAPTER 7

During the next few weeks life for Luciano returned to normal, or at least what was supposed to become his new normality.

Neither he nor his mother heard anything from the Police or from Detective Scala, who was conducting the investigation, and having requested not to have any mention about the details to the press. the Newspapers limited their articles to short columns about the news in the case.

If there was something Giulia always despised, it was the way some of the press tried to intrude into the private lives of common citizens, especially when a murder happened.

Certain things had nothing to do with the reporting of the news, and everything with the need for sensationalism that sold more copies of this or the other paper. She felt disgusted by the way they were feeding their readers with fabricated news and hypotheses, theories about who could have been the killer and why a man like Claudio Calvani was murdered.

Certainly, according to Giulia, a jerk like her ex-husband got exactly what he deserved, yet this was simply her own opinion driven mostly by the bitterness she feared would have resided in her heart for the rest of her life.

Nevertheless, that disgrace wasn't something she wished for her son, who obviously viewed his father as a god, a person to emulate, not for what concerned the way he treated his wife, but for the way he conducted his business. For the sake of her son, she'd step in to help with the funeral, once the body would be released by the forensics. One thing she was expecting was Luciano to receive the letter from the attorney with the invitation to the reading of Claudio's holographic wills. The firm had to remain in business and needed a leader who could take charge.

Returning from work, Giulia found two letters bearing the name of the Antonioni law firm in the mailbox. One, as she expected for Luciano, and the other was the invitation to the reading extended to her.

"Luciano!" she called from the main door as she entered the apartment. "There's a letter for you. It's the invitation for the reading of your father's testament."

Coming from his room, Luciano gaped at her as if he wasn't expecting anything like this to happen. "How do you know what it is?" he wondered, taking the letter in his hands.

"Because I received exactly the same one from your father's attorney, and there was the invitation," she replied, slipping her heels away with a deep relieving sigh.

With a puzzled expression frowning his brows, Luciano opened the letter and started to read. "It will be for Friday," a mumble escaped his mouth.

"Are you busy?" joked Giulia.

"No, I was simply wondering. What I am curious to know is who else had been invited. Should we tell this detail to the Police?" he wondered, following his mother to the living room as she collapsed on the couch.

Yawning and massaging her neck, she tried to recall what was agreed with the detective last time she met him. "I guess, at least Detective Scala should be informed. All the people who will benefit from your father's death are those who are most likely to be suspected of his assassination. As for me, I'm surprised to be invited, I was sure your father left everything to you and his new girlfriend." That last word was uttered with an unveiled bitterness tone in her voice.

Luciano sat down beside his mother, holding her to himself. A smile brightened up her face as she kissed his hair, "I'm sorry if my bitterness toward your father has spoiled your memories. The fact that it didn't work between us, shouldn't mean you had to take part in our divorce. You know he loved you as much as I do," she said, feeling elated to have Luciano once again back in her life.

They both remained holding each other in silence for a while.

"You have all the reasons to be bitter toward him. He hasn't been a model of fairness toward you. Regardless of whether he is now dead, we should forget about old grudges." He stood smiling at her.

"One thing for sure, is sooner or later, you'll need to step in and think about the business he'd been building up. It wasn't simply something he built for himself. He always hoped you would have taken over on leading the firm. Perhaps, after this reading and when the bureaucratic matters are solved, you'll have to make a decision about it."

Luciano nodded slowly, thinking about the way he would have approached the issue. His intention was not to sell the business, that was something he didn't want to even think about. Yet, someone needed to take the reins and start working in the same direction his father did.

Noting his thoughtful expression darkened by concern and perhaps, also fear, she understood he was probably far too young and inexperienced to completely run the entire business alone.

From the day they got married, she helped Claudio daily with the expansion of his company, helping with the bookkeeping, communications with the clients, and bureaucratic matters. She had her job at the administration of the National Postal Services, but she gladly sacrificed her free time to help her husband expand and fulfill his dream to bring the family business to its maximum potential.

She stood from the couch and walked to the bathroom, willing only to have a long shower and wash away all the tiredness of the working day, together with the weight of the memories the testament brought back to her mind.

We thought this was going to be something to bond us together; a project for our lives and for the future of our children, she thought as she enjoyed the warm and relaxing shower. *Everything changed when our lives settled into a routine and Luciano turned eighteen years old. Then, he met **her**, and our life together meant nothing anymore.*

She slipped into something more comfortable other than her business attire and her thoughts turned to informing the Police about the upcoming testament reading.

***

Maurizio was in his office, after returning from a well-needed chat with the employees at the firm Claudio owned. Besides the tension for the uncertain future of the business and the eventual redistribution of the working places, nobody seemed to have any problem of going along with Claudio.

"Every person I've spoken to would describe him as a very easy-going person, understanding and professional. This, at least, might take away any sort of jealousy in the firm." His voice resounded between the walls of the empty room. He raised his glance from the keyboard of his laptop, where he was putting in order his notes, and felt the loneliness of not having either Leonardo or members of his team to brainstorm with.

It wasn't the first time he was working alone, but certainly, it was the first time he felt lonely. Leonardo was finalizing the collection of the data from the apartment. Once it would have been completed, they would have gone through all the bits of information and get an exact idea of what happened that evening and what could have been the reason for murdering Claudio.

The ringing of his mobile phone resounded in the room, giving him a sense of gratitude, toward whoever came to rescue him from his loneliness.

"Scala," he answered with his usual firm tone.

"Good afternoon, Detective, this is Giulia Martini, Claudio Calvani's ex-wife. I'm not sure whether you need to know this particular detail, but I feel like it's better to know too much than too few in this case," she commenced as she walked to the kitchen to get a soda from the fridge.

Leaning on his chair, his expression relaxed. "Good afternoon to you, Mrs. Martini. How can I help you?"

"Well, today, as I came back from work, as usual, I had checked the mailbox, and between the regular correspondence, I received two letters, one for me and one for Luciano. We both have been invited this Friday to the reading of the holographic final will of Claudio," she explained, hoping this wasn't useless information that could be considered a waste of time. "I was surprised to receive the invitation as well; I was sure he'd left everything to Luciano and his new girlfriend."

Maurizio grabbed a pen from the desk and started playing with it as a smile opened up on his face, recalling how Leonardo found this way to release his stress: tapping any object he could find against the surface of the desk annoying. "That indeed is a very important piece of information and, if you permit me, I will need to be there as well. Do you have any idea of who else may have been invited to the reading?"

Shaking her head and scrutinizing the letter once again to check whether the names of those who would participate were listed, she replied. "No, Detective, I believe the only way you can find this information is to call the attorney who is handling this case. I wish I were more helpful."

"You have been very helpful with this call. One thing I would ask you is the time of the appointment and the address where you are supposed to meet. I will be there as well and, perhaps, I will get the opportunity to have a chat with the attorney who has taken charge of the will." He searched for a piece of paper where he could write down the address.

There was his laptop sitting on his desk, ready to take any sort of input, but Maurizio was still attached to the old-fashioned pen and paper method of note-taking. He felt like they were far handier, when it was a question of taking fast notes.

"Yes, the Antonioni Law firm is the one who's taking care of the case and you can refer to Silvia Antonioni, who is the attorney who sent us the invitation. I believe she took care of the legal business of Claudio. It might also be the law firm that was the one who was paid in case of legal issues with his business. We are supposed to meet there at three o'clock in the afternoon, and the address is '*via Cola di Rienzo, 100.*'" Her eyes browsed around the room and met the clock on the wall. With a grimace, she acknowledged that the time to prepare dinner was approaching.

Living alone, she never had to adhere to any timetable, but as Luciano moved into the same apartment, she returned to the routine of having dinner together at the usual time they used to have it, when they were once a family.

A melancholic sigh escaped her mouth, recalling those times, so far in the past to fool her as they belonged to someone else's life.

"Yes, thank you very much," he answered as he finished writing down the address. "Is there anything wrong?" Maurizio wondered, acknowledging her tone.

"No, Detective. I was thinking about preparing dinner," She giggled, amused, standing from the chair. "I'm no longer living alone, and this means timetables and routines have to be restored."

Folding the note, he placed it in his wallet. He nodded and recalled that probably he also was supposed to either call home or to consider the day over.

"You're right. I will have a chat with the attorney, and I'll be there for the reading of the wills," Maurizio stood from the chair, stretching his back. "Thank you very much for the information and I shall see you on Friday."

As he ended the conversation with Giulia, Maurizio thought he'd better tend to straight up the relationship with his wife. Therefore, he considered informing her that he was about to leave and prayed to be home as soon as possible. Later the traffic on the Tiburtine Road would have been unforgiving, and at best he knew he needed to get a head start.

He switched off the computer and walked away, trying his best not to even think about the investigation, at least until the morning after or until someone would have called him in the middle of the night.

As he entered his car, he decided to message Anna. "The important thing is that she knows I'm on my way."

The beeping of another message was coming in as he placed the phone on the passenger seat and made him regret his choice; he was risking an endless chat with his wife, but at the same time, he was glad she promptly replied. *'Whatever you do, don't take the Tiburtine Road to come back. There's been an accident, and the traffic is completely jammed. You'll spend the night there!'*

"Why am I not surprised about it? But that's a great piece of information, I will have to set up the navigator to find an alternative road." He typed a fast *'Thank you, sweetheart'* and started on his new route.

Every evening was the same old story, and many times, together with his wife they considered the possibility to move to another part of the city. Yet, every time they thought about it, either the real estate market was frozen, or the apartments were completely unaffordable.

"I'm afraid we should hire a real estate agent to search for something for us. This is not certainly the way we can go on," he mumbled. "It might take some time, but if we don't take a firm decision about it, we will live forever trapped by the confines of Tiburtine Road."

It took almost two hours for Maurizio to reach his apartment and considering the deviation he needed to take to avoid the accident on a route, which was supposed to be the fastest, he considered himself satisfied.

Coming inside the apartment and slipping off his shoes to fit into more comfortable house slippers, gave him a sense of peace, one that put a smile on his face, regardless of the day he had.

The scent of food coming from the kitchen and the television on made him feel that this was the only place on earth he ever wanted to be: his home, with the only people he would never have enough of.

"Maurizio, you just arrived in time for dinner— go wash your hands and join us!" The chanting tone of Anna's voice reached him like the trumpets of Heaven. He looked around and realized how lucky he was, and how he never appreciated enough of what he had.

Anna was the most amazing gift he had from life, with her patience to put up with his job that caused him to behave almost carelessly.

Returning from the bathroom, he hurried to the dining room, where everything was waiting for him, and almost with tears in his eyes, he reached Anna and held her tightly.

"What have you done?" she asked with a suspicious tone, parting from him. That was a behavior she was expecting when he had something to be forgiven for.

"I have never appreciated you enough, and I'm afraid I've also taken our relationship for granted, when instead I should have worked harder to make sure nothing could ever disturb this perfection. Yet, although I know, how important it is to remind you about my love, I never do so. I keep forgetting things, and let you wait."

There was a long pause of silence between them, when Anna tried her best to understand whether he was just kidding, as usual or he was serious.

She brought her hand to his forehead, "No, you're not feverish." Her voice started fickle with concern.

"I have been thinking about the argument we had, and you were completely right." He needed to take out all the right words coming out from his soul. "I don't take into account the effort you are putting into our life; the care for Giovanna, the care for the house, and your work..."

"Maurizio, Giovanna is at kindergarten from eight in the morning to four in the afternoon, and the home is clean mainly thanks to Ms. Pina, who comes three times a week to take care of it," she tried to explain that she wasn't by any means to be compared to Cinderella. "Of course, there are things I care for by myself here, but they are minor things if we compare to those who can't afford paying for a maid."

He closed his eyes and held her hands in his own, "I wish I had more time to spend with you two and be more present. I have chosen a terrible job to start with, but maybe I can try to make it up to you. I was considering moving us to a better part of the city, where none of us need to be stuck in the terrible traffic of the Tiburtine Road." He looked deep into her chestnut brown eyes.

"We tried many times, but without any success," she protested. Anna hoped they could move away, but only the thought of moving and packing everything made her feel tired.

"I will take care of everything; all you need to do is come with me to see the available homes. I'll call a real estate agent tomorrow, first thing in the morning, and from that moment on, you won't have to think about it," he assured. "This is the least I can do."

Her face brightened up, "Then we have a deal, but how about we eat our dinner, now? I'm starving!"

As they were eating, Anna scrutinized him, "How is the investigation going?" She hesitated a bit to ask about the latest case, because she knew the family requested the press blackout to protect their privacy, but sometimes there isn't the need for any press to make sure the news is spread around the population.

"We are still at the preliminary phases and gathering all the information about everybody, but we don't have any leads to anybody. The family wants to keep everything within the walls of their houses, and I can understand their feelings. It's not easy to be under the spotlight when you're mourning the death of a family member," he explained without coming into details of the investigation.

"I know. I was a bit curious, and I have been literally bombed at work and by people I know, about this case. I always say that you don't have permission to talk about it with me, so I don't know anything about it. However, sometimes it's difficult to keep them quiet. I wish there was more information about it from the press, but I'm afraid I will have to contain those news-hungry beasts. "An amused laugh escaped her.

"I know. I understand it mustn't be easy," he grinned sarcastically.

CHAPTER 8

On Friday, Maurizio reached the attorney's office a little in advance. He wanted to have a chat with Silvia Antonioni, who had arranged to summon the heirs.

She was a woman of an undefined age, possibly between thirty and forty. Her career would have suggested the latter, but glancing at the fire burning in her eyes, and the care in the way she chose her dress, she could have been younger. That was the kind of person Maurizio feared the most because there wasn't any chance to predict her thoughts, not at least based on the generation she'd been growing into.

Luckily for him, she wasn't one of the suspects, rather a possible ally, which made him more comfortable with the questions he needed to ask, before the reading of the testament.

"Thank you for granting me an appointment before the reading," he commenced, shaking her hand, and smiling amiably at her.

"There are no reasons for me to deny you some time, and I agree in this case, you will need all the information to find the person who murdered Mr. Calvani. Please, have a seat," she replied, inviting him to get more comfortable. "I have to admit the news of the death of my client came as quite a shock."

"Thank you," Maurizio replied, smiling. "There is one thing I constantly keep thinking, that being the time when Mr. Calvani gave you his holographic will."

She brought a hand to her mouth, thinking about it, and lowered her gaze at the pile of papers she had accumulated on her desk. "Let me check; I believe he changed it many times." She browsed through the folder. "He gave me the first version of the testament five years ago. At that time, he was still married to his wife, Mrs. Giulia Martini. A couple of years ago, he gave me a new one and informed me that he added three life insurances, one in favor of his son, one in favor of his mother who remained alone after the death of her husband, and another to a certain Madlen Fazekas."

At hearing her name, Maurizio froze, feeling he got a great piece of information that could have produced an important milestone.

"How much is the sum to be corresponded to each of those three beneficiaries?" His heart thumped in his chest.

"It was twenty million euros. However, since his mother died last year, her part will be divided between the other two beneficiaries, according to the contract he undersigned with the insurance company, so at the moment his son and Ms. Fazekas would receive thirty million each," she explained, raising her eyes back to Maurizio. She knew exactly what he was thinking.

He averted the glance from her and scanned the room to find a place to fix his attention on, a place that could have given him the chance to focus on his assumptions. The library at the right side of the desk where Silvia was seated grabbed his attention and offered him the best item to focus on.

Well, we have two winners in the lottery of life. One is the son, who would have inherited most of his father's wealth, so thirty million more or less wouldn't make a big difference in the whole jackpot. Yet, this is not a good reason for excluding him from the list of the people who had a reason to have Claudio Calvani dead. The other one is a stripper for whom the same figure would have meant a radical change of life. She was certainly maintained by her boyfriend, but we all know that relationships come and go, and he might have dumped her as he did with his wife. If this had happened, she would have had to return to her dancing career, but this time, considering her age, she wouldn't find another deal.

His mind was working like an overheated machine, and the possibility that Madlen had one of the best reasons to kill Claudio started to take over his mind, giving him a steady direction for his investigation.

I need to know more about this woman's background, where was she born, her family, why did she choose to come to Italy... I need everything, Maurizio pondered, caressing the stubbles on his chin, keeping his glance steady on the bookcase.

Silvia remained watching him, trying to guess what his thoughts were. It wasn't difficult to imagine he was contemplating the idea of having Ms. Fazekas accused of the murder of Claudio Calvani, and if she had to be honest, it sounded like the most promising lead to solve the murder. *Yet, there is still time and a long list of details, I'm afraid will come out from this case.*

"So, let me understand one thing," he turned his eyes on her. "He changed his will, and he added a life insurance policy to make sure his new girlfriend wouldn't have had to fight legally if the direct heirs contested the will, and they would most probably have won, leaving her without anything, back to where she started."

"That's a possibility, yes." She wondered where he was heading to, but she was waiting for him to clarify his train of thoughts.

"Yet, I don't understand the reason why a healthy middle-aged man writes a testament and in addition, he stipulates three life insurance policies, for which he might have paid quite a sum. What was he afraid of? Did he feel threatened and considered a murder something feasible to happen? But then, why to also include his son? He would have been the direct heir," he growled, biting his lower lip, hoping to find an answer to all those questions as soon as possible.

Silvia glanced at her clock and exhaled. "Those are indeed interesting questions, Detective Scala, but now we need to reach the room where my guests have arrived. Since Mrs. Martini has invited you, and you are investigating the case of Mr. Calvani's murder, I believe you will find some of the answers in the reading of the testament."

She stood up, gathering the folders on her desk, ready to reach the room designated for the meeting.

The air was already heated as they entered the room. The tension between Madlen and Giulia was tangible, and Luciano tried his best to act as a cushion between the two, who might have forgotten their ladyship and start fighting like wrestlers in the arena.

"Ehem." Silvia coughed gently to gather their attention, as she entered the room with Maurizio walking behind her. "Good afternoon, everybody. I would appreciate it if you could leave your arguments outside this office, so we can go forward with the reading."

It wasn't the first time that people who arrived to listen to the testament of a dear one, took the chance to take out old and new strife. It belonged to the process. After the mourning, they were ready to bury each other to get their hands on the inheritance. Regardless of whether it was for a pin or for a fortune, people always had to argue about who deserved and who didn't.

Giulia glared at Madlen with pursed lips, before turning her eyes to the attorney, and Madlen grunted, placing her chair as far as possible from her.

With a smirk, Maurizio grabbed one of the chairs available and went to sit down between the two opponents, to avoid any further action that would have taken place, thus allowing the reading to start in a peaceful manner.

His position also had a strategic value, as the young Calvani, who sat on the other side was clearly observable from the point he was. Madlen's and Luciano's reactions and behavior were what he aimed to observe. Giulia was certainly bitter, but it was clear she didn't have any reason or possibility to kill her ex-husband.

Silvia sat down at her desk and scanned, one after the other, the people in the room. "As you all know, I have invited you here this afternoon to read you the final wills of Mr. Claudio Calvani. Each of you has been mentioned in his testament, and I wish to have the chance to finish the reading without any interruption, and particularly to have this session proceed in the most civilized way." She glanced at Giulia and Madlen, who were obviously the only two people present in the room who were ready to start a fight.

She took a short pause, and when she was sure she had their spirits calmed, with a slow movement, she opened the folder, where the testament was stored. Taking another visual tour of the heirs, Silvia began the reading:

I, Claudio Calvani, hereby declare that this is my last will and testament. I declare that I am of legal age to make this will and sound of mind and body. It expresses my wishes without undue influence or duress.

Although I have divorced my wife Giulia Martini, I recognize that without her help, the family business would have never reached the point where it is now. She has been working hard to keep our family intact. Despite the fact that our paths have taken on different directions, I feel obliged to recognize her the ownership of half of the family business.

The other half is to go to my son, and I hope he will take advantage of the experience Giulia can offer, as to have a solid base for his career and one of future generations.

I possess a few real estate properties I have invested in, and they all will go to my son, Luciano. Certainly, we've had arguments in our life, but I hope he understood I never stopped loving him and never will.

Maurizio glanced at Luciano's reaction, and he was sure he could spot a slight twitch of his mouth, like a sarcastic grin that was forced back. His expression didn't transpire any sort of emotion, and he wondered whether this was something to be considered. Giulia, instead, looked surprised for being included in the testament. Her open-mouthed expression had rendered her speechless, which was completely fitting for the situation. Madlen was perhaps still waiting to understand why she was summoned there, as there hadn't been left anything for her share. Yet, she remained silently waiting.

The attorney went on:

In my life, I have also considered the eventuality that my business could drop and be crushed by the competitors and leaving a dead company wouldn't have sounded anything a parent should have looked for. For this reason, I have stipulated three life insurances. They all have the same value of 20 million Euros. The first one goes to my mother, the second one goes to Luciano, and the third one goes to Madlen Fazekas, my girlfriend. I understand if I had her included in the testament, my son wouldn't have accepted to share the firm with a stranger. Somehow, I sense some hostility toward Madlen, although, so far, they've never met. I believe it has to do with her being the reason for the divorce from Giulia. I hope this decision won't create any conflict between the heirs, and they will be able to keep any feelings of resentment aside.

Silvia slowly placed the paper on her desk and raised her eyes to her audience.

There was a long pause of silence, when nobody could find the right words to be spoken. Maurizio knew that was just a temporary situation and soon, all hell was going to break loose. Glancing at Silvia, he understood she was also waiting for the bomb to explode.

"That's the reason why you killed him!" Giulia yelled, standing from her chair glaring at Madlen. "You wanted his life insurance!"

Madlen was obviously still shocked by the news, and it appeared as if she had no idea of the existence of such a piece of the settlement.

"I had no idea! I loved Claudio, I would never have killed him, and I didn't know anything about this insurance!" She stood from the chair and felt the judging stares of everyone on her. Indeed, that was the most obvious reason for someone to kill, but she was ready to swear on everything she hadn't done it.

She glanced at Maurizio, who remained calmly seated on the chair, pondering on the situation, observing the reactions, and trying to get an opinion about it.

"Aren't you going to do anything, Detective?" Giulia wondered, outraged at his calm demeanor.

"Mrs. Martini, what am I supposed to do?" Maurizio furrowed his brows, knowing she was wondering why he hadn't already arrested Madlen for the murder of her ex-husband. "Having a good reason for killing Mr. Calvani, is not sufficient proof to bring her to jail. The investigation is still ongoing, and we need more than just a suspicion."

Madlen toured with her eyes Maurizio and Giulia as if to wonder whether they could have decided her fate right away.

Giulia threw her hands in the air in an exasperated attempt to be heard, or to have someone who could have listened to her. "That woman stole my husband, just to kill him!" She pointed her finger to Madlen, her voice trembling as old feelings appeared from a hidden corner of her heart; the same feelings she still held for the man she married. Despite the fact that she addressed him as a jerk and asshole, without the intervention of Madlen in their lives, she would still have addressed him with dear words. "Without her, my husband and I would have remained married, and he would still be alive today." Tears welled from her eyes.

"Claudio came to me, not the other way round. I had no idea he was married. When I met him, he told me he was planning a divorce."

Madlen tried to defend herself and her relationship with Claudio.

"Bullshit!" Giulia yelled at the top of her lungs.

"Mrs. Martini, please come with me, you need to calm down," Silvia came to offer her a friendly shoulder to cry on. Holding Giulia, she guided her outside, glancing at Maurizio, hoping he understood he needed to bring Madlen outside and try to calm the waters.

"I guess we all need to leave now," Maurizio announced, glancing at Madlen and Luciano. One thing baffled him; it was that Luciano appeared as cold as ice for the entire length of the reading. He had no idea whether he was a person who preferred to keep everything inside, even the tears and emotions, or there was something sincerely disturbing about his behavior.

"I will go to see whether my mother needs my help," Luciano whispered, and without greeting or waiting for any answer from Maurizio or Madlen, he left the room, walking in the same direction as Giulia.

"Detective, you have to believe me, I haven't killed Claudio. He never talked to me about any means to secure my future—we were not thinking about the possibility of dying. He was still young!" Tears started to flow like a river from her eyes, and Maurizio could understand the reason why he felt attracted to this woman. Scala didn't try to justify Claudio, but her beauty was something uncommon to be seen in everyday life.

"Ms. Fazekas, you certainly understand I have to consider this as proof. Yet, it doesn't mean I am going to arrest you only on this basis until we find who is responsible for the murder of Claudio Calvani." He locked his eyes on hers, trying to make her feel confident that despite the fact that there were a few suspects, there wasn't any steady lead on anyone at the moment.

"I loved Claudio," she wept, trying to wipe her tears away.

Gently Maurizio placed a hand on her shoulder, and guided her out of the room, and the building. As they were in the parking lot, she turned her glance at Maurizio. "Thank you, Detective Scala. I will return home now, and I will remain available to answer every question you need."

"Do you need a ride back home?" he asked.

With a fast shake of her head, she tried to smile, "No. Thank you, perhaps a bit of fresh air will help me to clear my thoughts. All I need now is to be alone."

With those words, she turned on her heels and walked away.

Maurizio remained there for a moment before deciding to take the car and return to the precinct. He looked at the clock; it was already four o'clock. He knew that returning to the office meant he had to write down his impressions and some notes about the new details obtained during the day. "I'll be late again, so it's better if I inform Anna about this. She can have her dinner with Giovanna and leave something for me," he mumbled as he started to write her a message.

Placing the mobile phone back in his pocket, he recalled he was also supposed to contact the real estate manager to start finding buyers for his apartment and another place to move to. *This is not something I can't take care of personally; they need to step in and make the deal for me.*

As he was reaching his car, his mobile phone started to ring. That was something he wasn't expecting, particularly because it came from an unknown number, and it was to his personal number.

"Scala," he answered.

"Detective, this is Berenice Moretti, and I happened to recall some details that might be of interest in your investigation," she kept her voice low as if she needed to hide from somebody.

Dumbfounded on how she possibly could have had access to his private number, he remained silent for a moment. "Mrs. Moretti, who gave you this number?"

"Never underestimate an elderly lady. I have lived longer and have seen many things you would never imagine. I have my ways to get the information I need," she giggled, amused. "There's a young lady working at the reception desk of the

Police Department who is my hairdresser's daughter. We've known each other since forever, and although she was a little reticent, she understood my information was of vital importance to the investigation."

"Well, if it's so, then I'm all ears..."

"You are not expecting me to tell you those details on the phone. You should know better than me that those devices are easily intercepted. I am not going to have indiscreet ears listening to what I need to tell you, so you'll have to come here," she kept whispering.

A deep exhale escaped him, making him regretting having ever talked to that woman. Nevertheless, she could have important information, and every road was worth trying, but perhaps not that day, as he already knew it would have taken almost an eternity and a half to go through all the details of the reading. "Would it be okay if I come by tomorrow morning?"

"Why can't you come right away?" she wondered, surprised that the detective seemed to underestimate the importance of her information.

"Because at the moment I'm busy and it will take at least three hours to have things ready for me to reach you. I would also like to return to my life for the evening," he explained with a smile on his face.

A short pause was necessary for her to think about what was better to do, "So it shall be. I will write down everything I need to tell you, so I won't forget overnight. I am sure I'll remember, but it's better to have a backup somewhere," she declared walking to the living room to find a notebook where she could write everything down.

"Brilliant idea. At what time would it be convenient for you to meet me?" he asked as he started to walk once again to his car.

"After seven o'clock, any time is fine for me," she replied, expecting him to reach her perhaps a bit later.

"I will be there at nine o'clock. It might take some time with the morning traffic on the streets," he considered, thinking about the best route from the Police Precinct to the apartment where she lived.

"I'll be waiting for you, Detective. Thank you for your attention, and have a good evening."

"Good night to you too, Mrs. Moretti."

Placing his phone on the passenger seat, he sighed. He wondered whether his life could have been easier without improvised detectives, who have seen too many Hollywood movies and considered themselves real investigators.

Shaking his head, he started up the engine, focusing only on what he needed to take care of once he would be back in the office.

He hoped he could count on the help of Leonardo, but he knew that for the moment, he would have been extremely busy with the results of the lab and wouldn't have the time to brainstorm together.

CHAPTER 9

That night, in the darkness of his room, Luciano couldn't sleep. The reading of his father's will brought many thoughts to his mind and he wondered whether the one who was supposed to die was Madlen, or maybe both together.

If it weren't for her, it would have been his job, his friends, another woman, or whatever other excuses. He never had time for me; I was just an accessory or a plan B, for those times when he had nothing to do.

He stood from his bed, and switched the lights on, to avoid being left alone in the darkness with his ghosts and demons. He wanted to call Irina as his glance met the alarm clock on the bedside table.

She's probably sleeping. I should have called her earlier, but I needed to calm down my mother, and from now on we will need to think about the running of the firm. That place won't run by itself, regardless of whether the leading team can go on for the general matters, they need to have a representative figure in place.

He tiptoed to the window, to avoid making any noise.

He slowly opened the window, to allow the nighttime buzz of the city to enter and break the silence taunting him.

The slight background noise of the few cars that circulated comforted him and, despite the cold night air, he considered the possibility of keeping the window open, so as not to be assailed again, by that agonizing loneliness.

Fearing that he had underestimated the consequences of his father's death, he felt a sense of oppression at the thought of the responsibilities that would soon be placed on his shoulders.

The following morning he should have returned to attend classes at the university. *I'm also wondering whether this would be the end of my academic career. I should probably get started immediately with running the business— after all, this is going to be my job from this moment on.*

The thought of having a job before reaching the middle of his studies, was something that comforted yet scared him. It was extremely difficult to create a career from nothing, and many would have paid whatever sum to be able to secure a solid career in the family business.

Most people had to struggle to find a regular job. Yet, he suddenly felt unfit for the role and wondered whether it would have been only a question of learning those managerial skills his father mastered to perfection, or that was something he was supposed to have as a natural gift.

With a slow movement, shivering from the cold, he closed the windows, as the world with its noises and struggles came to him as a barely audible muffled sound.

Once again, the silence dropped like a heavy curtain on the room.

"I need to sleep now. Tomorrow I will think about the rest, and perhaps Mom will help me, guiding me to this new chapter in my life." He walked to the writing table, and grabbing one sheet of paper, he started to make a list of things he needed to solve.

The first one being the work situation, second his academic career. Should he quit or try a part-time working schedule to fulfill at least the bachelor's degree? Another thing was to start the process to obtain the insurance money and secure the funds.

"Another important thing is to have a chat with Irina, and straighten up things as well with her. I wish I could say I would marry her, but if I told my mother I have a relationship with the daughter of the woman who stole her husband, it would cause a deeper scar in her heart," he whispered, staring at the ceiling as if to find a solution to solve his life from that bundle of emotions, complications and bureaucratic matters, clogging his mind making him unable to think clearly.

He closed his eyes, hoping to receive any sort of help or enlightenment, but nothing arrived. The siren of an ambulance from afar reached his ears and forced his eyes to open. He remained frozen for a moment to follow the wailing of sirens as it faded away.

That sound, closely related to that of the Police cars had his heart pounding in his chest. He wondered whether this feeling would have accompanied him for the rest of his life, or will there come a time when he could listen to Police cars arriving without fearing them. Time would have provided an answer, and probably it would have taken some time to fully recover from that feeling. "I need to sleep, before I lose my mind." He stood from the chair and decided to get some sleeping pills.

***

The morning after, Maurizio reached the address of Berenice exactly on time, and the presence of the Forensic Police car parked in front of it, gave him the idea to go and check what was the situation going on there. That was the perfect chance to kill two birds with one stone. He could have a chat with Leonardo about the reading he witnessed the previous day and having a visit with Berenice, hoping none of the two actions would have resulted in a waste of time.

He would have generally taken the elevator to reach the top floor, but on that occasion, he considered climbing the stairs, to get another perspective of the building and about the people living there. The building was not very tall, only four floors, but those seven flights of stairs felt like one hundred, and Maurizio reached the floor breathless.

Leonardo was coming out from Calvani's apartment at the same moment as Maurizio placed his hand on the wall to sustain his body, which wanted to collapse.

"Getting old?" he chuckled.

Maurizio glared at him. "Not today. The morning started to piss me off already, don't you get into it, too, please!" His voice, still gritty from the climb.

"We're a little edgy today." Leonardo raised his hands in mid-air, and went to the elevator, "by the way, for your information, it works."

A loud growl forced Leonardo to flee inside the elevator to escape Maurizio's rage.

Drawing a deep breath, Maurizio turned his eyes to the apartment where Berenice stood, tapping her foot on the floor, a disapproving frown darkening her features. "Detective Scala, I wish to remind you, this is a respectable and civilized neighborhood, and these types of sounds, belonging more to a caveman than to a civilized human won't be tolerated." Her voice echoed in the hall through the staircases, and Maurizio felt like a child caught by his mother doing mischief.

Pursing his lips, he peered at her. "I'm sorry, Mrs. Moretti, you're right, I should have behaved in a more considerate way."

Berenice's features relaxed at his apologies, and a smile brightened her eyes. "Well, let's not think about it anymore, I have something you might be interested to know," she said, inviting him into her apartment.

Closing the door behind him, she inspected the room as if she wanted to make sure nobody was in earshot. When she was sure she could speak freely, she commenced, "You see, I remembered Luciano, the son of Mr. Calvani, had a girlfriend. I've never seen her, but I know she visited him here every now and then, so I can't say who she is or what she looks like. One thing I do know for sure is she's a foreigner, and her name is Irina." She guided him to the living room, inviting him to have a seat on the same couch where they had a chat the first time.

Glancing around, Maurizio started to feel the environment familiar, as much as the scents of the old furniture, together with the aroma of the coffee she obviously just brewed for him.

"I'm going to get the coffee, a morning without it is not even closely acceptable," she giggled as she walked with fast little steps toward the kitchen.

When she returned, she was carrying a tray with biscuits and sweets together with two cups of coffee. Maurizio stood up immediately and helped her.

"Thank you, Detective, my movements are no more as prompt as they used to be when I was a teenager. Those were the times!" she complained, observing Maurizio placing the tray carefully on the small table and helping her to sit on the armchair.

"Let me understand one thing, how do you know so many things about this potential girlfriend, when you haven't ever seen her?" Maurizio wondered, fearing he would have regretted that question.

"Well, I might not have seen her, but when she was here, she didn't sound like your typical friend, if you know what I mean. These walls contain some noises from one apartment to another, but not everything, and particularly loud voices can be heard distinctly, whether you want it or not," she replied, sipping her coffee.

And certainly, there isn't anything you don't want to hear about the neighbors, he thought, amused. "I still don't understand why this is something you consider important for the investigation. After all, Rome is a cosmopolitan metropolis, and a university student like Luciano gets in touch daily with people coming from every place in this world. Moreover, he's a young man, and I can't see anything strange in the fact that he has a girlfriend."

He slowly reached the tray with the biscuits and grabbed one. He knew he wasn't supposed to accept anything when he was on duty, but how can one refuse the hospitality of a kind elderly lady? It would have sounded impolite not to accept anything, besides, his stomach was already complaining because he hadn't yet taken advantage.

"Detective, you seem to underestimate this detail, which is quite important. The fact that he has a girlfriend is irrelevant, but the fact that this girlfriend is a foreigner and probably coming from any of the states of the former Soviet Union, should ring a bell to you. If it doesn't, maybe you'd better check to see whether this girl isn't connected to Mr. Calvani's girlfriend, the one who, in my opinion, killed him for his money," she said, gracefully holding a cup in one hand and swinging a cookie in the other to underline her point.

Maurizio remained open-mouthed. Admittedly this could have been a possibility, that this girl had to do with the murder, if ever she was somehow connected with Madlen. He clenched his fist and placed it against his mouth, taking his time to ponder about it.

I haven't asked Madlen about her family, and perhaps this could be one path to follow, but what kind of relationship did this girl have with Madlen? She was obviously the same age as Luciano.

"Are you considering this possibility?" she wondered excitedly.

Raising a finger in mid-air, he opened his mouth to say something, but remained to ponder before giving an answer to Berenice.

"Mr. Calvani's girlfriend is much younger than him. What kind of relationship would these two women have in common with one another?" he wondered.

"How about being mother and daughter?" Berenice dared.

"We're going too far, I guess. The age might not match..." Maurizio shook his head, but there was again the nagging little voice that kept whispering in the back of his head that Berenice might have seen long enough.

*Well, this is a good point, but what in this world had any meaning if, and I repeat, **IF,** father and son were dating Madlen and her daughter? It would confirm that the world is small, but in terms of the investigation there isn't any meaning in those, eventual, relationships.*

He needed to be alone to ruminate on that detail, and perhaps he should also have a chat with Luciano to see whether he would hide the fact of having a girlfriend or he would openly reveal her identity.

Munching the last bit of the cookie, he grabbed his agenda and wrote down a note.

"So, to recap a bit the story," Maurizio raised his glance to Berenice. "Mr. Calvani senior has a girlfriend, a foreign woman who works in a night club. You've never seen her, but you seem to know more about her than everyone else in the family. How so?"

"As I explained, I have my network of friends and the walls don't retain all the noises. People around here talk about almost everything and the information is easily shared from one another," she giggled, understanding she should be minding her own business.

"Sometimes the information shared can be affected by a certain amount of distortion; and if I can't find a certain trusted source, I can't decode the distortion it went through to get the actual facts," Maurizio placed the agenda on his lap, getting more comfortable on the couch.

Berenice remained to think for a second, wondering whether she might have missed something, or could she counter his point of view. "So far, all my information was true, isn't it?"

With a cringe, Maurizio had to admit she was right, there was indeed a girlfriend coming from the former Soviet Union, and indeed she was working as a stripper. "You're right, but in my job, I need more evidence than rumors. I will go and investigate about Luciano's girlfriend, but I don't think this information holds any relevancy to the case."

A sigh escaped Berenice, who glanced at Maurizio with a saddened expression. "I understand, and I don't expect you to believe everything I'm going to tell you, but at least I wish that you'd consider everything I say as something that needs to be verified. Since I hear a lot of what happens in the neighboring apartments, you can consider me as a sort of **'black box.'**"

Maurizio's features brightened up into a chuckle; although she had to be considered like a broken black box, the value of her information was still high. "Sorry, Madam, I didn't mean to laugh at you, but I found it funny you being a type of 'black box.' Then, there's Luciano's girlfriend, a mysterious girl called Irina. She's also a foreigner and eventually someone he met at the University," he mumbled, almost to himself.

"Obviously, father and son, are more attracted by the exotic beauties," Berenice sneered.

He pretended he didn't hear her comment, which was probably supposed to be a loud thought. "Do you happen to know anything about his employees at work? Did you ever hear Mr. Calvani complain about the behavior of any of them?"

He did have a chat with the people he shared his working life with, but nothing conclusive came from them. Their relationship was quite relaxed, and nothing could have brought him to suspect that any of them had a reason to get rid of Claudio.

Everything turns around to this Madlen, but I am wondering whether she's just someone easy to set up. Certainly, with the death of Claudio she won a lottery, 30 million Euros in fact, many people would be ready to kill for such a sum.

Still chewing the details in his brain, the case seemed far too easy to solve, and by experience when the solution seemed too evident, there were some discarded details, which would have required a closer examination.

Almost absentmindedly, he stood from the couch and strolled to the window to catch a glimpse of the road, as if there was some sort of detail that could be found there.

Indeed, it wasn't a detail to be grabbed from the view out of the window, but he needed to take his eyes off the inquisitive stare of Berenice.

She remained on the armchair, observing every move Maurizio made. She knew she gave him a lot to think about. *My only hope is that, besides giving him some hints about the life and times of my neighbor, I could also give him a wider view of the players in the game.*

Inhaling deeply and closing his eyes, Maurizio turned toward Berenice, who was patiently waiting for him. "I believe I need to think about those details, if this was all you had to say, I would return to my office, and have them checked out with the forensic team, who's working in the apartment."

With a light groan, Berenice stood up from the armchair and offered him a smile. "Of course, *Commissario*. This was all, and if I happen to recall anything else, I will contact you."

"Thank you very much for your cooperation, but next time, don't call me on my personal number. If there's anything you need to tell me, use the number I gave you before. If I don't answer, leave a message on the answering machine. I'll get back to you whenever possible," he stated.

With a pout, she didn't like to be placed on hold, "I understand, but please, if I leave you a message, don't wait one week to call me back!"

"I promise I will treat your calls as a priority," he promised as he started to walk toward the door. "Thank you for your hospitality and your information. I hope I will find a solution to this mystery."

"You're welcome. Have a nice day," she greeted as he stepped out of the apartment.

"The same to you." With a smile, he walked to the apartment where the forensic team was ready to leave.

"How is everything going?" Maurizio asked as he spotted Leonardo.

"We are done here. All the important documents and data have been collected, and from this moment on, we can focus on analyzing, classifying, and start to reach some conclusions about the case. Of course, this doesn't mean we'll get the solution right away..."

Maurizio inspected the room where Claudio probably used to work from. Yet, he was sure most of the information was to be gathered from his personal life, following a hurt son, who desperately wanted to gather the attention of his father, to the woman who stole him from the apparently happy family life he had.

Almost whispering and glancing around to make sure nobody was in earshot he said, "Yesterday I attended the reading of Mr. Calvani's wills. Apparently, everyone won the lottery, as the son and the girlfriend found themselves richer of thirty million each..."

"WHAT?" Leonardo raised his voice, interrupting what Maurizio was going to say.

Grabbing him by the arm, Maurizio guided Leonardo to a farther corner of the room, "Shh for the Lord's sake! In this apartment all the walls have ears. That's why I was keeping a lower tone."

"Well, it's a good reason to eliminate someone. In this case, the list of suspects shrinks at two, most probable the son, girlfriend, and none of them has a valid alibi for the night of the murder. The son was sleeping here, so he could be the first one to be considered. The second one, the girlfriend, who could have lived like a queen forgetting to pretend to love him," Leonardo whispered back.

Those words sounded like the judgment bells and as if he had an enlightening, Maurizio ran toward the door, wanting to immediately ask Berenice something.

***

As he reached the door of Berenice's apartment, he hesitated for a moment to gather his composure back, and then he rang the bell.

"Detective Scala, what a surprise to see you so soon," Berenice giggled. "Please, come in."

"I only have one quick question," he asked, entering the apartment. "Do you remember if by any chance Luciano left the apartment that night after his father left for the first time?"

"Absolutely not," she replied certainly. "He listened to music and then switched on the TV until midnight. Then he went to sleep, or at least I think so because I didn't hear anything."

"Could it be he left the apartment, and you didn't hear him leaving? Perhaps he had been very careful by closing the door without making any noise," Maurizio started to be excited about the direction his mind was headed. He might have found someone else who could have been exactly at the crime scene— someone nobody thought about.

"No, Sir, and I can tell you why— please follow me." She walked outside her apartment and reached one particular spot in front of the apartment of Claudio. "See here—there's an irregularity in the floor. Every time someone comes and goes from their apartment, it sounds like a loud clang in my apartment. I would have noticed if he'd left the house."

Maurizio placed his foot on that spot but couldn't find anything that could have confirmed what she was telling him.

Understanding his skepticism, knowing she was telling the truth, she pursed her lips. "Go inside my apartment and close the door," she said. "Go to whatever room you like, even in the kitchen, which is the farthest room from here."

Maurizio hesitated for a second.

"Just go, I will walk about here, and you'll hear. I'm not imagining things!" she pushed Maurizio toward her apartment.

Squaring his shoulders, he walked inside and closed the door. With uncertainty, he walked to the kitchen and waited for something to happen. When he felt convinced, she was simply making up things to cover the fact that her purpose in life after retirement became spying on whatever happened in that condo, a creaking noise came to his ears. Indeed, it was something clearly audible. It sounded as if the pipes or whatever else for the matter, were bending and banging against the floor surface.

I'd be damned! This is definitely something as loud as an alarm, it doesn't indeed go unheard, he thought.

Walking to the door, he opened it and glanced at Berenice. "You were right, I could distinctly hear the clanging when you were walking there."

"Yes. I have tried, God-only-knows, how many times to raise the attention of the administration of the condominium on this problem. They never cared about it or came to inspect the problem," she grunted, disappointed. "Whatever the matter, this is the reason why I can clearly say Luciano didn't leave home after his father."

"Could it be that he left when you were asleep?" He didn't want to doubt everything she said, but he had to make sure the information he gathered was as accurate as possible to reconstruct the dynamics of the murder. He needed to place every player in a defined place to mark those who possibly could have been in the exact same spot with a weapon willing to kill Claudio.

"Detective, at my age, my sleep is as light as a feather. I get easily awakened, and that noise is certainly something able to break my sleep."

"Well, thank you, for now, that was enough. If I need anything..."

"...You will let me know," she continued his sentence with a giggle. "I'm at your full availability."

"Thank you, Mrs. Moretti, and have a nice day." He turned to walk back in the direction of Claudio's apartment, ready to tell Leonardo the news.

CHAPTER 10

That day, Madlen's thoughts turned to the reading of the testament. This was the first time that she could get her hands on a substantial inheritance and wondered whether there would be any problem getting the insurance settlement, since Claudio was murdered.

The ringing of her telephone brought her back from her contemplations and a smile appeared on her face when she recognized the telephone number of Irina.

"Hello darling, how are you doing?" she answered, relieved not to be left alone with her thoughts.

"Everything is fine here, I called to see how you are managing with all that is going on. "

"I'm still confused, today. Yesterday there was the reading of the testament. I was surprised to be invited and perhaps I should have sent someone to represent me. It hadn't been easy to be in the same room with Claudio's ex-wife," Shaking her head she walked to the living room, where she sat on the couch to get more comfortable. "I fully understand her hostility, but it wasn't because of me that their marriage didn't work out. If it weren't me, it most probably would have been someone else. Claudio was looking for a companion, and he was already considering divorcing her when I met him."

She raised a hand to her forehead, feeling the unavoidable sense of guilt for having ruined someone else's family.

"Mom, it wasn't your fault, but why were you invited?" She pretended not to know the reason for the invitation, although Luciano had informed her about it. She considered it important to have her mother convinced that she was still in Hungary.

"Apparently, Claudio subscribed a life insurance, and I was one of the beneficiaries. I am still shocked about it, but now I'll need to understand the bureaucratic steps to get the funds. I expect a long battle as there's a murder involved and its release might get blocked by the Police until the case is solved," she guessed, fearing she would never get her share.

"How much is the allotment you are supposed to get?" Irina wondered after a short pause, if there would have been a better way to ask this.

Nervously biting her lower lip, walking around the room at her father's home, Irina's heart started to race.

"It's a lot of money, thirty million Euros— can you imagine?" Madlen wasn't sure she knew how to spell that amount of money.

"Holy Shit!" Irina exclaimed aloud. She was aware of the testament being in her favor, but she didn't know the exact amount granted to her.

"Luciano, Claudio's son, had the same sum with another life insurance, moreover he got half of the firm his father was running. The other half went to his wife, as he said they had built it to succeed together, so he wanted to include her in the testament too." Madlen looked around and listened to her voice resounding in the apartment, and its emptiness daunted her soul. "I wish you were here; I can't stand this loneliness."

The last sentence was almost a whisper, mostly intended to Claudio, whose absence started to feel unbearable.

"You can contact the insurance company and try to come to a compromise. I understand perhaps they are going to wait for a statement from the Police, but they might be interested in having the chance to pay less than the agreed amount and pay immediately, ignoring the Police order of blocking the funds, if you are willing to bargain the compensation. Thirty million is a big sum, but so is twenty, for example," she cunningly suggested, glancing at her image on the mirror.

"I...I don't know," Madlen replied, hesitating, the soft leather of the couch gently crinkling as she caressed it with her hand. "I will have to call them, but first, I need to make sure I'm not suspected of the murder. There must be a way to make the Police understand that I had nothing to do with Claudio's death. I loved him."

Irina understood the situation wasn't going to be easy, particularly for her mother. *As for me, it would be impossible to connect me to the crime scene; the only two people the Police are investigating are Luciano and my mother. I need to act very carefully, perhaps leaving the country... I need to make sure my departure is as confidential as my entrance.*

The silence between the two women seemed to last for an eternity. "Is there anything wrong?" Madlen asked. It was rare for Irina to remain silent for such a long time. Generally, she had a lot of things to tell her. However, on that occasion, it was like the world stopped turning around and everything was on hold, waiting for a response from the Police or from the insurance company.

"No, why?" a nervous giggle betrayed her state of mind.

"Because you're never so silent," Madlen admitted. "But maybe it's just me? I'm still so shaken. The possibility of being accused of Claudio's murder is driving me crazy..."

Glancing around herself, Irina pondered carefully what to say. Certainly, she needed to regain her composure, or she might have ended up in trouble. For the first time, she understood the implications of dating Luciano, she was risking losing control of the troubled situation she put herself into.

Well, I guess it's too late to regret, now I need to go on and make sure to get out of this story. Then, perhaps Luciano and I could live our lives in peace and wealth.

She grinned, thinking about the possibilities that her relationship opened to her. "You think about getting the money, once you get it you can secure them abroad, so whatever will happen, you won't lose them."

"But I don't want anything to happen to me! I haven't killed Claudio!" Her voice raised, trembling in exasperation.

"Mom, you need to solve one problem at a time. At this precise moment, nobody has come to arrest you. They have no proof of your involvement. Therefore, the best thing is to secure the funds. Once this is taken care of, we will see what our next move will be." Irina clenched her fist, clutching the sheets of the bed as if to grab her only hope before falling into an abyss.

Indeed, Irina was right, and Madlen couldn't take care of everything at once; she had to think about what was the most immediate thing that came across her. In that case, it was the prize of the insurance. "You might be right; I'll contact the insurance company and see whether there's a way to get the money. Without Claudio, I am afraid I won't be able to keep up the expenses, and finding a job, after not having been a nightclub dancer for such a long time, won't be easy."

"True, but you don't have to worry about it right now, and if you need me there, you know you only have to ask." Irina didn't want to be recorded officially by the authorities in the National territory, but she felt she needed to be close to her mother.

"No, you stay away from this mess. I'll manage on my own, and besides, I need some time to reorganize my life and to secure my position with the Police. Although it's clear I was the last person who saw Claudio alive, it doesn't mean I am the assassin." She tried to convince herself about the strength of her position, but she could see the weak points in it. The only evidence in her defense was that she wasn't in possession of any firearm.

"I need some time to think about what my next move will be, but I want you to know I love you very much, and . . . well . . . I'm also sorry if I made you feel left aside," Madlen said. She wasn't sure why, but she considered it of importance to explain once again her position to Irina. For her entire life, she tried to protect her daughter. "I was afraid that if you had grown and had gone to school here, people would have harassed you because of my job. All I wanted was to give you a good life, one far from the judgment of those who have nothing else to do but stick their noses in business that doesn't concern them at all."

"Mom, you don't owe me any explanation. I know it would have been challenging for you to have me there, and I perfectly understand your reasons. I also think everything would have been far more difficult, if I had been there." For a long time, Irina thought about her mother, and considered her sacrifice.

For the rest of the world, she was only a stripper in a night club, but none of them ever considered that sometimes you don't have any choice. Her decision was, after all, better than begging at the side of the road or ending up in the hands of ruthless pimps.

"Take care of yourself, Mom. I love you," she assured.

A smile relaxed the concerned expression on Madlen's face. "I love you too," she whispered before interrupting the conversation.

With a grimace, Madlen scanned her surroundings as she placed the telephone on the couch. Certainly, Irina was right, and she should at least ask the insurance company about the modality and time frame to have the funds released. The money she'd been saving wouldn't last forever, and she needed to secure her finances. After the reading, everyone who was present received a copy of the testament and the details for the inheritance.

She went through all the information, but nothing conclusive came out of it. "One thing is clear— that in case of murder, it must be proven that the beneficiary has nothing to do with it," she muttered as she searched on the documentation received. "This is understandable and I'm wondering whether I can do as Irina suggested and bargain over the funds in order to have it unlocked. Otherwise, I will have to figure out a way to make a living."

Back in her room, Irina remained seated for a moment, then with a whine, she let herself collapse on the bed. She needed something she didn't have the luxury for— time. Time to think, plan, and act. Before any of those, she needed to have her mind clear from all the thoughts haunting her.

Closing her eyes everything got clearer. "I need to get rid of all the evidence," she whispered as if she feared someone could have heard her, although she knew it wasn't possible, as she was alone in the apartment at that time.

The noises of the traffic coming muffled through the closed windows, seemed to echo in the room along with the voices of the people passing by in front of the building. Even from the other apartments, everything was quieter than usual.

Her eyes opened wide as she grabbed a clear and steady thought. Getting rid of the evidence meant also getting rid of the pistol. That weapon should simply disappear, and she was certain she had found the right way to make sure nobody would ever find it. *Or maybe...* she grinned. . . *I'll have to make sure the Police **will** find it.*

Grabbing her mobile phone, she hesitated, wondering whether Luciano's telephone would have been tracked by the Police. Grimacing, she threw the mobile on the bed, *I will have to find another way. Concerning myself, I should probably leave the country.*

Without waiting any further, she stood from the bed, left a written message to her father on the table and rushed to get the car. She needed to arrange her departure, and another plan started to form into her mind.

Pushing her foot on the gas pedal, she sped toward the harbor of Civitavecchia. There she was sure she would have found the same people who helped her to reach Italy from the island of Corsica.

It took less than one hour for her to arrive at her destination, and immediately she directed herself to the dock, where the fishermen who were traveling between the two countries would have helped her one more time for the return trip.

Without any hesitation, she walked in the boat. "Anybody there?" she called, hoping to find at least one member of the crew.

Aldo's head peeked from the cabin, and when he saw Irina, he opened up into a bright smile. "I thought you would have enjoyed a longer stay here in Italy," he joked with a chuckle.

"That was only half an enjoyment, and I was here for business." She leaned against the baluster. "I need to leave right away. When is your next scheduled departure?"

"We can arrange it in a couple of days, perhaps on Monday at one o'clock in the morning. Do you need a ride?" with a confident stride, he reached her.

"Yes, I will need to contact Alec to get me from the international waters to the coast. We will need the maximum discretion, if you know what I mean." Her lips trembled anxiously, as she pursed them together.

With a light nod, Aldo agreed, considering how to make sure the two things would have combined. "Let me talk to Alec, once I have spoken with the rest of the crew, be reassured of it. We should agree together, so everything can run smoothly. The price is going to be the same as for the trip from there to here, and we'd prefer payment in advance." His expression toughened. The agreement was different, but he needed to also acknowledge the risks.

Narrowing her eyes, she clenched her fists, glaring at him, "That was not what we agreed!" she shouted, barely containing herself, coming closer to his face.

Her attitude couldn't impress a rough seaman like Aldo, although he knew what she was capable of and that it was better not to try her patience. Nevertheless, he was aware there wouldn't have been another way for her to reach the French coast, then to rely on their ride.

"The risk is getting higher. If we get caught by the coast guard, we will end up in trouble. I'm not going to risk any of my business for you. I need my insurance." His voice remained calm, but rage started to boil inside at the demands of this spoiled brat.

Averting her eyes from him, she considered her options. *Indeed, if I want to have everything cleared, I need to come to a compromise, although the deal has suddenly changed.*

She didn't have time for bargaining with anyone, so she inhaled deeply, trying to quell her rage. "Fine, you will have your compensation the moment we leave. In this case you will have to deal with another issue." What seemed to be a problem suddenly offered her the solution she was looking for. "My father will come with me, but he won't reach any of the coasts. His journey will have to end in the middle of the Tyrrhenian Sea."

"You're insane!" His voice started to get louder, and he didn't care that she was one dangerous girl— it wasn't even the question of the money anymore. The change in the deal she proposed wasn't something easily arranged. A dead body was always something difficult to conceal. It didn't matter whether they would have dumped him in the sea or taken care of him in an alternative way. Their connection to the murder wouldn't have been difficult to establish.

"We didn't agree on being charged twice for the service, so I guess I'm asking a fair exchange. You are going to have more money than you asked for, and I'm going to get rid of a nuisance that starts to get quite annoying, to be honest."

Shaking his head, in the desperate attempt to find a solution, Aldo turned his eyes to look at the clear surface of the sea. For a moment, he remained to listen to the waves lapping against the boat, letting his mind rest for a bit.

"It's too dangerous," he muttered.

A long pause of silence broken only by the water battering against the side of the boat and the far chattering of other fishermen, preparing for the evening, fell upon them.

He opened his mouth as if to say something, but he immediately closed it as a couple of fishermen passed by. One of them waved to Aldo and greeted him, to which he replied with a nod and a smile.

Aldo followed them until he was sure he couldn't hear what they were talking about. "Come with me, it's not safe to talk here."

Without waiting for her reply and expecting to be followed, he headed to the deck. "This is going to be far too risky for us. It's no more a question of money, it's that neither of us wants to be connected to a murder. We all have our lives, and smuggling a person, which is a European citizen, between two countries isn't a problem, but helping someone in getting rid of a corpse, is a fucking big problem. I don't need to explain this to you!" he hissed.

She smirked at him. "You look sexy when you get pissed, Aldo. It would be a pity if I needed to get rid of two corpses, instead of one." She came closer to him, whispering into his ear, as her hands searched for his skin under the oil-tainted shirt.

She was sure there was an easier way to get what she wanted, noticing the way Aldo always stared at her. He would have gone through hell and back to have the chance of holding her naked body, teasingly showing from the short dress she was wearing.

He closed his eyes, deeply inhaling the scent of her skin, counting the times he wished to have her as close as she was in that moment. She was dangerous, and perhaps that was what attracted him the most. When she promised death, it was something she wouldn't have failed to deliver. He was certain that when she promised pleasure, it wouldn't have been a joke—she'd be damn serious.

As her body almost glued to his through their clothes, his arousal overwhelmed his reason, desperately trying to warn him the danger lurking in the promise of pleasure. Slowly his hand lifted her skirt, caressing her soft skin traveling up to her panties. It was too late, and he knew he fell into her trap. If he didn't want to be a

148

victim of the 'mantis,' he had to do what she was asking, even being an accomplice to the murder of her father.

"I can be very generous with those who are loyal to me," she whispered, holding her naked body to Aldo's.

He barely heard her words, and he already regretted his weakness. He knew she wasn't supposed to stay. She was there like the morning breeze, easy to rise and easy to disappear, unless she would have turned into a storm, burying her victims to the bottom of the sea.

Opening his eyes, he glanced at her, "I still need to call Alec, but I consider it quite unfeasible for you to join us on Monday. We need to be coordinated down to the millisecond." His voice barely a trembling whisper.

"I knew you were a reasonable person. Call me when you have an answer— don't let me wait in vain." She stood from the bed and quickly dressed, ready to leave and return back to Rome, where she would have set up the trip with her father.

"This is no longer only up to me. You know Alec, and he has his schedule. Be prepared to hide in the Italian territory for another month or more. You know better than me how these things go."

Aldo remained for a moment to think about what he agreed to, and the more his mind regained clarity, the more he felt he'd acted in haste and was ashamed of how he handled the situation. He wasn't alone; there were the members of his crew who would have traveled with him.

"The only consolation is that none of us is an innocent angel from heaven," he smirked, shaking his head as he slowly dressed. "We've been taking care of many other side jobs, besides fishing. We all have our unpaid dues with the law, but this time..."

He stood and peered outside the window to the horizon. "This time we're dealing with a homicide." The creaking noise of the wooden structure of the boat rocking with the waves reminded him of the reason why he preferred to stay away from people and sought refuge at sea, where he didn't have to deal with the craziness of humanity.

CHAPTER 11

Time mercilessly slipped away from Maurizio, and yet too many pieces didn't fit together.

Maurizio arrived in his office a bit earlier that morning, his intention was to go through all the details on a list he compiled and try to place every suspect in the right place at the time of the murder.

His mobile phone caught his attention, diverting his eyes to where he kept it on his desk; for some strange reason, he wondered why Berenice hadn't called him anymore. *Certainly, If I hadn't asked her to call me unless there was something extremely important to tell, she would have done it more often.*

A whimper filled the emptiness of the room as he exhaled, collapsing in his chair. Caressing the smooth surface of his desk he let his thoughts roam free, whether to Mrs. Moretti, who hadn't called him in a while to her suggestion about Luciano's girlfriend.

"Why does she think this girlfriend is important to the investigation? What could be her connection to the murder, besides being sentimentally connected with the one who benefitted the most from Mr. Calvani's death?"

His voice was hardly a mumble as he followed his hand caressing the desk. A sudden thought forced him to stop the trail of his hand. His eyes opened up wide to focus on what his mind was formulating.

Like a little cloud on the summer sky, it started to take form, growing, and spreading through the blue. Its color changed suddenly and from the fluffy white cottony shape, it turned lead-gray and oppressive, kicking up a thunderstorm.

A bang like thunder was the loud noise caused by the landing of Maurizio's open palm to the surface that brought him to realize something he'd never considered, the implication of a third person.

He stood from his chair, rushing outside. Running to the parking lot, he was determined to reach the Forensic Department, where Leonardo had his office. He needed someone to confirm or debunk his newest theory.

Like a storm, he opened the door. "I need your help," Maurizio panted, slamming the door behind him.

"Take a seat, or you'll pass out," Leonardo smirked, amused.

Maurizio grabbed a chair and sat down right in front of Leonardo's desk. Generally, he would have reacted to the sarcastic comment, but on that occasion, it seemed as if he didn't hear what he said. He was still chewing an idea storming in his mind, and, he knew he wouldn't have any peace until he'd talked with someone or brainstormed about it.

"I was trying to put all the pieces together, when the observation of Mrs. Moretti returned to my mind. She was pointing out that Luciano, had a girlfriend." he commenced, hoping to get more clarity in his mind. "Now, I know a young man who is a student at the University most probably has a girlfriend or is in some sort of relationship. What tickles my mind is that the girl's name is Irina, and Mrs. Moretti is ready to swear she is somehow connected with Mr. Calvani's girlfriend."

"Hmm..." muttered Leonardo leaning on his chair. "So, we might have a case of a family date? The father is dating a woman, causing the divorce from his wife, and then the son starts dating the daughter of the father's girlfriend."

Leonardo crossed his fingers in front of his mouth and ruminated about it for a moment.

"This wouldn't be the first time that something like this has happened. What might be considered strange is that according to Ms.

Fazekas, she never met Luciano. I haven't said that this Irina is her daughter. This is what Mrs. Moretti suggested, but we need some confirmation, and to do so, we need to talk with Ms. Fazekas one more time. Come with me; I need a witness during this chat." Maurizio stood up and started to walk to the door.

As he noticed that Leonardo didn't move from his position, he turned to glance at him, "Are you waiting for something in particular to move your ass from that chair?"

"Belonging to different departments, and since you aren't my direct supervisor, I would have expected a 'please' to accompany your request." Leonardo remained seated in his chair. "Secondly, shouldn't you call her first to see if she's at home or anywhere else? Moreover, why me, and not one of your cohorts?"

Grinning, and clenching his fists, he understood that he might have a point with calling her before going to her apartment. "For the first question, you got a point, concerning my collaborators; I have given them specific tasks, and they are busy," he growled, pulling his mobile phone from the pocket of his jeans.

He sat down once again, followed by the amused glance of Leonardo, and dialed Madlen's telephone number.

Madlen was at the door, ready to leave the apartment and go to a meeting with a representative from the insurance company to obtain some information about the process to obtain the insurance settlement.

The telephone ringing startled her as she cringed, noticing it was an unknown number. It wasn't difficult to guess who was calling her and the reason for that call.

"Hello," she replied, trying to sound as natural as possible.

"Good morning, Ms. Fazekas. I'm sorry to disturb you; this is Detective Scala. May I borrow a moment of your time?" he greeted with a plastered smile on his face.

"Good morning, Detective, I'm in a bit of a hurry now, as I have an appointment in one hour, but if you need to ask me a question, I'm at your availability. Otherwise, we can set up a meeting in the afternoon." She hurried to the elevator.

"Can I ask you one question right now? I would also need to meet with you later this afternoon. Will it be ok if I come to your apartment at three o'clock?" he asked, avoiding glancing at Leonardo, as he knew he had that mocking 'told ya' stare.

"Of course. I will certainly be back home," she replied, checking one more time to have everything she might need during that meeting.

A smile relaxed Maurizio's frown. "So, I was wondering about your daughter..." She never talked about her family back in Hungary, and he was expecting that question to stir up the waters

155

a bit. That was the first personal question he asked her besides the relationship she had with the victim.

For one second Madlen's blood boiled in her veins, wondering why he was now questioning her about her daughter. "Do you mean Irina?"

Maurizio grinned victoriously at Leonardo, "Yes. Is she living with you?"

"No, she's in Hungary. After I divorced my ex-husband, I sent her to live with my sister. There she would have a more normal life than she would have had here with me." With a sigh she relived her memories, and the feeling of loneliness for not having her in her everyday life grew stronger in her heart. "She was very young, and I knew what her life would be like once she started attending school. Her classmates would surely come to know her mother was working in a night club and she would have been bullied constantly, shaming her for the career I chose for myself. She didn't deserve to suffer for my choices, so I agreed with my sister that she would live in her household and I would pay for her education and personal expenses. I called her every day to see how she was doing and to make sure she had everything she needed. I wanted her to know that her mother didn't reject her."

Maurizio turned serious as the only emotions he could clearly grab from her voice were regret and sadness. *Yet, I'm wondering whether we are talking about the same girl. Perhaps it's a coincidence that Luciano's girlfriend's name is Irina. Besides, it's quite a common name and I bet if I'm looking through all the exchange students at the University or at the daughters of immigrants, I will find at least a hundred girls with the same name.*

"I understand. Did she ever travel to meet you? How old is she?" Maurizio pursued, intrigued to know more about that woman and her past. Particularly, he needed to know something about her ex-husband, whether he could have had a jealous reason to kill Claudio Calvani.

"She is now 23 years old. Every now and then she comes to spend some time here, but never more than a couple of weeks for the holidays. She finished her studies and is now looking for a job, but also considering the possibility of going to the University." She reached her car, and switching on the hands-free system, she started to drive to the offices of the insurance company. "She has a double passport, so she thought perhaps it would have been better to study here and then return back to Hungary. She is young and needs some time to focus on what she wants in her life."

"Of course," Maurizio mumbled, crossing his legs. His eyes met a pen lying on the table, and he leaned forward to grab it.

Promptly Leonardo snatched it, knowing he would have, otherwise, started ticking it against the desk, something that could drive him crazy. A disappointed pout brought a shadow on Maurizio's face. "I guess that's all for the moment. I will meet you this afternoon at three o'clock, then."

"Yes, see you later, Detective," she said, ending the conversation.

"So, what's the news?" Leonardo wondered.

"She indeed has a daughter called Irina, but according to what she said, she's in Hungary, so I find it difficult for her to be the same girl Mrs. Moretti was talking about. Nevertheless, she also said her daughter comes home from time to time to see her and spends a couple of weeks in Italy. She's twenty-three years old, and she's still thinking about her future, whether she wants to frequent the University here in Rome or to find a job directly." Maurizio shook his head, still trying to fit that information together. "I also wonder about the father of the girl. She was married once, but she divorced. I guess I'll have to ask her about her husband. If he's still living here, he might have had a good reason for killing Mr. Calvani."

Leonardo nodded, "So, before we only had two possible suspects, now we have four. This is brilliant; I can't wait to see how many more had a reason to kill that poor man. Luciano wasn't missing anything and could have lived his wealthy life carelessly for another five years, and then slowly entering into the business of his father. Then there's the girlfriend. What kind of connection are you considering for her?"

Leonardo didn't get the idea behind her possible involvement and was curious to know Maurizio's point of view.

"I'm not saying this is the truth, but think for a moment. Luciano is a wealthy and nice-looking guy. He likes to show off his money, particularly when he secretly borrows his father's Lamborghini." Maurizio started to explain. "Now that's a car that doesn't go unnoticed, and a girl might be tempted to snatch the opportunity. I haven't seen her, but if she remotely resembles her mother, then she has more than one chance to reach the heart of any young man."

Shaking his head, Leonardo didn't consider it a good reason to kill. "If it's true, and I repeat **IF,** why wouldn't she try and get pregnant by Luciano, so to force him to marry her? What kind of advantage would she get from killing Mr. Calvani? Sorry, but this makes no sense!"

"That's true, but what if Luciano and Irina were planning together the assassination of the father?" Maurizio wondered. "No, you're right," he added after a short pause to consider the facts. "There's absolutely no reason that would lead to her involvement."

"Another thing to consider is the murder weapon, a 9mm pistol. Luciano doesn't have a license. His only way to get his hands on such a weapon would have been through illegal channels. Nevertheless, only experienced criminals have access to those channels. Firearms aren't sold in the same way you get hashish or marijuana. You don't get it from a friend of yours who knows a guy, who's got 'good stuff' from a friend at the disco." Maurizio continued.

"Following this train of thoughts, none of the suspects would have had the chance to get his or her hands on such a firearm," Leonardo objected.

Averting his eyes from Leonardo, glancing at the door as if attracted by a noise coming from the corridor, Maurizio said, "I figure it out to be easier for a stripper to get to know people in such an environment where she could easily get a weapon, more so than Luciano.

I think the most suitable suspects at this point are Ms. Fazekas, and eventually her former husband. We need to trace his position, because something tells me, he might have a role in this. He might be the one who would have had the opportunity to get the weapon."

In his mind, Maurizio placed everything in order, together with all the laboratory results obtained by the forensics on the car, the house, and the crime scene.

"The laboratory tests we performed on the suspects' hands to find traces of gunpowder resulted all negative, but this, once again, doesn't mean they are innocent, but they were wearing latex gloves... If only we could find the gun...." Maurizio pondered. "We have to deal with someone who has carefully followed all the Police procedurals movies."

Leonardo grinned. "Something meant to entertain gave an advantage to those ill-intentioned."

With a long exhale, Maurizio stood from the chair. "There are a lot of things we need to focus on. The most important part now is to answer the following questions: 'Who is Madlen's ex-husband and where was he on the day of the murder? Who is Luciano's girlfriend? Is she Madlen's daughter or another Irina? Was she in Hungary the night of the murder? Can we find her and have a chat with her?'" He counted on his fingers as he started pacing in circles around the room.

"One place to start, is to ask permission to track and record all the telephone calls Madlen receives. We also need to obtain the past call logs, who called her and from where. This will place the daughter to a precise unmistakable location," Leonardo pointed out.

As Maurizio returned to his room at the Police Precinct, he started immediately to search on the citizen's register for any information about Madlen's daughter. *She was born in Italy, but I don't know if her parents had been recognized with Italian citizenship. However, Madlen said that she has a double passport, therefore I can start checking that.*

He should have gone to the chief commissioner's office to have permission to track all the phone calls of Madlen and Luciano, but he knew it would have resulted in a massive waste of time. Chief commissioner Angelini was the kind of person who could have taken half an hour of chatter to make his point. Conciseness wasn't certainly one of his best characteristics. With a grimace, squaring his shoulders, he opted for an email.

His mind returned to Irina. *For all the times she returned to Italy, her passport, whether Italian or Hungarian, should have been recorded from the passport control.* All of this caused his head to boil. She didn't need any visa to cross two countries, as passport control between the EU isn't necessary. However, the authorities can request a list of the passengers.

He stared at the screen of his computer for a long time, immersed in his considerations, when a call arrived.

"Scala," he replied, without caring who was calling him.

"Good morning, Detective, this is Loredana DeSantis, from the Vitas Insurances." A soft feminine voice announced. He recalled that was the company Mr. Calvani used for his life insurance.

"Well, good afternoon, Ms. DeSantis," he replied. "How can I help you?"

"To be honest, I think I can help you this time. Yesterday we received a call from Ms. Fazekas, one of the beneficiaries of the life insurance stipulated by Mr. Calvani. We just had a meeting, and she left a couple of minutes ago, asking about the process to be followed to obtain the funds. By our rule, in this case, we need to have a statement from the Police about her non-involvement in the murder. Yet, she was quite anxious and willing to reach a compromise and get half of what she was entitled to."

That can be an interesting detail, he thought.

"At the moment, we don't have any concrete proof against Ms. Fazekas' involvement in the murder. Nevertheless, it's still too early to come to a conclusion." He needed some time and had to wait until he could talk to her in the afternoon. "Since the case concerns a murder, I would ask you to wait before releasing the settlements, both to Mr. Calvani junior and to Ms. Fazekas," he said, thinking about the changed situation. "Did he contact you?" he asked, hoping to get a wider image of the situation.

"He called once to understand the procedure to receive the allotment, but he never tried to get his hands on it. He was well-informed about the fact that until the case is solved, we're not willing to release anything," her voice quite categorical.

"So why did you have a meeting with Ms. Fazekas?" He narrowed his eyes, wondering whether they were trying to get a good deal on that, losing the rules in favor of paying less than the established amount.

"She wanted to talk with one of our representatives and didn't mention the reason why she wanted to meet. We don't have any reason to deny a face-to-face meeting when our customers ask for explanations. Some of them prefer to talk on the telephone, some are satisfied with an email, and others need to see a physical person explaining the procedure and the requirements."

According to the way she toughened her voice, it seemed as though she could have seen Maurizio's doubting expression.

"Fine, let me know when or if Mr. Calvani asks for his share. I understand perhaps this may never happen as it seems that neither he has any need for cash or any hurry whatsoever. Nevertheless, I would appreciate your cooperation." Maurizio concluded, ready to return to his speculations and get ready to meet Madlen in the early afternoon.

Smirking, Ms. DeSantis shook her head. It was true that as an insurance company, their duty was mostly getting the maximum profit possible. *For many people, this might sound unfair and could be seen as a way to cheat them. The reality is that most of the time we are targets of scams, and we need to shield our business from them,* she considered.

"We will let you know about every move any of the beneficiaries will make," she assured.

"That will be enough. Thank you for your call and have a nice day."

Placing his telephone back on the desk, Maurizio considered the new details. *This woman will have to explain her rush to obtain the money. However, there are also many things that don't fit and will be enough to take her out of the list of the suspects...I predict at least ten kilograms drop in my weight,* he considered as his stomach already started to complain about his delay in feeding it.

"Have patience, my friend; this evening Anna will prepare us something good," he promised, glancing at his belly.

CHAPTER 12

Madlen couldn't stop thinking about the upcoming meeting she would have with Detective Scala. She was sure he couldn't find anything to tie her to the murder, but perhaps he might have heard about her visit to the Insurance company.

Catching a glimpse of her image in the mirror, she could hardly recognize herself. That shade of terror and hopelessness darkening her eyes was something new to her. Never in her life had she thought she would have ever been accused of murder.

She walked to the bathroom and retouched her makeup, for her upcoming visit with the detective, hoping to conceal the stress, clearly transpiring from her eyes.

Slowly, she turned and leaned on the sink. Closing her eyes, she focused on her heartbeat, trying to use the same relaxation technique she used when she was a dancer at the night club. She needed to be able to detach from her daily problems in the same way.

Taking a deep breath, she started to hum the same lullaby she sang to Irina, when she was a child. That was the same one her mother sang to her and was a tune capable of soothing her soul. As the tune started to fill the room, she felt a bit calmer. That simple melody could perform real miracles.

Her life hadn't been easy and getting to know Claudio was her second chance for happiness. It wasn't the money she was after; it was the fact of having someone who would have been by her side no matter what. He was the man who could look beyond the appearances of a dirty job and see through her soul. She opened her eyes, and with a smile on her face she walked to the living room, where the balcony that looked over the main entrance was located.

Without going out, she peeked from behind the curtains waiting to spot the Police car arriving, wondering whether Detective Scala would have used an official or a civil vehicle.

Thinking about it, she didn't remember having noticed which car he had the previous time, so there wasn't any expectation for her.

With a sigh, she walked away from the window and glancing at the clock, she decided to have a coffee. Instead of making her nervous, it would soothe her. She was ready to let the rich aroma fill her nostrils as she reached the kitchen and started to prepare the coffee maker.

She sat on the couch, with her coffee. Reaching for the cup, she deeply inhaled the rich aroma, bringing the bland, bitter tones and the crisp taste to her lips. With the first sip, Madlen's expression relaxed in full enjoyment of the strong chocolaty flavors giving her a warm sensation of safety, able to soothe her soul while she waited for something she couldn't foresee. Coffee was her favorite drink and considered it almost a ritual. Every sip had to be enjoyed with the due calm, celebrating the flavors and sensations.

With a long exhale, she placed the cup back on the table and remained for a moment thinking about the situation she found herself in. With a slight groan, she stood from the couch and brought the cup to the kitchen, placing it in the dishwasher, when the intercom rang. With a startling movement, she closed the dishwasher and after a second of hesitation, she hurried to answer.

"Yes?" She asked, trying to sound as calm as possible.

"Ms. Fazekas, this is Detective Scala. I'm with Forensic Inspector Romizi. Can you please open the door for us?" Maurizio announced.

She pressed the button to open the main door. "Of course, you know how to arrive at my apartment," she confirmed, wondering about the reason to have another officer accompany him.

Knowing they were inside the building, she went to open the door to wait for them. The elevator in front of her apartment started to climb the floors and together with it, her heartbeat increased in her chest. The doors of the elevator finally opened, and Maurizio came out followed by Leonardo.

"Good afternoon Ms. Fazekas," Maurizio greeted, pacing toward her. "This is Forensic Inspector Romizi, he directed the forensic team in this case. His presence here is only a formality."

Maurizio wanted to clarify Leonardo's presence to avoid useless misunderstandings and uncomfortable feelings Madlen may have about any suspicion of her involvement in the murder.

"Pleased to meet you, come inside." She kindly invited them in, carefully closing the door behind her.

Maurizio and Leonardo walked behind her to the living room, without bothering to remove their jackets. They didn't have any intention to remain there for a long time, or at least this was what they both hoped.

As they were all seated on the couch, Madlen glanced at them furrowing her brows. "How can I help you?"

"I would like to get to know more about your background. As for now, I know you came to Italy as a seventeen-year-old girl looking for that kind of fortune and future you couldn't see in your country. What I don't know is what happened since the day you arrived." Maurizio commenced, trying to keep the discussion on a general tone, without entering into the details.

He hoped she would be open to willingly provide them with all the answers to their questions without the need to pursue and insist on what they already knew.

She took a deep breath. "It might take some time. Are you sure you don't want to take off your jackets?" she asked.

She wasn't an old lady, but she lived in Italy for a long time, and her life had been anything but boring. Exchanging a fast look between each other, Maurizio and Leonardo stood up from the couch and complied with Madlen's suggestion.

"After the death of my father in Hungary, the economic situation of my family deteriorated, making me an easy target of ruthless traffickers. At that time, it wasn't uncommon for girls coming from Eastern Europe to become victims of the prostitution network. For this reason, at the age of seventeen, I agreed with my mother to move away from my hometown. She had some friends here in Rome who could host me. Although I was to be considered underage, I was under her responsibility, and the Italian authorities didn't have anything to complain about it. My mother and her friends took care of the bureaucratic work. I started working as a waitress at the Venus Caprice, and later I was offered a job as a dancer."

She paused for a moment, thinking about her story and how lucky she'd been compared to other girls moving to Italy looking for a better life only to find themselves stuck into an endless nightmare.

"Here I met Ivan Leonov, an Italian-Russian citizen five years older than me, and we connected since the first moment we met."

"Is he the father of Irina?" Maurizio wondered, reaching for the notebook from his pocket, knowing this was the good time to write down the information before he might have forgotten.

"Yes, I got pregnant, and we decided to get married. Things seemed to go fine, but after the birth of Irina, the relationship with Ivan started to deteriorate. He became increasingly jealous of my job and wanted me to quit, but the salary of a waitress isn't quite the same as a dancer, and without that extra money, we couldn't provide for Irina. Therefore we realized there wasn't any other solution but to walk away from each other."

Leonardo remained silent, as he didn't need to write notes. He was able to memorize and keep all the details stored in his mind, and this skill was very useful for his work at the forensic department.

Irina was three years old, and I was afraid I wouldn't have had the possibility to take care of her. After a discussion with my sister, we decided it would have been best for my daughter to return to Hungary and live with her. She had a normal family, something I couldn't offer." Averting the eyes from them, she glanced at her entwined fingers on her lap, recalling that difficult decision.

Maurizio nodded. "Does your daughter return to visit you often?"

"There isn't a precise schedule, when she has time twice every year. Why does it matter?" Madlen tried to understand the reason for their interest in her daughter.

"Just curiosity— you mentioned she was thinking of coming to Italy to study or perhaps to find a job, and I was wondering whether her desire was due to a relationship with a young man here." He couldn't say there was a girl with her same name who'd been seen, or better heard, in the company of Luciano.

"Do you mean if Irina has a boyfriend here?" Madlen goggled at Maurizio, surprised at his suggestion. "We're always together when she comes to visit me. Of course, she doesn't need any permission to travel, and she's no longer a child. Yet, I know she would have told me if there was someone she was interested in."

Leonardo drew a long breath and exhaling slowly, turning his eyes to Madlen. "And what about your husband? What kind of relationship does he have with you and Irina?"

Surprised at his question, she remained speechless for a fraction of a second. Her lips twitched into a shy smile. "I have no idea where he might be presently. I know he kept in contact with Irina. The problem between us didn't involve her, and she wasn't the reason why we decided to divorce." She took a pause regaining her composure. "He wasn't a good husband, but at least I can say he was a good father."

"So, I assume he was also paying her child support? And what about the alimony to you?" Maurizio chimed in, writing in his notebook about checking the identity and the location of the man.

"We agreed he would have paid only the child support. I was able to earn enough to sustain myself and send some money to my sister. If he was going to pay his part for Irina and stay away from me, this would have been more than enough." Her voice turned tough, as she clenched her fists, grabbing onto the fabric of her skirt.

"Had he been abusive toward you? Was he ever arrested for domestic violence?" Leonardo inquired, leaning on the couch.

"No, he was not violent, but he was extremely jealous. He was always thinking there was another man trying to get me away from him. It was an obsession, which caused him to follow me wherever I went and check all the telephone calls I made. He never raised a hand to me, but it was impossible to live that way." She paused for a moment then, widening her eyes, unclenching her fists as she turned to look at them both. "You are not suggesting that he might be the one who killed Claudio for jealousy?"

"Why not?" Maurizio answered with a calm tone on his voice, raising his glance from his notebook to her. "A jealous man doesn't stop being obsessed with his wife simply because they aren't married anymore. To be honest, this was something you should have told us since the beginning, and we will check his alibi."

Averting her attention from them, she covered her mouth with a hand, considering Maurizio's words. They made sense, but she wasn't ready to believe he would have reached that point. "I... I personally don't think..." Suddenly all the words failed her.

"We're only trying to see all the possibilities. I'm not saying he is for sure the murderer, but he had a good motive for killing Mr. Calvani. Your former husband was a jealous man, and if he knew you had a new boyfriend, he might have lost control over this, and do something irrational. Did you ever notice him or his car around the night club where you were working?" Leonardo asked, trying to put her at ease.

"No," she shook her head. "I haven't seen him or noticed anything strange when I was at work, or with Claudio."

"We will find this out, but there's another question I need to ask you." Maurizio started flicking the pen between his fingers. "Why did you have a meeting with the insurance company? You should have been aware that until the case is closed, or we give permission to release the funds they aren't allowed to make any payments."

"I need money. While Claudio was alive, he paid me an allowance of 2000 Euros every month. Now I'm left with nothing at all, I'm not his wife, so I have no access to any social compensation or any inheritance. I don't have any other income, but I need to live."

"Have you tried looking for a job?" Leonardo's voice arrived like the screeching of nails against a chalkboard, leaving Maurizio and Madlen surprised.

Maurizio's face turned red as if it wanted to explode, and the veins on his temple got swollen and pulsed like crazy. "Romizi!" he yelled, his voice thundering through the room.

Leonardo wished the ground would swallow him up and tensed his shoulders, understanding he'd been tactless in his question. Moreover, he also knew his incautious words would have led him to the room of the chief commissioner as they'd reach the Police Department. He hoped there wouldn't have been any disciplinary measures.

Me and my big mouth, Leonardo cursed within himself. "I... I'm sorry, Ma'am, I didn't mean to be impolite," he muttered.

Madlen's expression relaxed, she realized that she had to start thinking about her life. She needed to get her hands on that settlement at any cost, and she hoped the chat she had with the representative at the insurance company would result in her favor. They said they would look into the situation and would give her an answer.

I hope Irina was right and they will be ready to pay half of my share. I wish I could leave this place forever and live my life with my daughter in peace. I swear I'll never mess up my life with any man ever again.

She felt bitter, not because of the rude improper comment of Forensic Inspector Romizi. She inhaled a deep breath. *After all he's right, and the only chance I have is to find a job at least to make sure I'm not going to live on the streets.* She glanced once again at Maurizio sending inflamed glares at his colleague.

"I understand you didn't mean to be offensive, and you're right, I should start to think about my life and taking it back in my own hands," she said.

"You'll be reported to your supervisor," Maurizio growled, as Leonardo's body tensed up.

Maurizio couldn't think clearly any longer. He scanned back through his notes taking a fast look at everything he'd been asking trying to figure out whether there were any other open questions. One thing he knew for sure, was that next time he was bringing someone to question a suspect, he would have made sure the man was mute.

So, to sum it up, there's a jealous husband we need to locate, and question. There's still the question of her daughter; I still can't say whether she's the same person as Luciano's girlfriend or not. According to what she said, she can't be the one, as she comes to Italy only to visit her once in a while. Yet, she might have kept her relationship with the son of her boyfriend a secret. I can see how the situation might be a bit bizarre.

He turned his back to glance at Madlen, "May I ask to see a recent picture of your daughter?"

Like awaking from a dream, she became startled. "Of course, hold on a moment," she said, standing and walking to a closet. From one of the shelves, she grabbed a picture album, returned to her seat on the couch and opened it to the latest page. "Here's a photo of her last birthday, five months ago."

Maurizio gently took the album in his hands to observe the picture. The first thing he noticed was the striking resemblance to her mother, and he understood that with her beauty, she could have turned many heads, including the one of younger Calvani.

"Congratulations, she's a very beautiful young lady. And you say she still lives in Hungary...."

"She's still looking for a direction in life, but she works part-time as a waitress in a pub. She still lives with my sister," she said with a smile.

Maurizio stood up, wearing his jacket, and placing the notebook back in its pocket. "Ms. Fazekas, thank you very much for your cooperation; we will let you know if we need to ask you any further questions."

Leonardo mumbled something that resembled another apology and thanked her for her availability, keeping his eyes lowered.

As they were in the elevator, Leonardo peered at Maurizio. "Are you going to tell what happened in there to the chief commissioner?" He cringed, expecting another thunderstorm approaching his way.

Shaking his head, Maurizio turned his eyes to look at Leonardo. "No, I might also have been too impulsive, but you need to understand it's not your duty to tell anyone what they should or shouldn't do. Particularly when you're wearing your uniform. We're representing the law, for Christ's sake, and if she were a more susceptible person, she would have demanded your name and surname and would have reported you to the chief of the Department. At that point, you would have been in trouble," he warned, placing a hand on Leonardo's shoulder.

"One thing to do now, is to call Luciano Calvani and have him interrogated one more time. I need to understand whether this Irina is the daughter of Ms. Fazekas or is another girl with the same name." He handed the keys of the car to Leonardo. "You drive, and I will give him a call."

***

Luciano was trying to focus his attention to the book he was studying. The exams were fast approaching, and studying was the best way to keep his mind occupied from the murder of his father and the decision he had to make about running the firm or continuing his studies.

There were so many thoughts swirling in his mind to keep him away from any academic or working duty. One important thing was that Irina had disappeared. He couldn't say whether she already returned to Hungary or was still in Italy.

Raising his glance, his eyes met the clock on the wall. It was half-past four, and he was far behind schedule with everything in his life.

The ringing of his mobile phone brought him back to reality, and not recognizing the telephone number, he answered, hesitatingly. "Hello?"

"Good afternoon Mr. Calvani, this is Detective Scala. May I steal a moment of your time?" he asked.

"Of course, Detective. Is there any news about the murder of my father?" he asked, closing the book in front of him. It was obvious that after that call, he wouldn't have any chance to focus on anything else.

"Not yet. I wanted to know whether you would be available for a chat, I could meet you right away, as I'm driving at the moment," Maurizio observed the road going by, as Leonardo started to drive in the direction of the Police Department.

Luciano wanted to tell him that he preferred not to have anything to do with the Police until everything would have been solved, but he knew he would have climbed up the list of the suspects. "Of course, I'm at home..." his voice hesitated. "Do you know where I'm living now?"

"Yes, we have the address of your mother's apartment, if that's still the place where we can find you." A chuckle escaped Maurizio's mouth.

Pursing his lips, Luciano grabbed all his strength and self-confidence. "Yes, I still live with my mother. I haven't yet received the keys to the apartment where I was living with my father."

Maurizio looked at the clock, and after a fast calculation of the time necessary to reach Luciano, he nodded. "I'm with Forensic Inspector Romizi, from the forensic team. We will arrive within half an hour, so he can tell you about the time required to return you the keys."

"That would be great. I'll be waiting for you. See you soon."

Luciano hung up the phone, without waiting for any answer from Maurizio. He was glad to know there was at least something he could clarify, and that was when he could return to the place, he called home. He loved to be with his mother, and during the time they lived together he had the chance to appreciate her better than he'd ever done so far. Nevertheless, the freedom of having his own space was something he started to miss. With his father, things were easier; he was rarely at home, so most of the time, it was like living in the apartment alone. His mother was completely different, she enjoyed spending her time at home, and they spent a lot of time together. It was good to have the feeling of being considered more than a roommate, as he sometimes felt with his father.

***

"We're going to the address of Mrs. Martini; it's *via Colfiorito 8,*" Maurizio said curtly to Leonardo. "And this time, try to behave, or I will be the one who reports you directly to the Chief of the Department and have you transferred on point duty."

Leonardo gave a fast glance at Maurizio and they both burst into a loud laughter.

CHAPTER 13

It took about twenty minutes for Leonardo and Maurizio to reach the building where the apartment of Mrs. Martini was located. The main door got opened as one of the residents came out, and they reached the top floor. Without any hesitation, Maurizio rang the bell expecting to see Luciano.

To Maurizio's surprise Giulia came to open instead. "Detective Scala, Luciano informed me about your arrival, please come in."

Her voice calm, and kind, returned a serene feeling to Leonardo, who still felt upset for his gaffe with Madlen.

"Good afternoon," Maurizio replied. "Please forgive this late afternoon visit. I understand you might have just arrived from work. This is Forensic Inspector Romizi from the forensic team."

With a shy smile Leonardo shook her hand, "Pleased to meet you Ms. Martini," he greeted briefly.

"There's absolutely no problem about it," she replied, guiding them to the living room. "Lucio! Come here, Detective Scala arrived!" she called.

Turning her eyes back to her visitors, she took their jackets and offered for them to sit on the couch. "He will come soon. He's preparing for one exam and he's always in his room studying."

"Ah, the life of a student; I miss it," Maurizio replied chuckling.

"Good afternoon," said Luciano appearing from one of the doors leading to a corridor that remained in the darkness.

Maurizio and Leonardo stood up to greet him, "Good afternoon, Mr. Calvani. We will try to be brief and not steal too much of your time. This is Forensic Inspector Romizi, and if you prefer to talk in private..." he explained peering at Ms. Martini.

Giulia glanced at them, understanding that probably they wanted to ask confidential questions, and included details of his private life, one she might not be aware of. They never spoke about a relationship, and she was afraid he was feeling slightly embarrassed to open up his private life to anyone, particularly to his mother. That was something she was aware of, and she accepted the fact that probably a daughter would have felt more comfortable talking about boys and relationships with a mother, meanwhile a son would have preferred speaking to his father.

"Oh, I was going to see a friend of mine on the second floor, you can chat freely here," she winked, feeling amused.

"Thank you, Mom," he smiled shyly at her.

Now alone, and seated on the couch, Luciano scrutinized both men, trying to guess their thoughts, and wondering exactly what they knew. "Is there any news about getting the keys back to my apartment?"

"We expect to have everything ready by the end of next week. We're sorry for the delay, we needed to collect as much information as possible," Leonardo replied in an apologetic tone.

He understood there had been several delays due to the lack of manpower at the laboratory, but that was a detail he wasn't willing to share with anyone.

"That's not a problem, I can certainly wait."

"I know you have already answered this question, but I would like to go into a bit more detail. How would you describe your relationship with the victim? I know there had been highs and lows, like in every family, but the neighbors were claiming having heard quite inflamed arguments coming from your apartment. Can you tell me a bit more specifically the reason why you argued with your father?" Maurizio needed to handle the question of the girlfriend with care.

He could not get straight to the point, in that case, besides being considered rude, it would have raised some suspicions from one of the potential assassins.

Luciano averted his eyes from him and slowly entwined his fingers on his lap. "Our relationship was sometimes a bit troublesome, I understand. The reason we were often arguing was because of his broken promises," he commenced, raising his glance shyly. "My father was a busy businessman, and that wasn't something new. The problem began when he started to be more serious with his girlfriend and had no time for me anymore. I felt like a useless presence in his life, and I tried in every way possible to spend some time with him."

"Did you ever ask your mother for advice?" Maurizio started to dig deeper.

With a sarcastic chuckle, Luciano tilted his head backward. "He divorced her because of his girlfriend, and I asked her for any advice on how to get my father back. She suggested to leave him, because it was a lost cause." Returning serious, his eyes glanced down to his hands. "Perhaps she was right, and I should have returned to live with her. She always listened to me when I asked her something."

"What about your friends, your girlfriend, did you ever talk to her about your problems?" Leonardo chimed in. He regretted it immediately and waited for another admonition coming from Maurizio.

Nevertheless, Maurizio nodded, considering his way of introducing the presence of a girlfriend, simply brilliant.

"Irina? Yes, she was the one who was always listening to my complaints. Sometimes I feel guilty for including her with my personal problems, but this is what a relationship is made of, isn't it?" Luciano asked.

"So, Irina is your girlfriend; that's a beautiful and exotic name. Where does she come from?" Maurizio asked, pretending to be curious.

"I met her at the University. She's originally from Hungary, but she has the double passport." Luciano replied, hesitatingly. He realized he'd made a mistake in telling them anything about his relationship with Irina and her citizenship, but it was too late, and he had to hope this information wasn't going to bring any trouble to either of them.

"Does she study here in Rome?" Leonardo pursued, intending not to let go of that lead for any reason in this world.

"No, I met her when she was trying to figure out what to do with her life. She is still deciding whether she's going to follow any course or not. She still lives in Hungary with her aunt and comes here only for holidays. She has a job as a waitress back in her country and can't come here as often as she'd like. Sometimes I go to visit her, so we can spend more time together." He desperately hoped this would have taken her away from the crime scene so they wouldn't think about pursuing that lead.

"When was the last time she was here to visit you?" Maurizio intervened. That would have been a good starting point and his heart started slowly to increase its pace, at the thought that perhaps this would have been another piece to be added to the puzzle.

"Hmm... Let me think, it was sometime in October. When my father was murdered, she asked me whether I wanted to have her here. I told her it would have been better if she'd remain away for a time, as I needed to take care of my life, and put the pieces back together. I still need to figure out what I'm going to do from now on." He peered cautiously at them, twisting his fingers.

After a short pause, Leonardo brought his closed fist to his mouth. "You said this girl, Irina, lives with her aunt. Where is her mother, or father? Do you know anything about them?"

He noticed Luciano's discomfort and knew it was because they were reaching a critical point.

"We never spoke about her family. I don't know..."

"How come? She knew everything about your family; she knew your parents divorced and your father was murdered. Yet, although you were in a romantic relationship, you cannot say where her parents are? Did she keep it secret, or weren't you interested in that detail?" Leonardo pressed. He didn't care whether his questions were impolite or not. He was smelling a dead rat, and by the look on Maurizio's face, the stench was so strong, they could almost see the rotting corpse.

"What are these questions about?" Luciano snapped. "I wasn't interested in her background, and if you had seen her, you would have understood that the last thing you come to think of is about her family."

"Do you happen to have a picture of her?" Maurizio's voice was calm and tried to sound as reassuring and friendly as possible, but he knew they were close to something big, something Luciano wanted to keep secret.

The reason for this secrecy, not necessarily was connected to the murder, as there could have been thousands of explanations, for example keeping secret from his mother the fact that he was having a relationship with the daughter of the woman who stole her husband.

Thinking about it, he realized there would be more than a good reason to hide his relationship, yet he should know that we are supposed to keep maximum confidentiality on every private detail of the people we are interrogating. It doesn't matter whether they are serial killers or witnesses, they all have a right to privacy. Maurizio considered.

Luciano relaxed his muscles and drew a deep breath. "Sorry for being rude, I have a picture in my mobile phone," he said with a defeated tone.

With a slow movement, he stood from the couch and pulled it from the pocket of his jeans.

Browsing through his pictures, he returned to sit and as he found what he was looking for. He handed the mobile phone to Maurizio. He was aware of the incredible resemblance to her mother and was waiting for their reaction. *Now I need to play my cards wisely. I can still win this game.*

Maurizio inspected the picture and immediately recognized the daughter of Madlen.

"She's indeed a very beautiful girl and resembles quite closely...."

"I know!" Luciano interrupted, throwing his hands up in mid-air. "How do you think my mother would react if she knew I'm dating the daughter of my father's girlfriend?" Luciano knew he just found the greatest escape plan from a hopeless situation.

"You should have told us, because hiding any sort of detail can be considered a way to misdirect the investigation," Maurizio warned, his brows furrowed as he handed him back the mobile phone.

"I...I" Luciano's lips twitched as his heart sank. "I didn't mean to hide anything. I was sure this was a detail that held no importance whatsoever. I'm dating Irina, who's generally is living in another country. What does this detail have to do with the murder of my father?" His voice trembled as tears started to form in his eyes.

He covered his face between his hands and felt hopelessly slipping into an abyss he'd never imagined possible.

"Mr. Calvani," Maurizio commenced. "We're not accusing you of anything, but you need to understand we need every single piece of information. Let us judge what's important and what isn't." He tried to keep his voice calm, although he wanted to run to the Department and start delegating the team to search for every member of Irina's family and their moves in the last three months, together with their backgrounds.

There was a pause of a few long moments, where Maurizio and Leonardo gave Luciano a chance to regain his composure and try to calm down. The silence in the apartment brought every noise in the foreground to take center stage. And so, the slight buzz of the fridge, almost imperceptible, took life, merging with the regular ticking of the clock on the wall, and the muffled noises coming from the other apartments.

They weren't there to arrest him. *Not yet at least, but there are so many questions open. I am afraid nobody here has told the whole truth, and Mrs. Fazekas, Mr. Calvani and this girl, Irina, will have to explain a lot once this puzzle will start to come together,* Maurizio bit his lower lip, scrutinizing every little movement of Luciano.

Leaning back on the couch, Luciano closed his eyes for a second to inhale deeply, recalling the fact that they didn't have any proof against him, *and certainly never will.*

He opened his eyes once again and scrutinized Maurizio, who remained almost frozen into the same expression and position.

"You're right, detective, and I'm sorry for not having considered this particular detail. I should have thought about the importance of this to find out who has killed my father and the reason why," he tried to explain and apologize at the same time for something that might have almost caused him to climb up the list of the suspects. "There isn't a person who wishes to know the identity of the assassin more than I do. We might have had our disagreements, we might have yelled at each other, but he was still my father. It doesn't matter whether he wasn't perfect— none of us are."

Closing his eyes as he nodded, Maurizio relaxed into a smile. "Mr. Calvani, I completely understand your position, and I can assure you we will do everything in our power to find the killer and make sure the culprit will pay for this crime."

With those words, Maurizio stood up to return to the department. Although he was sure that most of his collaborators had returned home, he needed to prepare the list of tasks and send emails to everybody to prioritize them.

Leonardo followed his example but remained silent. He was still trying to digest the details they received and started to formulate once again the crime scene, which began to get populated by people belonging to the international criminality.

"For the moment we have all the information we were looking for. We will let you know whether we will need to have another chat with you. Meantime, I hope you will call us whenever there is anything that comes to your mind that could help us to bring more pieces to this puzzle." Maurizio concluded, shaking Luciano's hand.

"I will try to recall every detail, even if it doesn't seem to have any importance, I will inform you about it. I guess I've learned my lesson today," Luciano said with a shy smile brightening his still wet eyes.

As they were ready to leave, the door opened, and Giulia returned. "That's what I call perfect timing, Madam," Maurizio chuckled. "We're sorry we've entertained ourselves a bit too long. I hope you'll excuse us."

Giulia smiled broadly, "Detective, there isn't any reason to apologize. Although things haven't worked out with Claudio, I hope you will find who is responsible for this despicable act. I would never have wished him dead."

"I know," Maurizio whined. "Not everybody is ready to walk away from an offense the way you did. Some people take revenge to the extreme, but we will find out who did it, be reassured. In the meantime, I wish you a pleasant evening," he added with a slight bow, as he grabbed his jacket.

***

"What do you think?" Leonardo asked as they were back in the car.

"I think we absolutely need to find out more about this girl and also about her entire family," he replied. "The father is a figure that intrigues me. I need to know whether he kept regularly paying for child support, what job he's doing, where he lives, and whether he could be the one who killed Mr. Calvani out of jealousy as his ex-wife started a relationship with him. According to the book, a jealous and oppressive husband, can turn into a stalker and murderer, if the wife walks away from his life," Maurizio started to count the cases on his fingers.

Leonardo kept driving, maintaining his eyes on the road. "I think we should keep an eye on the boy. There was something in the way he twisted his fingers that told me more than a wish to hide his relationship from his mother. He knew we would have kept every single word he spoke to us confidential."

Maurizio's mind started to formulate his own hypotheses, when his glance met the clock glaring 07:00 pm with a huff, knowing he would have stayed at the office for a few hours, he sent a message to Anna.

The reassuring tone of the answer he received back, gave him some peace of mind; he would have not been forced to sleep on the couch. A grin appeared on his face, as he realized another issue— he would have skipped dinner.

CHAPTER 14

Alone in his room, Luciano's hands still trembled, and his heart found no release from the pounding that had begun during the chat he had with the two officers. He needed to talk to Irina, wondering whether the Police were tracking every call he was making. Shaking his head, he grinned. *If they got suspicious after this chat, it would still take time before they can arrange any tracking. I need to act fast.*

Grabbing his telephone, casting away every hesitation, he called Irina's number, hoping she'd answer right away.

"Hello?" her voice, at a whisper.

"Hi, can you talk?" He also tried to keep the tone of his voice lower, to avoid being heard by his mother.

She turned her eyes, spotting Igor's figure in the living room, she narrowed her eyes, and tiptoed to her room, where she could reach the balcony, hoping for some privacy from her father. "I can talk now, but I don't have much time. After the initial delay, due to some coordination problems between Alec and Aldo's team, we might be ready to leave next week. Do you have any news?"

"Police came to ask a few questions. I have no idea how they figured it out, but they were aware of our relationship right from the beginning, and they knew you're Madlen's daughter. I seriously doubt they are suspecting you of any involvement, but we need to be very careful from this moment on. This should be our last call." Adrenaline rushed in his blood, the last thing he wanted was to be accused of murder and having his life ruined. "The Police need a suspect, and we need to fabricate one," he added as he waited for Irina to react.

A few interminable seconds passed without an answer from her. She needed to understand at which point they were, and which were the possibilities open to them. Making sure that only Igor got accused of the murder was perhaps their only chance to get out of this mess.

"What else did they know? Did they ask anything about my background? Do they know about my father?" Her voice started to flicker as she clenched her fist, grabbing the baluster of the balcony. The cold touch of the cast iron sent shivers through her body.

"I'm afraid they went to see your mother before coming here. Do you know whether they might have had any reason to see her? Could it be so, and she told anything that could have brought them our way?" Luciano's paranoia became unmanageable. He knew this would have happened, yet he let himself get tangled in the story. *That was supposed to have an easier outcome.*

"I have no idea about it, but I can find it out. However, it's better if from this moment on, I quit using this phone. If you need to contact me, use the same messenger we used before. I can check it through another country's VPN. I will use my father's phone to call mom, and see what she has to say about it, but now we all need to keep our nerves steady," she proposed. "Concerning the culprit, I have thought about it, and arranged everything. All you need to do is keep your poker face. Can you manage this?"

"Of course, you don't need to worry about me." The corner of his mouth twitched thinking about the consequences of any faux pas from that moment on.

"I'll let you know when I'm safely outside the Italian territory. I'll return back to Hungary, and then I can call you. Nevertheless, this is going to require a longer journey than simply flying there; I need to avoid any border control," she considered releasing the baluster from her grip. Her mind recounted all the things she had to do. The first one was perhaps that of calling her mother, but to do so she needed the telephone number of her father. From his number, only Igor could have called her, *and soon he will also be history, and not a word will come from his mouth,* she thought, clenching her teeth.

"Then have a safe trip. I'll miss you." That last sentence sounded almost foolish.

"I will miss you, too. There'll be a time when we can enjoy our life together— we won't need anyone else," she whispered, relaxing the tension from her expression, melting into a smile.

Ending communication with her felt like placing thousands of kilometers dividing them. Distances grew endless and time froze into a single moment.

A lump formed in his throat, thinking this was perhaps the way it feels when you have to say goodbye to a loved one. In the silence of the room, he turned his face to look around, feeling lost in a place he couldn't recognize anymore. The fear of being apart from her in case they would be considered both guilty for the murder of his father grasped his heart with clawed hands, stopping every beat.

He gasped breathlessly, almost collapsing on the bed. "I need to get a grip on my emotions. If the Police keep seeing me this way, it won't take long before they'll figure out everything. I can't allow this to happen, not to me or to Irina."

He whispered, hoping not to be heard by his mother or by anyone in the world. He wondered whether there was a place where he could have been safe from the view of that nosy Detective Scala and his lousy sidekick.

At that thought he grinned, with the confidence of the man who knew how to get out of this type of situation, sneaking like a shadow in the darkness.

***

Igor reached Irina's bedroom, knocking at her door. "Are you still there?" he questioned.

Opening the door, she offered him a broad smile, "I am, and you shouldn't be here listening to my business," she replied with a pout.

"I wasn't listening, I wondered whether you wanted to join me for dinner?" he asked.

With a sarcastic giggle she narrowed her eyelids, "Are you asking me to come to dinner or to prepare it?" She knew he wasn't any good as a cook, the best he could do was to warm some ready-made meal. She didn't have any memory of them being a family, and the only daily family life was the one she lived with her aunt in Hungary. Nevertheless, this had never been something she missed. Her mother had always been there with her daily calls, her regular visits whenever her job allowed her and with the money she kept sending for her education, clothing, and personal expenses.

She wasn't bitter with her father, for he took care of her as well as always being present. What she couldn't forgive was the stalking, oppressive, and psychologically stressful behavior forcing her mother to cut the bonds with him and search for safety in the arms of Luciano's father. Her experiences with the world of males had been nothing but bitterness, and the time for revenging them all had finally arrived. Luciano was probably the only one she still had some respect for.

"You know me, I'm a disaster in the kitchen, but we can order something from the restaurant. I'll bring you back to France, and I have no idea when I will be able to see you again." Although the relationship with Madlen didn't go the way he'd hoped, he still loved both his daughter Irina and Madlen. Certain that if it weren't for the guy who intruded in their relationship, they'd still have been a family. *He deserved to die; nobody gets in between Madlen and me.*

"Then we might go out to a restaurant. Let's have at least one decent meal together. After what happened, I'm not sure I want to be seen here for a long time. It was a risk to return, but it was also necessary to set up everything," she walked to the door, grabbing her jacket, ready to go out.

Igor followed her, watching every move, and taking in every word she spoke. Irina was completely different from Madlen, as he could see himself in her determination and desire. She was a dangerous concoction between the beauty of Madlen and his willpower.

If you add her own personal unpredictability to this, you have a bomb ready to blow, and if or when it does, she'll be able to transform into a cold-blooded killing machine. Nothing and no one can stop her. Shivering at that thought, he wondered whether he should also keep his eyes open on that ticking bomb.

With a fast shake of his head, he put on his coat and opened the door for her, ignoring the little voice in the back of his head, warning him about his daughter. He considered himself safe, as partners in crime, generally tend to stick together.

***

It was half past ten, the lights in the Department were dimmed, except for the one in the room of Maurizio.

Leonardo left a few minutes before, and the stillness of the place was interrupted by the noises coming from the streets, the random creaking of old furniture and the flipping of the pages, as he compared his notes.

The noise of footsteps, walking in his direction sharpened his senses. Fewer officers were working at the precinct at that time, and generally they were on the other block, or watching position outside the building. Raising his head, almost holding his breath, he stared at the door, figuring out the direction from where the footsteps were approaching. With a slow movement, he switched off the main light in his room, allowing only the small desk lamp to illuminate the environment.

Slowly he opened the drawer where he kept his Beretta 92FS, and trying to be as silent as possible, he grabbed it.

He stood from the chair, and silently walking in slow motion, reached the door, which was left ajar by Leonardo. The footsteps crept closer, clicking on the tiled floor, echoing through the walls, as if they were right behind the corner that connected to the main corridor. The intruder seemed to know where his target was.

Maurizio tightened his grip on the gun, and with his left hand, he reached the main switch of the lights in the secondary corridor.

As he got a glimpse of the foot of the intruder, he switched on the light: "Freeze!"

A loud shout came from the man who turned his face at Maurizio, pointing the gun at him. "For fuck's sake, Detective Scala, are you going to kill me?" Gennaro, the guy from the cleaning service whimpered breathlessly.

"Gennaro, what in the world are you doing here?" Maurizio released his breath, lowering his Beretta. "I thought you were an intruder!"

"I'm doing my cleaning rounds; I should ask what you are doing here? It's half past ten." he regained his breath.

Maurizio glanced at his wristwatch, "I must have lost track of time, I wasn't considering it was so late. I'm sorry I've scared you."

A relieved smile on Gennaro's face creased his aging features like a rubber mask. "Commissario, shouldn't you be home, enjoying the company of your wife and children? The bad guys won't be stopped by a tired cop, and a neglected wife won't add an extra bonus to the package. Go back home and rest."

Grimacing at the thought of Anna, Maurizio shook his head. "You're right," he yawned. "I'm going home. Will you take care of the rest?"

"As usual, *Commissario*. Good night, and I hope I won't see you again like I've seen you tonight," he waved his hand and continued his rounds, whistling in the hope that if there was someone else, he won't be risking being shot or having a heart attack.

With a long exhale, Maurizio returned to his room, paused his computer, and grabbed his coat, switched off the lights in the room, ready to leave, and bid goodbye to the assassin who was still free to do whatever he wanted in the streets of Rome.

Reaching his apartment at almost midnight, a lump formed in his throat as he crossed the door to the room immersed in darkness and completely still. Although he knew his wife and daughter were already sleeping, that image forced his blood to run cold.

It wasn't the first time he returned later than usual at home, and certainly it wasn't the first time he found everyone else sleeping. That was part of his job, and he thought he was used to it.

Without switching on the light, he remained for a moment in the darkness, until his eyes got accustomed to the dim illumination coming from the windows. Tiptoeing, he reached the couch, slipping off the jacket, and sat down; he wasn't ready to go to sleep. The thousands of thoughts and unanswered questions would have kept him from falling asleep, resulting in tossing and turning on the bed.

Leaning on the couch, reclining his head, and closing his eyes, he tried to visually reconstruct what had happened the night of the murder. Like in a movie, he could almost see Claudio coming inside the apartment like he did a moment ago, in the darkness, trying not to wake up his son.

A telephone call, from a hidden number from a foreign prepaid sim card, he started to recall. *Fuck! There must be a way to know who owned that prepaid sim card!*

He clenched his fist in the desperate attempt to understand the dynamics of the murder.

Calm, stay calm, he repeated to himself. *Now the caller must have been a person he knew and for whom he would have left immediately. Madlen comes to my mind. At that time of the night, nobody else could have given him a good reason to leave the house.*

His eyes opened wide, realizing a thought he might have missed.

Madlen's ex-husband! What if he told him he was going to kill Madlen if he wouldn't have come immediately to an established place? That could be the only solution, therefore we need to get our hands on the man before it's too late.

He stood up from the couch and reached the room he used as a studio. There, he switched on the computer, and connected securely to the main server of the Police Department.

He searched the full log through the archives of the mobile phones, hoping to find something in Madlen's one. The idea that her ex-husband was guilty, not only of the psychological abuses and stalking but also of the murder of Mr. Calvani, started to make sense.

Going through the whole list would have taken the rest of the night, but on the other hand, there wasn't any chance he could have done anything else but think.

It's useless, here— there isn't any telephone number which... hold on! he thought as his eyes stopped at something interesting. *Here's another unknown number. Another prepaid sim card...*

Getting closer to the screen, he searched for more information about the call. Of course, the owner couldn't be traced, but according to the search, the location was in Rome. He went through all the contacts he could find in Madlen's phone directory, and that particular number wasn't stored. Nevertheless, she received several calls from that number. *I'm wondering why she didn't save it. The provider is foreign, but according to the GPS, the phone was indeed in Rome. Could it be a glitch or perhaps it was the number belonging to her husband? Who else could have been the caller? Her daughter? Why?*

He held his head between his hands, clenching his fists, grabbing, and pulling his hair. *I'll go crazy! Why didn't I choose an easier job? Why a Police Officer, and why would I even want to pursue a further career to become a detective?*

Listening to his heart racing in his chest, his eyes raised once again to the screen and his attention was caught by the clock, which read 02:00 am.

***

Like every morning, Anna woke up at seven, at the insistent ringing of the alarm clock, perfectly corresponding with the calls of Giovanna from the adjacent room.

With a curse, she opened her eyes and noticed that Maurizio didn't come to bed at all. "I'll figure out this one too, but first, I need to get the second alarm switched off," she muttered, standing up from the bed. "I'm coming, I'm coming!" she said sleepily, limping to the room where Giovanna was insistently calling for her.

"Would you ever give me some time?" She groaned, taking Giovanna in her arms.

With a sigh, she needed to figure out what happened to Maurizio. Reaching the living room, she noticed his jacket on the couch.

"At least he returned home," she said, glancing around. "Let's see if we can find him in the studio."

"Bingo!" she said aloud as she spotted Maurizio asleep on the chair in front of the computer.

"Detective Scala, are you sleeping on duty?" she yelled.

With a jolt as if he'd been tasered, he stood from the chair like a spring, "No, Sir!" he replied.

Realizing where he was and Anna laughing at him, he relaxed his posture and expression. "Fuck! You almost gave me a heart attack."

He glanced back at the chair, "I fell asleep and didn't realize it. Yesterday evening I almost killed Gennaro, one of the workers of the cleaning company."

"Why? Did you fall asleep at work too?" She giggled, playing with Giovanna's hair.

"No, I lost track of time, and when he started his rounds, I thought he was an intruder."

"How hilarious, an intruder at the Police Department," her sarcastic tone was palpable.

"You can laugh about it, but this wouldn't be the first time that some punk got caught trying to intrude on our premises." He switched off the computer and started to walk to the bathroom to have a shower. He kissed Anna and caressed Giovanna before leaving the room, "I love you two, madly."

"And we love you back; isn't it so, Giovanna?"

The little girl gave a giggle and nodded, watching her father leaving the room.

CHAPTER 15

It took a couple of extra strong coffees to get Maurizio started the next day before he arrived at the Department, allowing him to be ready to add more pieces to the puzzle. Before reaching his office, he directed himself to the room adjacent to his own, where senior officer Sandra Milani and officer Carlo Silvani, the two agents helping him, were trying to get through the long list of data.

"I need your help, urgently!" he commenced, justifying the reason for his irruption into the room. "I need to identify Madlen Fazekas' ex-husband. I need his present location and telephone number, and I needed them yesterday! I want to talk to him as soon as possible."

"I'll be right on it," Senior officer Milani said. "As soon as I get the info, I'll forward it to you, although this might take longer than yesterday."

A smirk appeared on Maurizio's face, "Let's try it anyway, ok?" Without waiting for any reply, he rushed to his room. He wasn't sure what he wrote last night, before falling asleep, but certainly the notes he remembered having written would have cast some light on the case.

From the glass wall, he spotted Leonardo as he was walking to the common room to get a coffee. "LEO!" he yelled as he quickened his steps to reach him.

"What's wrong with you. Have you been sampling coke confiscated by the anti-narcotics?" he chuckled, watching Maurizio.

"I barely closed an eye last night; I've been working until late evening and I continued from home until I fell asleep on the computer. I'll take a holiday when this is over," grimacing he recalled the incident.

"Yeah, I just met Gennaro, who was going home. I guess everybody should know how you almost gave him a heart attack," his finger poked teasingly at Maurizio's shoulder. "However, what have you found out?"

They resumed the walk to the common room, "I haven't found out anything yet, but I noticed a few phone calls from a mobile phone here in Rome. The number is from a foreign operator to the number of Ms. Fazekas, probably from Russia. I bet everything I have it's a prepaid sim card, so finding the owner won't be possible, I guess we could ask Ms. Fazekas about it. My first thought was that it could belong to her ex-husband, which I ordered Senior officer Milani to identify." Maurizio's tone of voice was feverish.

"So, I think we should start to put the pieces together, including that man," Leonardo added. "Everything considered, he could have the best motive of all to kill Mr. Calvani.

With a nod, Maurizio entered the common room and went to the vending machine, trying to fit the new pieces to the picture that started to form in his mind. "Another thing to consider is whether the daughter has something to do with the story. I am also keen to believe the whole family created this plan together to get to the money of the victim. Even twenty million divided by three people would be a good reason to plan a murder in detail."

"Then, you need to locate and track all the movements of the girl from three months before the murder." Without averting his eyes from Maurizio, Leonardo reached the vending machine to get his coffee too.

The silence between them, although interrupted by the chattering and the noises coming from the corridors, overwhelmed Maurizio, but he could hardly hear anything else but the voices of his own thoughts as he reconnected everything together like a braid.

There must be a red wire that brings together the actions of every single person involved. The discomfort of Luciano's behavior, his relationship with Irina, this elusive possessive ex-husband, and the apparent innocence of Madlen, must be related to one another.

The ringing of Maurizio's phone brought him back from the depth of his considerations. He peered at Leonardo, who was also mentally placing the pieces together, and grabbed his mobile.

A slight groan escaped him as he realized Berenice was the caller.

"Good morning, Mrs. Moretti," he greeted with a hardly concealed annoyance in the tone of his voice.

"Good morning, Detective. I know you told me not to call you using this telephone number, but I needed to talk to you. Do you have the time to see me?" her voice was far from being apologetic. When she was certain to have good grounds to call Maurizio, she understood she had to overcome every bureaucracy or formality.

"What's your emergency?" he asked, sipping the coffee before it would have gotten cold. *And unless I order an iced coffee, this isn't the way I enjoy it.*

His mood got slightly offset at the call, but he also knew that as the case would have been closed, even Mrs. Moretti would have become a distant memory.

"I was going through my morning routines, when my attention was caught by some noises coming from the apartment of Mr. Calvani. Did you return the keys to his son, or should I presume there is an intruder?"

At those words, Maurizio froze, and turned his eyes in the direction of Leonardo, and almost forgot about Mrs. Moretti waiting for an answer.

"Detective, are you still there? Do I have to presume you're on your way? Should I keep an eye on what's going on in the apartment?" Her voice reached an excited tone.

Surprised to hear her voice coming from the telephone he kept glued to his ear, he almost startled. "Oh, Mrs. Moretti, can you wait a moment so that I can check on something?" He muted the conversation he had with Berenice.

Creasing his forehead, Maurizio looked at Leonardo. "Someone's in the apartment, and unless it's someone from your team, we might have the stereotypical assassin who returns to the crime scene. Come with me, we need to find out and to make sure Mrs. Moretti won't intrude in this matter."

That being said, Maurizio turned and started to walk toward the exit, expecting Leonardo to follow him. Unmuting the conversation, he took a deep breath.

"Mrs. Moretti, are you still there?" he asked.

"Yes, but what's going on? What am I supposed to do?" her voice lowered the tone as if she didn't want to be heard.

"Remain where you are and don't go to the apartment. We're coming to check what's going on there, whether there's a thief or it's Calvani

213

junior, who's trying to fetch something he might have forgotten there," he warned as he reached the parking lot and entered the car.

"Ok, Detective, but what if the intruder leaves?" she asked.

"Keep your eyes on the door, and if he leaves, you'll take account of the time, and we will take care of the rest, but stay away from the apartment." His voice growled inside the car, as Leonardo entered.

Pursing his lips, Maurizio shot a cold stare to his colleague, who kept his annoying nagging expression. "Not a single word!" Maurizio warned.

He was going to tell him everything, but he needed to have Leonardo silent for a minute. That was the moment when his sarcastic comments were the most unwelcomed. The night he spent sleeping in the home office didn't help improve his mood, which went on deteriorating by the minute.

"It was Mrs. Moretti, the woman living in the apartment adjacent to the one of Mr. Calvani," Maurizio explained, trying to focus on driving and to calm down his spirits. "She called to inform that she'd heard some noises coming from the apartment. Now, I am to believe Mr. Calvani recalled some detail he hoped we didn't notice."

Leonardo's expression changed and turned serious in a matter of a second. That wasn't the time indeed to nag at his old friend. "Interesting, and in this case, he might have a lot to explain, as the whole apartment is seized, and its access is restricted only to the forensics. I hope he knows what he's doing, because he won't leave the building with his own car; he's coming with us for an interrogation."

The rest of the journey went on in silence, with the Police radio as the only background to their thoughts.

Reaching the building in *via Giuseppe Luigi Lagrange,* they couldn't recognize any vehicle belonging either to Luciano or to any of the suspects. *Unless he parked in the underground garage? Well, we'll find out soon.*

The gate of the building was open and, as they reached the main door, it buzzed open. "The efficiency of Mrs. Moretti is surprising." Leonardo chuckled, amused.

At the elevator, Maurizio hesitated for a moment. "You take the stairs in case he decides to leave using the other escape route."

Without objecting, Leonardo started to climb the stairs; it wasn't more than four floors that wouldn't have caused much of any delay to the operation. And besides, he was in better physical shape than Maurizio.

They met again in front of the apartment, where Berenice was waiting for them.

"There hasn't been any other noise coming from there, but I haven't seen anyone coming out either," she whispered as she saw them.

"Are you sure you heard correctly, and the noises came from this exact apartment?" Maurizio whispered back, trying to make sure they weren't going to arrest a mouse or creaking furniture.

"Well, there isn't any other way to find out, but to come inside," Leonardo added, extracting a couple of sets of latex gloves from his pocket, and plastic protection for their shoes.

As they were ready, Maurizio tried to open the door, but finding it closed, he turned to Leonardo, hoping he had the keys to the apartment with him. "Were you looking for the keys?" he whispered.

The unavoidable *clicks* of the door lock echoed through the entire building, regardless of its metallic sound. Entering as silently as possible, Maurizio turned his eyes at Berenice, whose breath was almost at his neck.

"You can't come in. This is an official Police operation. Stay here," he whispered, fearing that he had to leave Leonardo there watching her, avoiding any intrusion. With a pout, she backed up a couple of steps without saying a word.

Of course, she knew she wasn't allowed to enter the apartment, but the curiosity was too strong to resist the temptation of following the two officers inside.

Maurizio remained to listen to any possible noise coming from any of the rooms, but it seemed as if whoever was there, if any, had left already. A silent home not necessarily meant an empty one, so, he started to move toward the corridor leading to the bedrooms as Leonardo remained close to the entrance, ready to block anyone who might have tried to leave the apartment. With a slow movement, keeping his eyes in the direction of the corridor where Maurizio disappeared, he closed the door behind him, careful not to make any noise.

It took a few minutes before Maurizio returned once again in the living room. "Nobody's here," he declared, slowly strolling toward Leonardo.

"So, this means we came for nothing?"

"I haven't said this; I said *presently* there isn't anyone in this apartment, but the window in the bedroom of Calvani junior was open. Do you remember leaving it open or is it possible to find out who forgot to do so?" Maurizio's heartbeat kicked up a few paces. He knew Leonardo and every member of his team. None of them would have made such a rookie mistake, but he needed to hear the confirmation of it from his mouth.

Shaking his head, with a grimace. "You know me, and you know my team. We would never keep any possible ways for contamination open." Creasing his forehead, he grabbed his mobile phone, and called one of the officers who took care of the collection of the data.

Meantime, Maurizio returned to the room, hoping to find something that would have cast some light on the case. *I have to admit, it was pure luck to have Berenice to keep her eyes and ears open to this apartment. Without her call, we would have given back the keys of the apartment to Luciano, possibly losing some traces that might give us more data to analyze.*

He reached the window and leaned out of it, trying to figure out a possible way from where an intruder could have come inside or left.

His attention was caught by the cornice. *Hmm, it's quite narrow, but not too much to impede a thief or a murderer from entering or to use as an escape route. I'm wondering where it might lead to.*

Without thinking about it, he decided it was time to get into action like the good old days. The noise of footsteps approaching the room from the corridor stopped him momentarily from his purpose, and as Leonardo appeared from the door, he got a brilliant idea.

"I called my team. None of them recalled having left the window open. According to them, and also to my memory, we didn't open it; it wasn't necessary to the investigation as the murder happened in the garage," Leonardo informed, placing the mobile phone back in the pocket of his trousers.

"Then, I guess we might search for every trace and see whether we can get more information about the visit of our intruder. However, I'll need your help as I intend to walk the cornice and see where it might lead. I don't recall having seen it, but if there's an emergency ladder somewhere, this might be another place where we could focus our research," Maurizio replied, crossing the window seal, trying to avoid looking down.

Leonardo cringed at the idea, but perhaps that was a good one. Although he was in better physical shape, Maurizio was shorter and had smaller feet, which could fit in the span of the cornice. "Be careful," he warned with a whisper.

Taking a deep breath, Maurizio raised his eyes at the sky, as if to ask for some blessing coming from somewhere. Then, collecting all his determination he began to move carefully, his first steps along the walls of the building. Every sort of dramatic movies came to his mind, but trying to focus his mind on his task, he kept going without letting those thoughts distract him.

Easier than he thought, he reached the corner of the building. There, a couple of meters away, was the access ladder to the rooftop. He considered the missing of the security cage was something to point out, because in that case the intruder would have been forced to find another access, or escape, for the matter.

Peeking from the corner, he glanced at Leonardo. "There's a service ladder. I'm using that to reach the ground floor. Meet me downstairs and call your team to gather here immediately with the complete equipment. We need to find out whether the intruder left any traces which we can analyze."

Without waiting for his answer, and already dreading being hung from a narrow cornice, he hurried to walk to the ladder and climb down.

Never in his life, he recalled being so happy to have his feet on the ground. However, he rushed to the main entrance of the building, waiting for Leonardo, who arrived at the same time. The expression on his face revealed how he felt having to explain everything to Mrs. Moretti.

"I know," chuckled Maurizio. "She knows how to get the information she's looking for."

"What's more disturbing is that she knew who my mother is and where she lives. She also asked me to greet her, next time I see her. How's it possible that she—" Leonardo wondered, unable to put in words the confusion Berenice could bring to his mind.

"She knows everything and everybody. She lived longer than us and has more connections than the organized crime itself."

With bouts of laughter, they returned to the car.

"I have called the entire team. They'll be here in a few minutes, so, perhaps we should wait for them. They don't have the keys to the apartment,"

Leonardo recalled, so they waited in the car for the forensics van to arrive.

CHAPTER 16

Aldo and the crew were seated at the table in the small common room of the boat. It was as if a thick curtain had fallen between them, offering an odd silence, which was palpable as none of them dared to make a sound. The slow movement of the lamp, in harmony with the tidal waves of the sea, oscillated to and fro, providing ample light alternately to different sides of the table.

The creaking of the vessel and the ropes which kept it anchored to the dock broke the silence every now and then. The onset of quiet caused a nervous twitch on Aldo's lips.

With his hands on the table, fingers entwined, he mentally went through the details of the plan for that night, the way they would have murdered Igor and concealed his body to the bottom of the sea. *He will be in good company with all the other unfortunate souls who found their resting place among the waves.*

Time seemed to pass slow, and every minute brought more restlessness to the members, wishing for something to happen that would have saved them from the plan they had to agree to. Suddenly, the weak whistle returned them to reality, and like the flip of the switch, they all stood up simultaneously to get ready. Irina and Igor arrived, and that was their signal they were waiting for.

Wearing his jacket, Aldo walked to the bridge, and his eyes caught sight of the two visitors. A weak nod with his face, keeping his grave expression, was all he could offer them.

"So, is everything ready? Are we late?" Irina asked, trying to break the ice, as if to warn Aldo to behave more naturally.

An uncertain smile formed on Aldo's face, concealing the turmoil in his soul. His body tightened up with a shiver when the face of Igor appeared in the light of the boat as he moved out of the shaded position he had been in.

His pale skin and blond hair already caused him to resemble that of a corpse. *That might make things easier, at least from a psychological point of view,* Aldo considered. "Please, come inside, we're leaving immediately, before the tide will become unfavorable," his voice, hardly a growl. *I still don't like the whole situation.*

Expecting to be followed by Irina and Igor, he turned his shoulders to them and walked toward the same place, where a minute before his crew, which were now busy with the routine operation to leave the dock, idled.

Without saying a word, Irina and Igor walked behind him, and as they reached the common room, they took a seat at the table. The feeble light of the lamp barely illuminated the entire room, leaving some corners immersed in darkness, where shadows tended to stretch like the hands of demons, waiting for their victim.

The ship began its route. Aldo kept his eyes on the pitch-dark sea, hoping to arrive at the designated place for the murder in a short time.

The door opened, which startled him, "Captain, we'll reach the place in a while." Mario's voice trembled. "Are you sure we're going to get out clean with it? Isn't there a better way?"

"There isn't." Aldo clenched his teeth, hissing at Mario's remark. He'd rather be somewhere else, and find another solution, but that wasn't an option— Igor had to die. "I don't like this idea either, but we can't turn back anymore. The best way is to go on with the plan and forget about this day."

Nodding, Mario raised his hand to smooth his hair. Like a beast in a cage, he restlessly glanced around unwilling to leave the cabin. His blood pumped faster through his veins as he stumbled back against the wall.

"You're going to put all of us in trouble," growled Aldo. "Take my place and don't move from here until I return. You know where you should stop."

Arching the corner of his mouth downward, Mario lowered his head, averting his gaze from Aldo's furious eyes. But it wasn't rage that moved the captain; Aldo's heart raced too, with all the thoughts swirling in his mind. Going to jail for the rest of his life accused of murder, wasn't what he had planned. That wasn't what he searched for when he sought refuge in the sea.

There's no other way, and a life is a life, whether it's that of a tuna or the one of a human being, he tried desperately to reason and find justification for his future action. He wasn't the one supposed to get rid of Igor directly. Mario was the one who stepped in and volunteered for the job. *We're all fishermen, and none of us ever killed anything other than a fish. We smuggled goods and people, alright— but to kill?*

He took a deep breath, allowing the night's scent of the sea to fill his lungs, hoping it would soothe the storm building in his soul, as it did in past operations. He closed his eyes. *It should be a matter of a few seconds, go there, kill him and together with the rest of the crew we'll take care of the body and the cleaning. Come on, Aldo, you need to do this— it's his life or yours.*

Choosing between murdering a stranger and having his life taken away should have been an easy decision. *Of course, I prefer my life— who is he, after all?*

His eyes opened wide and clenching his teeth with a savage growl, he grabbed the harpoon he used for the tuna and stomped toward the common room. That was something he rarely used in recent times; it was an item that could come in handy for many occasions.

That night, the best would be the murder of Igor, Irina's father. Something was off and the nagging voice in the back of his head didn't want to shut up, repeating that this would have given more complications than the promised solution.

Swallowing the tears welling to his eyes, Aldo growled. "For fuck sake, stop it! I know it's wrong, but I can't turn back, and you know better than me."

He didn't believe a word of what he said, but at that moment, as he felt the engine of the boat slowing the power, he realized the time had come, and there wouldn't be a second to waste.

Holding the harpoon tightly in his hand, with tears filling his eyes, and thousands of thoughts fogging his mind, he reached the room and without any further hesitation he attacked Igor who was seated with his back toward the door. A loud scream coming from Aldo's mouth shook the silent sea. Igor didn't have the time to realize he was drawing his last breath as the spear pierced through his heart. His life ended abruptly without the time to say goodbye, or at least a last prayer to ask forgiveness for all his sins.

Aldo fell on his knees, sobbing for his life and his soul. He wasn't a man who had a firm belief.

What he believed was the sea, it was his religion, his church— his heaven.

Through the blurred sight of Igor's body, that same heaven became his hell, and he promised himself that his life would remain bound to the sea. He wouldn't return to the mainland ever again. From that moment on, he would belong to the tide, to the place where for the first and last time, he killed another man.

The harpoon fell from his hands lying beside him on the rocking floor of the boat. Wiping his eyes from the tears he looked over at Irina, whose trembling lips revealed a pleased smirk at the amount of blood covering the floor and the table.

"Curse you," he whispered. "Curse you!" he yelled once again. Standing from his position he ran out, needing to puke away the dread and remorse he knew would accompany him for the rest of his life.

The crew, unable to speak, silently gathered to the room, ready to clean the mess and prepare the body for its eternal resting place.

Wobbling, like drunk on fear, Aldo reached the command deck, where Mario was petrified; his eyes staring at the darkness in front of him.

"You can go and help the others. I will resume the navigation," his voice a broken whisper.

Turning to Aldo, Mario didn't reply, releasing the grip on the boat's wheel.

Muted by sheer terror, Mario left the cabin as if he was sleepwalking in a nightmare waiting for the morning sun to release him, reassuring it was a dream. No murder had ever happened, and he was still in his bed.

Aldo remained alone; his shirt still marred with Igor's blood. *What am I doing? I can't keep these dirty clothes; I need to clean up everything, including myself.*

Sobering up from the shock, considering that at least he had to keep himself out of jail, and delete any connection with the crime, he walked to have a shower. Cleaning the clothes was the most challenging part, as he needed to delete any trace of DNA. He'd watched enough crime movies to understand this would have been the first thing he had to get rid of. Therefore, he brought on board a good amount of oxygen bleach to clean not only clothes, but also the surfaces from every DNA residue. The boat required an intense cleaning, and the corpse had to be safely concealed at the bottom of the sea.

The spot they chose to get rid of the body was far enough from the route they would have taken during a regular fishing campaign. That was also away from every other fishing route because of the less favorable condition and fish availability.

The crew worked incessantly and hard for three hours, when they could finally resume their journey. All the lights and signals should be turned off, relying only on a maritime compass;

nobody else had to spot their presence, nor the fact that they were returning from an unusual route.

At half past four in the morning, they reached Alec's motorboat, and never before had Aldo been more relieved, as that marked the last time he would ever have to see Irina again.

"So, this is the time to greet each other," Irina's voice was grave as if he never heard her before, as she handed the due money for the service. "We will be in touch if I need your services to reach Italy."

Shaking his head, knowing the gazes of the rest of the crew were upon him, he replied, "Alec can find you another contact from now on. We'll all resume our original fishing activity. This money is not enough for the nightmares we all will continue to have for the rest of our lives, and we would prefer to keep ourselves far from each other."

Flaring her nostrils in anger, she wished to kill Aldo. Nevertheless, she understood that it was the time she had to accept a defeat and get on with her life. *After all, after this one, I won't need him anymore,* she considered.

Trying to keep the beast at bay, she smiled. "So it shall be, this is then a final goodbye. It is a pity, though."

Without waiting for any reply, she turned and walked away, climbing down from their boat to

Alec's motorboat, which would safely smuggle her inside the French territory from where she entered regularly. He knew perfectly how to avoid the national coastal guard, and also in the unfavorable case of being spotted, he had all the cards to avoid troubles.

***

It was a fair March morning, when Luciano was awakened by the ringing of his mobile phone. In his half-sleep, almost mechanically, he grabbed the phone lying on his bedside table, and without caring to check who was calling him, his eyes still closed, he answered.

"Hello," his voice hardly a mumble.

"Bonjour!" the chirping voice of Irina echoed in his ears, causing him to fully wake and sit up in bed.

"Well, I thought you weren't supposed to call me for some time," surprise filled his voice, as his eyes made contact with the alarm clock.

"I know, but we were able to reach the coast of Corsica a couple of days ago. From there I was able to arrive in Paris yesterday evening, so according to the immigration, I haven't moved from here since I arrived in December. I'm calling you from a telephone in a cafeteria. The owner was very kind, when I told him my mobile went off and I needed to make an emergency call. This also means I might call you again, but our conversations need to be very casual from now on," she warned, glancing around her, to make sure there weren't other indiscreet ears listening to what she was saying.

A smile brightened his face and like a stone that fell from his heart, he stood from his bed like he had no more weight. "I love you, Irina, and I can't wait until the time comes when we can live together. Soon we'll be free to live our lives the way we always wanted to, no interferences from anyone— just you and me."

"I love you too. It has been a difficult period, but we will go over it. I promise. I will call you once again from my mobile whenever possible. I plan to return back to Hungary and remain there until the situation is cleared; then we will plan our life in more detail," she proposed.

A sigh, followed by a long pause alerted Irina, as she sensed some troubles were still on their horizon— the kind of trouble she wasn't hoping for. "Is there anything wrong? Why, all of a sudden have you become silent?"

As his attention focused on the reflection of the sunrays, filtering through the shutters against the wall, he tried to recollect his thoughts and find a good way to explain his concerns. "I went back to the apartment." His voice turned lower as if he didn't want to be heard by anyone.

"Did they give you back the keys? Is the data collection over?" She wondered, glancing around to check whether someone was coming to the little room where the landline telephone was located.

"No, not yet. The problem was more connected to a doubt I had," he began to explain, hoping there was nothing to be afraid for. "As you know, last week, Detective Scala and one of his coworkers from the forensic department came to ask some questions about us. They were supposed to return the keys by the end of this week. Yet, when they left, a thousand thoughts started swirling in my mind, and the doubts of having left something important there started to become more and more obsessive. I tried to think about every possibility until one thing came to my mind. That was perhaps the most important one and I couldn't recall whether it was destroyed, if I brought it with me, or I gave it to you."

"Stop changing the topic. You're driving me crazy!" she hissed. "What the fuck did you forget there?"

At her sharp change of tone, Luciano backed up on his bed. The hair stood up on the back of his neck at the swift shiver crawling along his spine, as if to retract from an attack that could have come through the telephone.

"I'm talking about the prepaid sim-card I used to communicate with you previously. That was supposed to be destroyed, but I couldn't remember when or whether it happened." His voice started to shake. He closed his eyes, trying to get a grip on his emotions. His right hand clenched into a fist, grabbing the sheets of the bed. His heartbeat started to increase, his chest tight, as he knew perfectly well what she was capable of.

"You fool! Don't you remember? You gave it to me to be destroyed! How could you forget this detail?" Releasing the tension from her toughened expression, she almost felt like laughing at his zeal and worries.

"I couldn't call you and ascertain this detail, so I needed to find a way to find out. I reached the apartment using one copy of the key nobody knew I had." His fist released the sheet, as he stood from the bed and began pacing around the room. "That was one of the copies my father and I used when we forgot the keys inside. Of course, I made sure to wear gloves, not to leave any trace. However, our neighbor might have called the police, as she might have heard some noises coming from the apartment. I have no idea how she always knew about every move we made. It's like she'd been spying on our family forever." He narrowed his eyes at the thought of Berenice nosing once again in matters that didn't concern her at all.

"So? Did they find you there?" Her tone was alarming, but on the other hand his presence in his own apartment at the end of the data collection, wasn't something that worried her too much.

"No, as I noticed the police car parking in front of the building, I ran to my room and got out of it using the ladder for maintaining the roof. There wasn't any chance to be spotted, because there aren't balconies, or neighboring windows. I seriously doubt anyone has seen me coming out from there, and even so, my face was covered, so it could have been a thief, knowing the apartment was empty."

A long pause allowed them both to recollect their thoughts and consider the situation.

"Call the police and ask when you can get your keys back. They will tell you if there had been an intrusion in your apartment or whether they had spotted something suspicious. If they will return you the keys without any mention about it, there's a good possibility they didn't find anything relevant. Otherwise, if they suspect something, they'll call you in for further interrogation. In that case, I suggest you find a good alibi." She was still shaken, but she knew his intrusion wasn't confirmed by any proof.

They still have nothing against us. "Don't you worry, everything will be solved; you should have recalled that detail, so you wouldn't have to reach the apartment one more time. The only thing now is to stay calm to avoid raising any suspicion. I made sure the weapon will be found in Igor's house, hidden in one of the drawers. There are only his fingerprints, and I believe they will be more than satisfied with that outcome. They have the assassin, and they have the motive. What else they could need?" A broad grin opened up her face.

"Sure," Luciano muttered still shaken for a mistake that could cause him some unnecessary headaches. A grin twisted his face as there was nothing connecting him to the crime.

As he ended the call with Irina, he walked to the window and lifted the shutters. The light filtering through them, forecasting a fair day, and that promise got confirmed as the bright sunlight forced him to narrow his eyes.

Yet, it was brighter, with the knowledge that everything would have turned for the best. Irina's father was probably already dead, otherwise he couldn't explain her happy tone of voice, nor the fact that she was in Paris.

Nothing in the world could have ever disrupted the inner peace he was experiencing in that precise moment, not even the nosy Detective Scala would have been able to get the truth out of that story.

With a loud yawn, he walked away from the window, and decided to call the Police Department. They were supposed to return the keys by the end of the week, but so far, he didn't receive any news.

The thought of having to speak with Detective Scala wasn't appealing to him; he always felt tensed when he heard his voice, and wondered whether he could have simply talked to the call center or information desk to deliver his message.

CHAPTER 17

Maurizio was in his office. Time seemed to have stopped as he worked on his computer. His hand slid across the table's surface, searching for his cup of coffee.

"Nothing conclusive has come out from any of the clues we've collected," he said slowly bringing the cup to the mouth. With his right hand on the mouse and his eyes steady on the computer's screen, his senses still looked forward to the hot coffee to give some relief to his thoughts.

A disgusted grimace contorted his face as the coffee, already cold, reached his mouth, bringing him back to his office and to reality. "Shit!" he exclaimed.

Shaking his head, he stood from his chair and walked to the common room to throw away the evil liquid.

Oh, well, if I want a perfect coffee, I need to go to the bar downstairs.

Likened by his enlightened thought, he threw the cup and the coffee away and foretasted the fine aroma of the espresso served at the cafeteria. Maurizio left with a broad smile on his face.

On his way back from the main corridor he noticed senior officer, Sandra Milani, coming from his office, holding some sheets of paper in her hands. Rushing his steps, in order to reach her, he called out, "Milani!"

At his call, she turned herself in the direction of Maurizio's voice, and opening up into a bright smile she paced toward him. Her eyes shone with excitement as if she was burning from the need to tell what she'd found out.

"I have some very interesting news for you, but let's go to your office; we need some space," she raised mid-air the bundle of papers she carried.

"Fantastic, because after a great coffee at the cafeteria, I'm not ready for bad news," Maurizio replied as they kept walking toward his room.

Closing the door behind him, he gestured for Senior officer Milani to take a seat at the table he had in the middle of the room, where he generally hosted brainstorming sessions with his team.

"So, tell me what you've got. I'm all ears and eyes," he commenced as they were both seated at the table. Carefully placing the papers on the desk, her hands spread the sheets like the cards of a fortune teller, and with a grin, she took a deep breath before starting to explain.

"I have two different pieces of news, and all of them are very interesting. Let's start with the one you asked a while back. I have been searching the call log of Luciano Calvani for the last six months. Like every young man, he has quite a long list of friends. However, I focused on two particular numbers, which I presume belong to the same person."

Taking a pause to let her words sink in, she turned one of the sheets closer to Maurizio. "You see, this is a Hungarian mobile telephone number, belonging to his girlfriend, Ms. Fazekas' daughter. If we check the frequency they call each other, we can immediately notice there are periods where those calls have a distinct break." Her finger moving through the log to the places she'd been marked with a red pen. "During those periods, he received and called this prepaid number. Does it ring a bell to you?"

She watched Maurizio carefully as he was staring at the sheets she gave him. Like under the effect of a hypnotic order, he froze for a second and slowly raised a finger to the air as if that call log had something familiar.

He stood from his chair and went to his computer, checking another call log he had saved and selecting a part of it, he sent it to print. With the printed sheet, followed by the curious glance of Senior officer Milani, he reached the table and compared the two papers.

"It just doesn't ring a bell—it's like the whole damn St. Peter's belltower complex on Christmas Eve. The same prepaid number called Ms. Fazekas recently as well, but not before." Maurizio's heart started to race as his adrenaline pumped in high gear.

He grabbed one pen from the pen tray at the center of the table and swung it before landing on the paper. "This is the telephone number of Irina, even without the need of asking for any confirmation. I don't have any proof about it yet, but I bet ten years of my life, that it was hers."

Senior officer Milani giggled at his expression, "Be careful what you bet on!"

"If this was hers, we need to find out where exactly she was calling from. This is simply a call log displaying telephone numbers. I need to understand which operator was connected to for the roaming. Was it an Italian one? Was it Hungarian or whatever other country? We cannot get the name of the person who owned the sim card, but we can find it out in many other ways."

Maurizio stood from the chair once again and paced the room, keeping the paper in his hand. "If this was her number, and she was in Italy, this means she was here in October for a week and in December before Christmas for another week. What strikes me as odd, is why Luciano told me he hadn't seen her since October?"

"Another question is, why didn't he receive any calls from any of her numbers during January and February? Did she use another telephone number? Did they both use other foreign prepaid cards during that period? Did they keep silent? Why? Two months of not speaking to each other is quite strange for two young lovers..." Senior officer Milani commented still following Maurizio in his walk.

At her remark, Maurizio stopped abruptly as if an imaginary wall materialized in front of him. "What about the emails? Did you check the messages through their email? We need them. Let's ask Leonardo. He should have a copy of the hard drive of Luciano's computer, and they should still be on that log."

Without hesitating a second further, Maurizio hurried toward the door, determined to find out that little detail in the shortest time possible. It was half past noon, and people were either going to the canteen for lunch or returning from there. Maurizio didn't feel his stomach complaining. He wouldn't have had the time to eat, and besides, he wouldn't have been able to stay away from the case.

Senior officer Milani followed him, trying to keep up with the speed as he was walked the corridor. She was trying to avoid stumbling into other people, meanwhile in Maurizio's case, it was the ones who tried to stay out of his path.

Taking the car to the Forensic Department, he stormed into the room where Leonardo was working, "I need Luciano's email log!" he demanded.

Not impressed, as usual, Leonardo hardly raised his eyes from the computer, "Hey, easy does it, man!"

Narrowing his eyes, hardly containing the rage that started welling from his guts, Maurizio clenched his fists. "Please, would you be so kind and give me the files with all the emails of Mr. Calvani junior?" His teeth clenched together as if to contain the demon wishing to exit his body and kill Leonardo.

Slowly raising his glance to Maurizio, he smirked. "You look like a mad dog. Cool down man, and breathe, or you'll pass out." Standing from his chair, Leonardo chuckled, amused. He loved to tease Maurizio every time the occasion was presented to him, and in their job, with a hot-tempered co-worker, these occasions happened regularly.

With a low-pitched growl, Maurizio remained silent, waiting for Leonardo to hand him the material, and as Leonardo approached him with the memory stick, where he copied the email log data, he snatched it from his hands and without any other word spoken, he left the room, not caring whether Senior officer Milani would have followed him. To be honest, hearing her giggles, made his blood boil further, and he hoped she would have remained there until he was ready to return, once a civilized human being again.

Remembering the call received from Berenice about a thief, Maurizio tried to calm his hot temper and returned to Leonardo's room.

"Just one question, though. What about the intruder in Calvani's apartment, do we have any results?" he asked.

"Oh right, I almost forgot about it. Yes, we have the results, but nothing conclusive came out of it," Leonardo replied. "Apparently, whoever came inside the apartment that day had been extremely careful of not leaving any trace."

"So, nothing to report," Maurizio pointed out, with a grunt.

"Unfortunately not, but we can say that at least someone intruded in the apartment as nobody from my team left the window open." Leonardo shrugged.

Knowing the discussion wouldn't have led anywhere, besides him getting sourer than he was before, Maurizio, turned and hurried to the door, mumbling curses meant to be heard only by himself. Pacing through the corridors, his mind got clearer with the increasing distance between him and Leonardo, and as he reached his room, instead of slamming the door behind him, the way he planned, he closed it gently.

He completely forgot about Senior officer Milani, and at that moment, it didn't even matter whether she would have reached him in his office to continue what they started. Nevertheless, as he sat down at his desk, he recalled she'd mentioned having two good pieces of news to give. He was almost tempted to go and ask her about it, but focusing on the little black memory stick, he reconsidered it.

It's better if I'm now going through this log and solve it whether they exchanged emails during that period of telephone silence. If I don't find any emails, we'll need to go through all the most recent call logs and see whether we can find another prepaid number he'd been calling or from which he has received calls.

He turned to the window, observing the soft rain falling with its gentle trickling against the glass. Looking at the sky, he could predict that shortly the sun would have shone again, as small patches of blue started to appear here and there, promising fairer weather for the evening. With a sigh, he released the last bits of bitterness left from the encounter with Leonardo, and with a relaxed expression he opened the file, and started going through all the recipients.

It didn't take much time to spot the email address of Irina and isolating them from all the others; he started to go through the entire content. Something that didn't sound right was the change in the tone of their emails from October onward. They sounded more like the ones he was sending to his mother-in-law for

Christmas or birthday greetings. They were forced, stiff, unnatural.

"Then, without even saying goodbye, or having a reason that could indicate a rupture in their relationship, the email communications quit. The last phone call was recorded in December, before Christmas. The last email was dated the second of January. If they ended their relationship, this would have happened by phone or in person, and after that, there wouldn't have been any other connection, not by email or telephone or any other means," Maurizio mumbled as he went through the emails between the supposedly lovebirds.

With his eyes fixed on the screen, it was vital for him to go deeper into their relationship. "It's clear enough they are hiding something. I don't dare to say you were involved in the murder, but your position is fairly suspicious."

Grabbing the phone on his desk, he dialed Senior officer Milani's number.

"Hello, I thought you wanted to remain alone," Senior officer Milani justified herself as she answered the phone call. She knew that in other cases, she was required to follow Maurizio to continue from where they interrupted, yet she knew that when he had an argument with Leonardo, it wasn't safe to come close to him without wearing protective armor.

A smile showed up on Maurizio's face; he was aware of the way he looked, and it was true when he said that he looked like a *mad dog*. He also felt like one.

"There's no need to apologize. I was going through the emails between Luciano and Irina, and I would like you to collect all the call logs from yesterday to and from Luciano's mobile phone. Do you think you can manage this task for tomorrow morning?" His contrite tone was something Senior officer Milani wasn't used to. During demanding cases like the one they were working at, he was constantly in a bad mood, and there wasn't any chance for him to admit he was wrong.

She hesitated for a moment, trying to understand whether she was still talking with Commissario Maurizio Scala, or to someone who'd taken his place. "Umm, I think I can do better," she stated. "I can give you the phone call log until the end of February and ask to have a more recent one. You will have it by tomorrow at noon, probably."

"Oh, that's fantastic. Please send it to me, and let's make sure we'll get it in real time."

"Sure, I'm doing it right away..."

"And one more thing...." Maurizio recalled she had something more to tell. "You were mentioning another bit of news, but then we completely forgot about it. What was it?"

"Yes," she recalled. "It was about Igor Leonov, Ms. Fazekas' ex-husband and Irina's father. Together with the sheets I gave you today, there's his address, mobile phone and so on. I could find and gather all the data about him together with the criminal records." She took a pause to give Maurizio the time to digest the information she was giving. "It seems like he wasn't an angel, and during his youth, he'd been in jail for drug and weapons dealing. However, after he married Ms. Fazekas, he wasn't charged nor suspected of any illegal activity. The only time police had been called to intervene was prior to their divorce. Ms. Fazekas accused him of repeated stalking, oppressive behavior, and psychological violence. Therefore, she asked for divorce and obtained a restraining order, after which things regained some sort of calm for a certain period. He never took any action besides calling her once or twice asking about him. Everything is filed in the papers I've printed for you."

Open-mouthed, words failed him, except, "Do you realize we have just found a person who was close to the crime scene, had a good motive to kill Claudio Calvani, had the chance and connections to get the murder weapon?" Scratching his head, he stood from his chair and reached the table where the sheets of paper given by Senior officer Milani lay. "I will ask for an arrest warrant; this man is as guilty as sin."

Without waiting for her to reply, he ended the conversation and gathered all the papers. Taking a fast look at them to understand what he had in his hands, he rushed to the chief commissioner's office. At that moment, he'd felt so close to the solution of the case and the fact of bringing another criminal to justice, which in that particular situation would have opened a case with the Russian embassy too as Igor, had double citizenship.

Without hesitating for a moment, he arrived in front of the door of chief Commissioner Angelini. He gave it two hard knocks.

"Yeah!" He growled from the room.

"Sir, we need to ask for an arrest and search warrant. We might have found the person who has murdered Mr. Calvani!" Maurizio blurted, coming inside, and closing the door behind him.

"Well, that's good news, and may I also be informed about the identity of the man or woman we need to ask it for? I would also appreciate having a good idea about the grounds for such a request," Angelini replied with a grin on his face, placing his hands on the desk, fingers entwined.

Shaking the sheets of papers mid-air, he placed them on the desk in front of the chief commissioner. "This man, Mr. Igor Leonov, Ms. Fazekas ex-husband," Maurizio began to explain, taking a seat on the chair in front of the desk.

Crossing his legs, he continued, "As you can also read, Mr. Leonov arrived in Italy with his family as a teenager. He'd been quite restless since then, coming in and out of jail for small crimes, in the beginning, and onto drugs and weapons dealing after. The encounter with Ms.

Fazekas seemed to be the event that led him on the right path of honesty. Yet, his restless soul couldn't be contained, and he'd been depicted as a possessive, oppressive husband that caused them to divorce after the birth of their daughter, Irina. That time Mr. Leonov was once again brought to the attention of the police for stalking, which presented him with a restraining order. Because of Ms. Fazekas' job as a stripper in a night club, they decided to send the daughter to live with her aunt back in Hungary."

Maurizio stood from the chair and, as he generally would do, started to pace around the room. "We have a man whose jealousy could have led him to extreme acts of violence, who could have access to the murder weapon, and who was living in the same city as the victim. Do you need another reason for asking for a warrant, or do you consider yourself satisfied with these?"

Creasing his forehead, chief commissioner Angelini, lazily grabbed the sheets of paper in his hands, and started to read what Maurizio had just explained in words.

A few moments of silence lasted for almost an eternity, torturing Maurizio's thoughts as if there was the chance that his superior would have found a detail to invalidate his reasoning.

Slowly placing the papers back on the table, Angelini looked to Maurizio. "Detective Scala, you're making progress. I will provide you the warrants you're asking, and in the meantime, I wish you will try and locate him. If there's a telephone number, call it. Find where his family lives and his circle of friends. Try to search for something more about him from those people close to him. Also, the most dangerous terrorist has someone to love and friends who care. Find them and let them talk about him. By the time you've found the man, you will also have the warrants in your hands, not only to arrest him for interrogation as the main suspect in the murder of Mr. Calvani, but also the means to search his house."

Like a stone falling from his heart, Maurizio felt intoxicated by his words, and didn't have any other desire than to follow the orders and find that man as if that was the last thing he'd done in his life. "Will be done, Sir."

Quickening his steps, he returned to his room and started to coordinate the tasks among the members of his team.

CHAPTER 18

The warrants arrived quite soon, even before Maurizio or anyone on his team could connect with Igor Leonov. The man had simply disappeared into oblivion, which gave him the feeling that either they were on the right path and the man decided to flee, or like the little voice from the back of his head kept yelling the situation was far more complex than they could have thought.

"I think there's no other way than to go and search his apartment. So far nobody answered, when our officers reached there," he said to himself, staring out the window. With a growl, he stood from his chair, from which he felt like having spent his whole life and walked to the room where senior officer Sandra Milani and officer Carlo Silvani were working.

He was looking for someone to go with him to try once again ringing Igor's doorbell, and in case nobody would have answered, they would have come inside anyway. They had the warrant for searching the entire place.

Generally, he would have asked Leonardo to come with him, but since Chief Commissioner Angelini usually frowned at that decision, Maurizio considered asking one of those who stood by the rules were supposed to go with him.

He considered whether to call the forensic team or not. So far, we don't have any clues to determine the need for their presence, and the louder we are, the worst it can be for the whole operation.

The room was silent, as he came inside, and officer Silvani was alone organizing the files on the database. As he saw Maurizio coming in he stood up from the chair, standing at attention. Carlo Silvani was one of the youngest recruits in Maurizio's department, and he was still keeping himself adhering to the strict discipline he'd learned at the Police Academy from which he graduated a few months ago.

"Sir," he promptly greeted.

"At ease," Maurizio replied. "You're coming with me. We need to reach Mr. Leonov's apartment, and if we don't find him, we'll need to enter the place one way or another."

"Yes, Sir," officer Silvani marched to get his jacket.

He paced toward the car as officer Silvani remained silent for the whole journey. His discomfort was palpable, but Maurizio had his own thoughts to focus on rather than on the feelings of his subordinate. He was sure he would have loosened up with a bit of experience in the Police Corps.

Parking the car in front of the building where Igor's apartment was, the first thing that came to Maurizio's mind was that he wasn't in the residential area where wealthy people used to live. It wasn't the Parioli quarter, that was Esquiline, and crimes were their daily bread in those places. Suddenly something forced Maurizio to stop in his tracks. It was a smell he could recognize in a heartbeat, and a noise capable of shaming him in the noisiest situation. The first was a whiff coming from a bar, where they served his favorite Porchetta sandwich, and the other was the reaction of his stomach to the stimulation.

"Hush!" Maurizio reproached as if he was talking to someone.

A confused officer Silvani furrowed his brow, "Sir?"

"Never mind, officer. Maybe one day I'll explain. Let's hurry up, we don't have time to waste." Quickening his step, already regretting losing the chance of the only meal of the day, he paced toward the entrance of the building.

Having done that job for many years, he trusted his instinct, telling him to call and have in place already a fire brigade's team. Something told him that they would find the house empty, as nobody ever answered when he dialed Igor's telephone number.

Meeting them outside the building, Scala greeted them: "Good afternoon, the apartment is on the third floor, but I can't say which one of those windows belongs to his or the neighbor's home."

"If nobody is inside, we can figure out a way to let you in, and force the front door open, if necessary," one of the firemen answered, as they entered the building.

Followed by officer Silvani, who kept silent for the entire time, they walked toward the stairs. That building, like most of those in the area, didn't have more than five floors, so it was uncommon to have elevators. However, Igor's apartment was located on the third floor, so there wasn't any need to have one.

Despite that detail, as they reached their target, Maurizio's breath was slightly labored. His first reaction was trying one last time to ring the bell, hoping someone would have opened it, and better if it were Igor himself.

Luck wasn't on their side, and although the ringing of the bell was clearly audible, nobody went to open the door. "I guess we need to force the door," muttered Maurizio, glancing at the firemen.

Opening the door didn't require extreme measures and as they entered the apartment, officer Silvani could close it behind him.

They both immediately realized something was off. The apartment was empty, but not in the way suggesting the occupant left for good. It was as if the owner left one day, intending to return in the evening or at least the following day.

"Something happened and either he decided to leave, or someone forced him not to return..." Maurizio considered walking around.

"Sir, do you think he'd been..." Officer Silvani didn't know how to put the possibility to have to deal with another murder, in the same case.

"Murdered? Possible, officer... very much possible, but this is something unconfirmed; this is one of the many hypotheses at the moment," he explained, exploring the rooms of the apartment. The first room he visited was the kitchen. "The fridge is full, meaning he plans, or he planned to return."

Officer Silvani walked to the bedroom. "Sir," he called from there. "His clothes are still here. I'm not sure whether he took some of them, because he planned to stay away for a short period. Certainly, he's coming back, eventually."

"We need to call the forensics. We need..." he said opening another door to another bedroom. "...Hmmm."

"Sir," officer Silvani piped in, as he stepped into the other bedroom, interrupting his thoughts. "I think I found the weapon that killed Mr. Calvani. It was a 9mm pistol, wasn't it?" he said, holding a Beretta APX in his hand.

An ear-to-ear grin opened up on Maurizio's face. "Brilliant, officer, simply brilliant! Yet, he might have had a guest, and perhaps they left together. Perhaps it was more than a guest; it was the partner in crime, or the assassin himself."

Maurizio grabbed the pistol and, opening a clear zip-lock bag, he sealed it in. "Someone placed a suitcase on the bed, its clear shape can still be recognized there." He went to open the wardrobe, but it was empty, likewise all the drawers and other chests in the room.

Narrowing his eyes, Maurizio slipped the notebook from his jacket, and started to scribble some notes. "Whoever was here, didn't mean to leave any trace, he or she, was supposed to leave permanently or perhaps was here only for a visit. This brings to my mind the possibility that this one could have been no less other than his daughter Irina," Placing the small notebook in his pocket, he rubbed his hands together, pursing his lips at the knowledge that all the missing pieces were probably coming together.

"Sir, could it be so, and she was also involved in the assassination of Mr. Calvani? But why?" Officer Silvani wondered.

"Interesting point, but still not sustained by any proof." He paused, roaming around the room. "We need to understand the location of this girl day by day since last October. That was the last time Luciano said she was here. But this is contradictory with what Ms. Fazekas claimed. According to her version, Irina was here in October for the last time, and they spent all the time together." He grabbed the notebook once again, and tapping the pen against it, Maurizio looked to Officer Silvani as if to ask him his opinion.

"We need another person to tell us what's going on, and that is the sister of Ms. Fazekas, the woman who hosted Irina like her own daughter. She might give us better information." He wrote a note on the paper. "Then we need an accurate status of her passport. Somewhere it must have been recorded. If it hadn't, but she's been here, we can consider her one of the major players in Mr. Calvani's murder."

A twitch moved officer Silvani's lip as he dared to speak his own opinion about the case. "But, sir, why would she be involved in the murder of the father of her boyfriend? Why do something that would have given such grief to the man she supposedly loved?"

His voice trembled with uncertainty, and regretted having asked something like that. He was expecting Detective Scala to burst into

257

laughter at his stupid remark, but instead, Maurizio didn't find it funny at all.

As if he was transformed into a salt statue, he remained frozen in a single moment and slowly, after a bunch of endless seconds, he turned his head toward officer Silvani. "Unless he was the one who ordered the assassination of his own father."

Open-mouthed, eyes wide opened as if someone just shot at him, officer Silvani remained speechless. "Sir, this is more than a conjecture," he objected as there weren't any leads to the reason why Luciano would have had any interest in killing his own father.

"We're all making conjectures here, officer; the only certain thing we have is that a man has been killed. All the rest are hypotheses, theories, and nothing else. Indeed, we have the weapon, but was this the one that fired the deadly shot? Conjectures, once again. Only the forensics can answer this question, and that's the reason why we are calling them now." He grabbed his phone and entered Leonardo's number.

"Darling, were you missing me?" Leonardo replied, chuckling.

"I'll never miss your ugly face, but we have a situation here, and your team is required to do their job." Maurizio nagged back. "We are at Leonov's apartment, and we've found a weapon similar to the one that shot Mr. Calvani. We also found traces of a guest he had, so we need to understand who his guest was, and whether there were more than one."

"We're coming right away," Leonardo replied, ending the communication immediately.

A stern glance was offered to officer Silvani by Maurizio, "Show me where you found the weapon."

With a fast nod, Officer Silvani turned on his heels and paced toward another bedroom. Despite the afternoon sun filtering through the blinds, Maurizio walked to the window and opened them in order to see even the smallest of the details in a better light.

The officer paced toward the wardrobe and opened it. "Here it was, sir," he pointed at a small opening of a secret compartment at its bottom.

"Hmmm, if this was the murder weapon, a few questions come to my mind: Did he act alone? Was this a way to get rid of a man who was around the woman he was still jealous of? How did he enter the parking lot of the building where Mr. Calvani kept his car? Was it him who called that night? How did he elude the surveillance guard and how could he know there was a lapse in their recording?"

Officer Silvani didn't reply, but simply observed in awe at his supervisor trying to find answers to questions he didn't think about.

After a moment of hesitation, Maurizio decided to question the people who were living on the same floor. He hoped to be lucky enough to find another Mrs. Moretti, who would have held the right knowledge or at least understand how many people lived in the house. Taking a fast glance at the mirror at the entrance, Maurizio tried to comb his hair, he stepped out of the apartment. He noticed there were five other apartments to which he could have visited, and having slipped away the latex gloves, he rang at one that was the immediate neighbor of Igor.

The door opened ajar and from the chain that locked the door the eyes of a young woman peeked through the opening.

"Sorry to disturb you, Ma'am, Detective Scala here. May I ask you a couple of questions?" Maurizio said, showing her his badge.

The woman hesitated a moment, and after a fast glance over her shoulders to check that whoever was in the same apartment with her, didn't have any objection, she opened the chain that locked the door.

She didn't allow Maurizio to come in, but simply stood there waiting for the questions he needed to ask.

"Do you know the man who's living in this apartment?" Maurizio asked, pointing at Igor's door.

Her expression tensed and her body stiffened, clenching her fists. "I don't know anybody here, and I mind my own business." She attempted to close the door, but Maurizio didn't want to desist.

"Madam, please, I need to ask only a couple of questions. It's important, will you help me?"

The door opened once again, with her eyes wide open, he noticed the terror depicted in her face, and taking one step inside he peeked around, "Are you alone?" he asked.

She whimpered at his reaction. It wasn't anything or anyone she was fearing, but everybody knew Igor was a dangerous person, and nobody wanted to be associated with him in any way. "Please, I haven't done anything bad; I try to live my life in peace here."

Maurizio wiped his forehead. "I only need a couple of questions, nothing more."

She nodded weakly lowering her gaze and tracing a couple of steps away from the door, she allowed him to enter the apartment, closing the door behind him.

"It won't take long, and we can remain here in the entrance. Do you know whether Mr. Leonov had any visitors recently? Did he receive any guests?"

"You will never tell anyone, about what I tell you, will you?" she trembled.

"The door is closed; nobody will know anything. Whatever you tell me is going to be more confidential than the sins you tell the priest." Detective Scala wanted to ensure her that in any case her safety would be considered a priority. If she had information that could have jeopardized her life, he would have taken all the necessary steps to keep her identity secret.

"Like I said, I tend to mind my own business. In this part of the city it makes the difference between keeping yourself alive or not. Anyway, I met him with another woman, as I was going out or coming in a couple of times. I didn't mind listening to what is coming from other apartments. Here, everybody is more or less noisy." Her features relaxed as she talked to the detective, yet she kept her eyes away from him.

Scala slipped his notebook from his pocket. In the middle of those pages, he still had a picture of Irina, the one he obtained times before from Madlen. "Do you recognize the woman in this picture? Was she the one who was with him?" he said, handing her the image.

She grabbed the picture in her hands and nodded. "That's her! Is she in danger?"

"No, I don't think so. I just wanted to know who was living with him or if he was alone. Can you tell me whether she had been here for a long time? When was the first time you noticed her?" He gently retrieved the picture and placed it within the pages of the notebook.

"Hard to say, I thought she'd been here for quite some time. It can be months, but whether it's two or ten months, I can't exactly say."

We need permission to listen to all the telephone calls between Luciano and his girlfriend. We need to know whether there are any clues that can nail them both to the crime, only one of them or it was something Igor planned, and executed on his own. I'm still baffled by the reason why any of these two lovers would have done anything like that.

The clacking of footsteps on the floor, suggested the forensic team had arrived, and perhaps it would be better to reach them.

"I think this is enough for now. Thank you for your cooperation and I wish you a pleasant day, Ma'am," Maurizio smiled charmingly as he opened the door ready to leave the apartment.

"Thanks, you too," the woman replied quietly, almost whispering, hurrying to close the door behind him.

Hesitatingly, Maurizio remained to think about the clues that started to populate the puzzle in his mind. He closed his eyes for a moment allowing those pieces to come together to form the first draft of what could have been a possible scenario. Yet, he couldn't find a place for Luciano.

He didn't have any reason for killing his father. He had access to everything he wanted: money, luxury cars, and a brilliant career in the family firm. The emotional path and jealousy of having his father shared with another woman shouldn't be a real reason for murder. He was married even before.

263

Opening his eyes, he shook his head. *The one who still had a reason and showed ill intentions was Igor. The fact that a similar weapon was found here should be enough to close the case and release an international arrest warrant for him. Nevertheless, there's also the position of Irina. She's been quite an intriguing and controversial figure in this whole puzzle.*

I feel like she has an important role in this situation, but what could it be? Her mother assured me she didn't come to Italy after October. Why would Irina lie to her mother? Was her mother lying to us? Is she also involved in the murder together with her ex-husband and daughter?

He grabbed his head between his hands. The puzzle still had too many holes, and despite the vital clues coming up from that last visit, they failed to make any sense with each other.

Drawing a deep breath, he looked toward the door behind which the forensic team was already getting started with scraping every bit of evidence, collecting items to be analyzed in hopes to get at least a confirmation about the Beretta being the murder weapon.

CHAPTER 19

Once again, he remained working in his office. The days were getting longer and the weather fairer with the onset of Spring. This meant that he'd be working with the AC on, rather than the heaters blasting. That was the only difference for him as he remained later, sometimes for most of the night studying the case. The ticking of the clock brought him to the realization that it was time for Giovanna and Anna to go to sleep. A smile curled his lips, tasting the bitterness of missing precious moments in their life for not having the chances he wanted to spend time with them.

He grabbed his phone and sent a goodnight message to his wife, asking for the umpteenth time to be forgiven for leaving them alone.

The usual clicking of Gennaro's footsteps on the tiled floor, raised a weak chuckle resounding in the silence of the room, recalling at the time when he almost shot at him. *The entire department is still giggling at the incident,* he thought, staring at the door, where a large A3 paper sheet bore the red inscription "DON'T SHOOT GENNARO!"

Another pair of footsteps echoed together with the ones of Gennaro, and from the window he could see Leonardo walking in his direction.

In the dimmed lighting, his face looked paler than usual, as if he was already dead. His pace, as he walked toward Maurizio's office was labored, yet almost mechanical.

The door opened and Leonardo, unusually silent entered the room, his expression blank as if he saw a ghost. "What's wrong?" Maurizio wondered, standing from the chair at his desk.

"It doesn't make sense..." He collapsed on the chair in front of Maurizio's desk. "We're lucky to have the DNA of Igor classified in our archives by all the times he got arrested. The DNA on the Beretta matches his, so he was the one who pulled the trigger. Yet, in that case, I was hoping for more traces. A man who's holding a gun to kill someone else tends to sweat, so there should have been more than the faint traces we'd found. A killer doesn't hide the murder weapon inside his house—he gets rid of it, carefully cleaning it to remove any DNA traces— bleach, oxygen bleach, and other products available that even children would know how to use. Yet, we have a consumed criminal who goes and kills a love rival and keeps the weapon uncleaned in his own house... Why?"

"Hah!" Maurizio jolted as if he heard a joke. "What about the fact that he doesn't seem to have

266

left the country, yet he's nowhere to be found? What about his car? Where is it?" Maurizio raised his hands mid-air, exasperated by the abundance of clues which proved to be completely irrelevant.

At that same moment, Senior officer Milani arrived. "Am I late for the party?" she asked with a giggle.

"There's no party. Why are you still here? I thought you were home," Maurizio replied, surprised to see her coming there at that time.

"I was going home, when a notification about an abandoned car grabbed my attention. I remained at the office a bit longer to go deeper in that piece of information," she said, swinging a sheet of paper she had in her hand. "The car is parked at the Civitavecchia Harbor, and do you want to know who the owner is?"

He grabbed the paper, where the details of the car were listed, "Igor Leonov," he muttered. "How about going for an early swim to Civitavecchia?"

"If my presence is not extremely necessary, I'd like to go home," Senior officer Milani whined, feeling overly tired.

"What about Leonardo?" Maurizio knew there wasn't any need for her to be there, as he only wanted to reach the location and in case he'd found the car, order a towing to the Forensic Department. "I think his presence is required."

"I don't have my swimsuit..." Leonardo chuckled.

"We go commando." Maurizio stood from the chair ready to drive to Civitavecchia and have the car in question towed to the Police Department for the joy of the forensic team to examine. "I know the Chief Commissioner isn't happy when you accompany me, but in this case, you might need to get some evidence. C'mon, get your little chemist's kit."

Leonardo grimaced, "Very funny."

***

It was about half past midnight, when Aldo woke up from a nightmare in his berth on the boat. So far, he kept his promise and never touched the mainland with his feet. Yet, that night he needed to get some supplies for the fishing gig and having forgotten to tell anyone on his team to bring them, he would have been forced to go himself to the storage, where he could find whatever he needed. He hesitated for a while, glancing at the concrete slab on the harbor, where his boat was moored. Less than one month had passed since the day he murdered a stranger, and from that moment, nightmares continued haunting him in his sleep. The blood, the face of the man when he arrived and his eyes— those clear blue eyes still looking at him from the depth of his dreams, still wondering why he killed a man he'd never met before; just following the orders of a young woman who didn't mean anything to him, more than a swift pleasure. Not a single day went by where he wanted to end his life but didn't have the strength to do it.

Yet, those eyes kept watching every move, waiting for him at the bottom of the sea. His heart raced as his feet slowly touched the mainland. Gathering all his strength, he walked to the places where all the fishermen had their storages, with repairing gears, spare parts, and other supplies.

His eyes steady to the nothingness, immersed in his own thoughts and consideration. He hardly acknowledged what was happening around him. At that time of the night, there wasn't anything particular going on anyway. Many fishermen had left; many others would have departed in the morning depending on the kind of fish they were after and their schedule. As for him, the best time to raise the anchor would have been between one or four o'clock in the morning and unwilling to wait for one of the crew to bring everything he required. He had no other choice but to take care of that detail personally.

"Sir!" a male voice abruptly interrupted his thoughts. He knew there weren't other people at the dock, so, whoever was calling out, was certainly directed at him. His stomach churned at the sole idea of having to interact with someone else but the members of his crew.

His blood ran cold when he noticed two men approaching and one wearing a forensic police vest. He couldn't tell for sure, but there were a few doubts about the reason for their presence there.

The turmoil in his mind slowly brewed into a storm and tightening the muscles of his whole body he forced a smile. "Yes," he replied with a frown.

"We got a notice about a parked car around this dock. Maybe you can help us with some directions," Maurizio commenced explaining the reason for their visit at that time of the night.

Aldo backed away from them as they approached. "I don't know. I rarely leave my boat— that's my home. Perhaps if you tell me the place where this car should be, I might be more helpful."

His feet wanted desperately to run in the opposite direction and be as far as possible from the two policemen. He wouldn't be able to hide his discomfort, and sooner or later they would have understood the reason why.

"We only know that a white FIAT Punto has been parked in the same spot for about three weeks around the Roman Dock." Maurizio didn't want to ask about the location of the car. When he saw Aldo hesitating to climb down the boat and the way he stepped as if the floor was on fire, caught his attention. Something told him that man had to be questioned, whether generally or specifically.

Drawing a deep breath, Aldo scanned the dock area and shrugged. "There are many places where a car could have been left abandoned." He turned himself toward the other side of the dock and pointed his finger in the direction of a building. "There's a larger parking lot over there behind that building— you might want to check that first."

Changing the direction of his finger, tracing the distance along the dock line, he continued. "Following the road, there's a smaller one. Perhaps the car's there. I can't say, but those two places are where you might start." His voice flickered.

"Is there anything wrong?" Leonardo wondered.

Aldo closed his eyes, swallowing his tears, "I'm tired... very tired, and my day has just begun, so if you'll excuse me, I have to get some supplies for the night." With those words, Aldo left, hoping not to be disturbed any longer.

The presence of the police never led to anything good; not at least for those ill-intentioned or those who have something to hide. Increasing his steps, he reached the storage without turning back to the two officers.

"Why did you have to ask him anything?" Leonardo wondered as they traced back their steps in the direction of the parking lot where the car was located.

"Because that man... I can't explain it, but there's something in the way he kept his gaze lowered as he walked. Something bothered him before he saw us, but got terrified, when I called him," Maurizio replied, keeping an eye on the place where Aldo disappeared. "Then the flicker in his voice when he claimed being tired. It was as if he was on the verge of a nervous breakdown. He might know something about the car or its owner."

Leonardo shrugged. "We generally make people get restless, particularly when they meet us in the middle of the night."

They reached the car and Leonardo started to take photographs of the location, and other traces he could add to the archive as they were waiting for the tow truck to arrive.

Wearing his latex gloves, Leonardo tried to open the door, wondering whether it had been left open—it wasn't. Besides, the car was supposed to reach the Forensic Department, and from that moment on his team would have collected every sort of evidence to answer at least a couple of the most important questions: Who was driving the car? Was he alone? Were there traces of blood, which were cleaned up? Any other body fluids?

While they waited for the tow truck, Maurizio kept an eye on the place where Aldo went and waited to see him coming out. The parking place wasn't the closest one, and the view to the dock was restricted. Nevertheless, if there would have been anything that attracted his attention further, he could have moved away.

The truck arrived at the same moment as Aldo got out of the storage. "Take care of this; I'm going to follow our friend," he said without taking his eyes off Aldo.

Reaching a good position, he noticed a group of four people walking in the direction of the boat where Aldo was. Something was also off with them. They were walking in a group, but none of them exchanged a word. They all appeared to be mesmerized...scared even; nothing to do with the fishermen he always remembered from the time when he went to the very same dock as a child with his mother to buy fish.

For as long as he remembered, fishermen belonging to the same team, charmingly chattered together, exchanging jokes or orders, and most of all they were all quite vociferous and loud. *These men seemed as though they were walking inside a church, as if they were going to a funeral. And perhaps they have witnessed one,* he considered. He took note of the name of the boat and decided he would have reached the closest canteen. Some places were open during the night, planned just for the fishermen who were leaving late. If nobody had given him useful information about that strange ghostly crew, he would have tried the morning after until someone would have

273

explained to him what was going on with these people.

The group reached the ship and went in without greeting the one who Maurizio considered being the captain.

"Anything interesting?" Leonardo's voice interrupted his inner considerations.

Turning his face to him, he grinned. "You bet there is. Have you ever had any experiences of members of a crew being silent, and barely talking to each other?" he asked as they started to walk back to their car.

Shaking his head, Leonardo had to admit it would have been the first time he'd heard something similar.

"I took note of the name of the ship; either we find someone ready to tell us what is going on with those people, or we will have to find out, our way." Maurizio kept walking in the opposite direction, turning his face every now and then to check the boat.

A loud yawn from Leonardo's mouth echoed in the silence of the night. "I guess we won't have time to go to sleep, will we?" he complained.

"I would like to ask around first, then we can return home, and tomorrow we will take care of the rest. Believe me, I'm dead tired too, and thinking of driving all the way back to Rome and home, is already killing me."

They reached the closest canteen, which was still open. Maurizio wasn't familiar with the town or the places, but he required information for his own peace of mind.

The place was ready for closure, as there weren't any customers, and the personnel started to clean up. The man behind the cash register was going to tell those who entered to go out, but his mouth froze as he saw the two officers coming inside. The first reaction was whether they were performing a routine check of the business activities for any irregularity, but noticing the forensic police vest, he relaxed immediately. "Good evening," he greeted. "What brings you here at this time of the night?"

Maurizio looked around to get familiar with the environment. "Good evening to you too. Is this a place where the fishermen come to have dinner or lunch?" He didn't have time for pleasantries, and he went straight to the point.

"There are many places where they go, but this is the closest one," the man replied as the other two kept tending to their cleaning chores.

"Do you know anything about a fishing boat called, "Sea Rider?" Maurizio asked.

"Aldo's boat? Sure, he came here every day for dinner. However, it's been a few weeks. I see it there, but he doesn't get out of it anymore. Sometimes I walk around, I have some good friends among those fishermen, and Aldo was one of them."

Narrowing his eyes, Maurizio glared at Leonardo with a barely perceptible nod. "What happened? Did you have an argument?"

Shaking his head with his hands raised he said, "That, I'd be damned if I know what's going on. To tell the truth, detective, the whole crew became like ghosts. None of them frequent any of the bars or restaurants they used to. They hardly exchange any words with the other fishermen. Some talk about an ancient curse, a tale whispered by the seamen, but you know those are just legends, and there isn't any curse, or any evil creature that can steal the soul of a sailor," he chuckled, amused recalling that story.

"I don't believe in those stories either, but sometimes those legends can hold a foundation of truth. Do you recall anything that took place recently, which could explain their change in behavior?" Maurizio inquired.

He was aware that in such a small environment, if someone had some trouble with any irregularity, the last person they would have talked to it was a police officer. Yet, if the case was perhaps more serious, like the case of a murder, they would have been more likely to talk.

"I can't say whether there had been anything that triggered their sudden change of behavior. The only thing I can say, and I know, is from one day to another, they quit coming to this restaurant to eat, they became all silent, and Aldo refused to leave his boat. I have asked the others, but none of them could understand what was going on." Some fishermen smuggled either drugs or weapons between the coasts of Corsica and Italy, but that was a detail he wasn't going to mention for no reason in the world. If that was the reason for Aldo and his crew to change their behavior, it would have been something the officers had to find out on their own.

I'm their friend; they all have families, and I'm not going to reveal anything that could bring such a financial catastrophe. Fishing is not an easy job or something to get rich with, and those people are trying their best to survive.

Maurizio nodded, understanding that what he revealed was only a part of the truth, the rest he had to figure it out on his own.

"Another question if I may—we received a notice of an abandoned car in one of the parking places. It was a white FIAT Punto. Have you noticed anything strange around? You said you walk around to chat with the fishermen, perhaps you've noticed the car too, or you've heard someone talking about it?" Maurizio needed to get all the information possible from him. Certainly, he could have asked around the day after, but his curiosity had to be satisfied; he didn't have time until the morning after.

"No, I haven't noticed anything about any car. I'm sorry."

As his lips pursed, Maurizio remembered having the pictures of Igor and Irina with him.

Perhaps that was information the man was willing to share. *If so, they might have left the country relying on the help of those fishermen, and perhaps their departure relates to the behavior of this Aldo and his crew.*

Maurizio searched his pockets, extracting the pictures, drawing a long breath, "Have you ever seen any of these two people around here? Did they ever come into this restaurant or have you noticed them passing by?"

Unwilling to give away too much information that could have harmed any of his friends, he took the pictures in his hands and examined them carefully. He certainly remembered having seen the girl roaming around Aldo's boat, but he was sure this information could have given him more trouble than the one he was dealing with; the ones that turned the whole crew into a ghostly bunch of lost souls.

With a weak shake of his head, he returned the picture to Maurizio, "I'm sorry, Detective, I haven't seen any of them around here. You should ask whether the fishermen had seen anything; they have better chances to be outside around the dock, either when they are taking care of the boats, or when they are unloading their ships."

Taking back the pictures, Maurizio looked at Leonardo, and back to the man behind the register. A long, exhausted exhale escaped his mouth as tiredness won over frustration and stamina. "Thank you very much. We'll try to find our own answer. Have a good night." He turned and motioned to Leonardo to head out of the restaurant.

"So, perhaps Igor and Irina were here, because the car was still in the parking lot," Leonardo commenced. "They had probably been seen them, because the man was obviously lying, and the most important thing is that this most likely had to do with the change in mood of the crew of the Sea Rider."

"And that's exactly what we will find out. I'm sure with the right pressure this Aldo will be ready to talk." He took another look at the dock, and with a grimace he noticed the boat was no longer there. "We will have to wait until tomorrow morning or afternoon, whenever they'll be back from their fishing gig."

Tilting his head backward Leonardo whimpered, "I can't wait. I need to sleep, or I will collapse here. It's two o'clock."

"We'll have to continue tomorrow. First thing in the morning you will go through the examination of the car, and I'll be back here with officers Milani or Silvani to find out more about those fishermen. I wish I had a search warrant, but that might require time, and it's something I don't have. Oh well, let's go to sleep."

CHAPTER 20

Maurizio arrived in zombie mode the following morning to his office. He had no idea how he was able to reach the Police Precinct with his car in the state he was in without having any kind of accident. A coffee wasn't simply a must, it was a civic duty, and for that kind of emergency, it should have been the one offered in the common room by the vending machine. That tasted like the nastiest rat-poison in the world; the kind of beverage necromancers use to wake the dead.

The morning didn't start off on the best premises, but recalling what was at stake, he gathered all his strength after gulping the murky brew, like a medicine. He paced toward the room where Officer Silvani and Senior officer Milani were supposedly working.

"Milani, come with me, we need to arrive at the Roman Dock in Civitavecchia," he said without even a simple greeting, slamming the door open.

Officer Silvani, as usual, stood at attention like a tin soldier, "Sir!" he greeted.

"At ease, officer... at ease," Maurizio smiled. Perhaps it was excessive, and not being in the army anymore, that kind of stiffness wasn't required, more than standing up as he came in with more natural moves, like senior officer Sandra Milani did. Nevertheless, it was something that pleased him.

Grabbing her jacket, she smiled, "Good morning, Detective Scala." She turned to Officer Silvani, noticing he had sat down, continuing his duties.

"Last night, Romizi and I reached the Roman Dock, where we found the car and had it towed to the Forensic Department, so I guess Romizi's team is playing the little chemist on it today," he chuckled with an evil grin on his face, as they walked to the parking lot.

"Interesting, but I also have some news for you," she commenced. "When you told us to have Mr. Calvani's call logs, we found out something interesting. Recently, he received a call from a cafeteria in Paris, besides those from friends and family members in Rome. Then, there was a couple of days of silence and then a regular call log from Hungary. The number was the same as the one he used to receive calls from his girlfriend, Irina Leonova."

"So, this means she's back in Hungary," he muttered. "As we return from Civitavecchia, we will have to pay a visit to Ms. Fazekas. We need her to call her sister and have her answer a couple of questions about whether she knows anything about the girl's hangouts. We will also ask what her mother knows about Irina." He took a short pause before entering the car, to explain what he was thinking. "Ms. Fazekas has always said her daughter didn't come to Italy if not to visit her. She also was sure Irina didn't have any boyfriends, not here or in Hungary, because she was sure she would have told her about it. Now, I don't have any experience about it, because my daughter is only four years old but perhaps you can help. Would you have told your mother if you're dating the son of her boyfriend?"

She placed her elbows on the top of the car, her eyes locked on Maurizio, and thinking carefully at his question. "I don't know. I mean, there's nothing wrong with dating the son of the boyfriend of your mother, but it might make the situation quite bizarre. Perhaps she doesn't feel comfortable telling her this detail; not at least until she's sure she wants to spend her life with him. In her place, I would have done the same."

"That's exactly what I was thinking," he said, pointing his finger at her, and entering the car. "The problem is, in this case, we have a murder, and there are a few options we might think about. The first is Igor Leonov, jealous of Madlen's relationship with Mr. Calvani, decided this has been the time to show her she belonged only to him, and if he couldn't have her, then nobody would. He didn't want to kill her, because deep inside he still loved her. Yet he was ready to make sure that everyone who came too close would be eliminated. So, strong of his previous connections with the criminality, he got a weapon and carefully planned a way to murder Mr. Calvani."

Senior officer Milani followed him without saying a word, focusing on the possibilities he was going to present her.

Starting to drive, he continued on with the list of his suspects. "Then we have Luciano, he doesn't need to murder his father for money. He has the funds already, together with fancy cars and easy life. Yet, the father doesn't have much time for him. Mrs. Moretti, his neighbor, confirmed there had been a tensed relationship between the two, and it often transpired into frequent arguments."

With a slow movement, Senior officer Milani turned her glance at him, "Oh please! This is not a reason to kill. In that case, I should have killed my father, bring him back to life, re-kill him and repeat the sequence at least ten times, for all the times we argued!" She raised her hands to her chest. "Sir, haven't you ever argued with your father, and yelled at him that you wished he was dead?"

The sudden roar of his laughter relieved the heavy atmosphere created by the conversation. "Indeed we argued, and once I also punched him on the nose... That wasn't a good move from me. You might be right; a fight can happen, and this doesn't mean he could have killed him. Yet, there's the controversial figure of Irina, despite the turbulent relationship between her parents, she has a good relationship with her father— so close to have her going to see him and staying at his place. The fact that she didn't tell her mother about her intention to spend some time with her father, could be a good explanation for Ms. Fazekas not to know about her move. But then..." He recalled what he saw last night. "Then the car of Igor was found in Civitavecchia abandoned in a parking lot. Eventually he agreed with some fishermen to bring him to the coasts of Corsica. Perhaps he had someone who could have smuggled him eluding the coast guards and the border police."

Senior officer Milani pursed her lips, twisting them to the right side. "Was his daughter, Irina, with him?"

"Probably, yes. In his apartment were found traces of DNA belonging to him, and some sporadic traces most likely belonging to a woman. The neighbors confirmed having seen a woman resembling Irina, going in and coming from his apartment. I consider her presence strange enough because, according to the border police, none of her passports were recorded after the time she left Italy in October. Although coming from a Schengen area, you won't necessarily have to pass for the passport control, the authorities would have the list of the passengers on a flight, boat, or train. If you come by road, the passport control can't be eluded. What did she have to hide, if not her involvement in the murder? Why murder the father of her boyfriend?" He grinned, knowing the answer was right in front of him, but he couldn't grab it.

"What if her father asked her to help him? What if she had the connections to help him reach France or any other country like a ghost?" She pondered, weighing all the possible explanations.

"That's the reason why I call her figure controversial, and her relationship with Luciano more suspicious. If you are in a relationship with someone, the least you want to do is make them suffer, so you are not going to kill the father... I can't place her anywhere with any certainty," he said, his eyes steady on the road. "There's more," he added. "Last night, we met a very strange crew of fishermen. The captain is a man who used to frequent one of the restaurants on the dock, but suddenly, he's reluctant to even step foot outside of his ship. The rest of the crew arrived later, only exchanging murmured words between each other. It was as if they were going to a funeral..."

"Well, that's weird," muttered Senior officer Milani.

"Would you consider it a coincidence that all these facts happened at the exact same time? I mean, Igor disappears and his car has been found at the dock. This captain and the members of his crew suddenly turn into zombies, without an apparent reason. Irina returns to regularly call

Luciano from Hungary, and Igor? Well, he simply disappeared, probably in South America with a fake ID. Obviously Igor is the killer, but is there a role in this for Irina too? What about Ms. Fazekas? Was it a well-orchestrated plan to get her hands on 30 million Euros of insurance allotment? Even if you divide that amount of money in three, it's enough to make them all rich."

Silence dropped in the car, as the noise of the engine and the beeping of the radio filled the gap. Maurizio's heart started to race, populating his mind with thousands of questions, which answers he knew would have created other questions, until there wouldn't be any more of them. His head was about to explode without having reached any solution, besides the responsibility of Igor, for which the Interpol, the French, and Spanish Police had been alerted.

Despite this, the case couldn't be closed until all the other players would have found their place in the crime scene, and they would be given to the judge to confirm their responsibility or to acquit them.

One thing for sure, he needed proof to arrest any of them, and suspicion alone wasn't enough. *I will have to ask for a request to interrogate Irina. She has too many things to explain and to prove. After the call with Ms. Fazekas' sister, I will call Luciano one more time and according to their answers, I'll decide how to act. I will make sure the press will be informed about the incoming closure of the case having Mr. Leonov accused of the murder acting alone. This is also something I can reveal today to Luciano.*

A grin appeared on his face. "You know what? I'm going to release the funds from the insurance and keep a very close eye on what everybody is doing. I will also invite Irina here for a final statement, as the killer is her father; we need her to testify and to clarify her position. Once they have the assurance that the case is closed, they'll loosen up and lower their guard."

Stopping the car in one of the parking spaces around the dock of Civitavecchia, Maurizio drew a long exhale, and turned to Senior officer Milani. "So, first we're going to see whether the *'Sea Rider'* is in the dock. In that case I'm sure I'll find the Captain there— if it's true as he said and he never leaves it. Let's hope something interesting comes out of it."

With those words, he rushed out of the car and started to walk to the harbor.

***

Aldo and Mario were the only ones from the team who remained to clean up after the fishing trip. There was a lot to be done, and the only thing they were looking for was to go to sleep after the long night spent on the sea. In silence, hardly exchanging a glance as if they were invisible to each other, they kept on with their duties, and didn't notice the arrival of Maurizio and Senior officer Milani.

Observing the two men silently working, Maurizio hesitated to grab their attention taking a second to understand whether this was to be considered normal behavior. Other boats arrived in that same dock, and although the members of the crew were clearly tired and looking forward to rest, they still had the strength to exchange a chat with each other, and divide the tasks to be done for the day, before they all could go and rest for the night.

Different than the previous night, when silence seemed to be almost deafening, during the day, the noises of the boats, the lapping of the waves, and the voices of the fishermen filled the air. The breezes ushered in the smell of salt, fish, engine gasoline and oil that blended together into a pungent scent— one which allowed them at times to come to their senses.

Only the 'Sea Rider' created a gap of silence between one ship and the other.

Shaking his head, as if to return from his inner considerations, Maurizio walked a few steps toward the boat. "Good morning," he greeted, making sure the badge he kept hanging from his neck was clearly visible, as Senior officer Milani kept herself at a certain distance to keep an eye on whatever was happening around.

Aldo turned his gaze in the direction of the owner of the voice and recognizing the same detective he saw the previous night, he froze in the same position, waiting for him to come and arrest him. He didn't fear ending up in jail, nor the shame of being arrested for the murder, after all he knew he deserved to be punished for something he hadn't pondered with the right clarity of mind. What he *was* afraid of was the future for the rest of his team. Those were the people that, although they agreed to the murder, had to lose the most from his imprisonment.

"Good morning, detective," he replied, walking closer to him.

"Do you mind a couple of questions?" Maurizio asked.

A weak smirk, moved the features of Aldo's face, "If I know the answers..." With a swift gesture he invited Maurizio to climb to the boat.

"Thank you, it won't take long. I can see you're busy here." He commenced taking the pictures of Irina and Igor out from his pocket. "Have you seen any of these two people around here recently?"

The trembling hand of Aldo reached for the two pictures; he noticed and recognized them as Maurizio handed them to him. The torturing feeling of having no idea where to hide, and that Maurizio knew what happened to Igor, forced him to lower his gaze, focusing on those two images.

The eyes of Igor, watching him from the photograph took life, asking him once again the reason why he had to agree to such a deal. With an almost imperceptible twitch of his lips, he placed the picture behind the one of Irina, hoping to find some shelter from those questioning eyes.

Yet, the only thing he found was the memory of the pleasure with which she convinced him to agree with the deal of having her father murdered on their way to France.

"I have no idea who they are, I don't remember having seen any of them around or perhaps I haven't noticed them," Aldo said, handing the images back to Maurizio. "There are many people coming here every day as we tend to sell directly to the customers our fresh fish when we return at seven o'clock. During the day, people are coming and going, and it's difficult to remember or to pay attention to anyone, unless they have some particular trait that grabs the attention."

"Hmm..." muttered Maurizio, placing the photos back in his pocket.

"Who are they, by the way?" Aldo tried to pretend being interested in their identity, because he wanted to know whether they had any idea about the murder.

"The man is accused of murder, and we're looking for him, hoping he didn't make it to France, or Spain..."

"Have you checked on the ticket sale for the cruises? Could it be so and they both took one of those cruise ships?" Aldo tensed his shoulders, considering that, perhaps the police thought Igor escaped abroad. *And without a corpse or any other evidence, there's no way they could discover what happened that night, when I brought her to meet with Alec.*

With a deep exhale, Aldo felt relaxed, and despite the turmoil with his conscience, he felt confident the police weren't after him, and perhaps they never would be.

"I see ... well, thank you anyway. I won't waste your time any longer, but if you happen to remember anything, I would like you to call this number." Maurizio handed him a business card with his name and telephone number. He seldom used a business card, but in that particular case, he needed to be the one he'd contact directly.

I'm not a psychologist, but I know when someone has something to say and can't find the words or the courage to let everything out, he thought.

Grabbing the card, he placed it absentmindedly in the pocket of his trousers, "I will. Have a nice day, detective," he muttered as Maurizio turned his shoulders to him and climbed down the boat.

"They are hiding something," Senior officer Milani whispered as they were leaving. "The other man almost tried to hide, fearing being questioned. I don't know whether they have something illegal in their activity or it was something connected to the case, but we need to keep an eye on them."

Maurizio didn't reply immediately, he was still processing in his mind the chat he had with Aldo and the vibes he had from his elusive behavior. He didn't' notice Mario, but what Senior officer Milani said about him fitted perfectly with the impressions he also had and shared with her.

His phone ringing startled him, and he almost was tempted to turn his face, wondering whether it was Aldo calling him. A slight disappointment darkened his expression as he read the caller ID, noticing the number of Leonardo.

"Tell me your news," he answered, in a busy tone, walking toward the car.

"We've completed the search of the car, and we couldn't find anything suspicious. Nevertheless, it was clear there were two people in the car and he was driving." Leonardo replied without minding at the formalism. "Since Irina was with him in the apartment, we can conclude she was the passenger, and they have probably left the country together."

That conclusion hit Maurizio right in his gut. Not that he didn't have the same feeling, but he hoped he could have stopped them before. Although the Interpol together with the French and Spanish Police were alerted, they'd wasted precious time allowing Igor to be safely hidden, but God only knew where. "I know. We asked the same guy we saw yesterday at the dock, and according to him, he hasn't ever seen either Igor or Irina. He suggested we check the cruise ticket office, but we all know their passports hadn't been recorded at any of the border control. Therefore, one option that comes to my mind is that they left the country illegally."

"That's the most feasible one but doesn't give us any chance to get them back." Leonardo grimaced, knowing they shouldn't have underestimated the ease by which moving through the border could have given so many troubles when dealing with a crime. "What are you going to do now?"

"We need to play smart," Maurizio looked around as if to grasp an idea from somewhere. "I'll mobilize a few officers to follow every single step, track every phone call of Luciano Calvani and Madlen Fazekas. They are the only two who didn't leave the country. I will release the funds for the insurance, and we'll see what will happen. If any of them are connected to the crime, we will know and act immediately. We might have the chance to get the position of either Irina or Igor."

Maurizio walked to the car mentally filing a list of things to do in the next few minutes. Turning to Senior officer Milani, he frowned, "Call Officers Mariani and Siri. Tell them both to follow Calvani Jr. like shadows. Never leave him alone, not even in the bathroom. I want a detailed report about what he's doing, where he's going, the people he's meeting and his telephone calls at the end of each day. Nothing should be left unreported, and if anything suspicious should arise, I want to be notified immediately, so as to order a warrant to arrest him. Tell them to be ready to bring him in at any time. Also, order the night shift for Officers Cattaneo and Marchesi. I will organize the same surveillance for Mrs. Fazekas in the meantime."

"Yes, sir," she briefly replied, grabbing the radio.

"Now we're going to the apartment of Mrs. Fazekas, and let's hope she'll be there willing and ready to solve that little mystery for us," Maurizio added as they reached the car.

CHAPTER 21

Maurizio and Senior officer Milani returned to the Department after three o'clock in the afternoon. The two teams of officers were already on duty to follow and report everything happening with Madlen and Luciano, but Maurizio just received other pieces of the crazy puzzle from the visit to Madlen.

In his office, together with Senior officer Milani, they began to put everything together and clarify the situation. "So, let's start with Irina," Maurizio began spreading the dossier on the table, where he collected all the evidence.

"She was raised mostly by her aunt and studied in Hungary. The relationship with both her parents was smooth, like those you could expect in a normal family. The mother called her every day and went to see her every time her work allowed her. Madlen described her as a quiet girl with great determination and sense of humor. Her aunt describes her as a restless child, who cooled down with age. She didn't seem to have had any trouble, either at school or frequenting wrong companies, I mean the typical lively child, who turned out to be a normal teenager. At school she'd always been a proficient student and started to work part-time during high school to earn some small money for herself."

Senior officer Milani kept her eyes on the papers, following what Maurizio said. Resting her elbows on the desk, she crossed the fingers of her hands. "When she reached the age of fifteen, she started to travel to Italy, to spend some time with her mother, and other times with her father. Those were all recorded by the border passport control at the airport," she continued. "But one day, something happens, and she meets Luciano. According to him, they met at the university, when she was looking for a course to follow. The flame sparks, and they fall in love with each other. Yet, we have no idea whether she knew Luciano was her mother's boyfriend's son. This is something we can only imagine. According to Luciano, she didn't know in the beginning, and she found out later." Maurizio continued, standing up from his chair.

Following him with her gaze, Senior officer Milani continued. "Indeed, and from that moment on, her visits to Italy become more frequent, but they aren't all recorded from any border control. According to Luciano and her mother, she was here in October. In December, none of her passports were recorded entering the Italian territory, but she was in Paris traveling with a friend of hers, this is according to her aunt as well.

However, her presence was testified by a telephone number from a prepaid sim card. The card has a foreign operator, but the roaming was recorded in Rome."

Maurizio started to pace around the room. "Yes, but these aren't the only times she arrived in Italy. For an unspecified period, she was living with her father, but her passport was recorded only in Paris. According to what her aunt told us today, she's now in Hungary, and we should move forward to get her here. The chief commissioner has provided grant permissions with the Hungarian government. We're eagerly waiting for a reply."

"Why would she try to enter Italy illegally?" Senior officer Milani shook her head.

"The first thought is that she didn't want to be tracked, but she made too many mistakes, like showing herself around. The second one is that she might have been aware of the plans of her father to kill Mr. Calvani, and she tried her best to stop him, in virtue of the fact that he was the father of her boyfriend." Maurizio tried to reason.

"Or perhaps she came to help him, because she was the one who had connections to allow them both to leave the country as fast as possible and without leaving any trace. But who could have been her contact?" Senior officer Milani wondered.

Maurizio stopped pacing and remained frozen. "The captain of the *'Sea Rider'* for example.

They were leaving for a fishing excursion. What if on that occasion they brought her to the coasts of Corsica?"

Shaking her head, Senior officer Milani's hair, secured in a ponytail swung from side to side, "How would they have been able to elude the coastal guard? They need special permission to enter the territorial waters of another country, regardless of whether we're talking of the EU, which has a special agreement."

"This might be true, but it would fit with the strange behavior of the crew. Yet, this is just a theory and we have absolutely not a single clue in that direction. To be honest, there isn't a single proof that Irina and the captain knew each other, and the connection to reach the French coast could have been through other sources. Nevertheless, this could be one possibility we might take into account," Maurizio returned to sit down in his chair and started to add some notes to one of the documents spread on the table.

"I guess we have the culprit. Igor Leonov killed Mr. Calvani out of jealousy. Was Irina also involved? Did she help her father by giving him the contact of the person who would have smuggled him far from the Italian territory? Did she pretend to fall in love with Luciano to obtain information about the garage where Mr. Calvani kept his car?" Senior officer Milani continued.

With a smirk, Maurizio leaned in his chair. "We'll need to have those members of the crew questioned either as witnesses or as suspects. Then we will need to have Irina here to listen to her version of the facts, as a suspect. If the Interpol, the French Police, or the Spanish Police will find Igor Leonov, we will have him here as the man who committed the crime."

"So, the case is closed?" Senior officer Milani asked.

"No, the case isn't closed until all the suspects have been interrogated. Once we are sure that there isn't anyone else who can be connected to the crime, we can close and archive the case," Maurizio explained. "But we are close to it, and it took a reasonable time to reach this stage."

He realized they were once again among the last to leave the office. Nevertheless, there was a positive note in it, and it was that although they were the last ones to leave, he could still make it on time to have dinner at home, instead of skipping it one more time.

"We'll continue tomorrow as we wait for any news about Irina, the Interpol about Igor." He grabbed his jacket and put his computer on pause. He was supposed to check on the reports of the surveillance teams who were following Luciano and Madlen during the day, but he considered that a task that could have been carried out from the computer at home.

He wasn't expecting anything new to happen in the immediate future. *Generally, it takes some time before obtaining interesting news.* A smile brightened on his face.

"See you tomorrow, Officer Milani," he said, greeting Sandra.

"See you tomorrow, Commissario!"

He sent a fast message to his wife, Anna, and rushed to the parking lot.

***

Since he returned to live in the apartment he shared with his father, Luciano didn't seem to have regained any ease in life. Browsing the TV, the sounds seemed to echo louder within the walls.

I thought I was accustomed to being alone in this place, as you have always been away for one reason or another. Yet, the knowledge that you're not going to be back brought a feeling of loneliness, I'm not yet used to, Luciano thought, still zapping from one channel to another.

Leaning his head back on the couch, he closed his eyes, remaining to listen to the noises coming from the streets and other apartments. Everything was quiet as if the whole world held its breath, waiting for something to happen.

It was a week since he decided to enter gradually in leading the family business. The help offered by his mother and the close cooperators of his father was priceless. Without them, he would have been in deep trouble, understanding all the details and the secrets to run it successfully. He hadn't yet come to a decision whether it would have been reasonable to quit the University studies and focus entirely on the family business.

"There shouldn't be any problem to keep going in this direction. I can continue my studies and work part-time on the firm..." He opened his eyes, almost surprised to hear his voice in the emptiness of the apartment. "I don't know, but I need to make a decision soon, and perhaps tomorrow I can have a talk with my mother and also with my mentors in the firm."

Standing from the couch, he walked to the window to watch the city, slowly falling asleep. "I miss her," he whispered, thinking about Irina.

The new responsibilities forced him to withdraw from the social life he'd enjoyed before the murder of his father. Although this wasn't the way he'd expected his life to turn out, he was also aware this was the way it was supposed to become sooner or later. And in this case, it was absolutely better to be sooner, than later.

His eyes searched the room and met the telephone lying on the table in front of the couch. Hesitatingly, he grabbed it and remained staring at it for long moments, wondering whether it would have been too late to call Irina.

As indecision stopped him from dialing her number, he decided simply to send her a message, and considering that the morning after he needed to be at work earlier than usual, he reached the bedroom.

Walking in front of his father's bedroom, he stepped inside. All of his belongings were still there in a box, as he didn't have the time to put them back in order, after the police concluded the search. There wasn't a steady thought in his mind, but he sauntered to the bed where the boxes were and found Claudio's mobile phone.

Holding it in his hands, he found it surprising that he didn't have any particular feeling at its touch. Slowly, he went through his father's belongings, something he didn't have the time to do before, or perhaps he tried to find all the possible excuses to avoid that task in the past days, since he got the keys returned.

There were all his clothes, the expensive watches he liked to collect... "All those things need to be gifted to some charity organizations. Someone might need those more than I do," he considered almost whispering within himself.

With a long exhale, he stood from the bed and walked to his room, ready to end the day, hoping to have the chance to talk to Irina soon. That forced separation was something he wished to bring to an end.

From the civil police car parked outside the building, Officer Cattaneo and Marchesi kept an eye on the movements inside the apartment. As the lights switched off, Officer Cattaneo smirked, lowering the binoculars on his lap. "He probably went to sleep," he said.

"Good for him, I wish I could do the same," growled Officer Marchesi. "I'm wondering what we are doing here? It has been a couple of nights and days that Mr. Calvani has been followed in every single move. Nighttime we place ourselves here and wait until the morning after. If you ask me, we're wasting resources uselessly."

"Well, at least I know this won't last forever. The case is coming to closure, so we will be assigned to something else. Personally, I prefer to keep an eye on this guy— it's an easier task."

Suddenly, the noise of the ringing of the phone interrupted the monotony of the night. Switching on the recording device, Officer Cattaneo jolted in his seat, "The girl is calling him!"

Luciano was sleeping when the telephone started to ring. He didn't need to know who was calling, as there was only one person who would have had any reason for that late night, or early morning call, for the matter.

Without switching on the light, he grabbed the phone, flashing and scattering its light in the darkness. "Hello, I thought you were sleeping." He climbed out of bed, turning the alarm clock to check the time.

"I wasn't sure whether to call you or not. I talked to my mother earlier, and she hopes the case will be closed soon, so she can have access to the money she inherited," she replied casually.

"I wish everything will be closed soon as well. I haven't received any news from the detective, and I'm wondering the reason for their silence. I wanted to call you because I started missing you. I can't wait until we can finally live together," his voice merely a whisper.

A giggle escaped her. "We haven't been apart recently, but I understand what you mean, and I feel the same. Returning here in Hungary, after such a long break felt a bit strange. My aunt has been asking me a lot of questions about my journey. I'm afraid the police questioned her too. It might have been a mistake revealing our relationship. We should have kept this detail to ourselves."

Luciano shook his head, "I was forced to. I have no idea how it was possible, but it seemed as if Detective Scala knew about us, and then it would have been worse trying to deny it. Someone must have seen us together and told him about us... Moreover, I tried to delete all the emails between you and me from my computer, but those things leave a trace in the server and they might have retrieved them, revealing our relationship."

For a few moments, none of them knew what to say. "There isn't anything wrong in being together and not wanting anyone else to know. Why are you so worried about it?" He was aware of the risk involved in being connected to each other.

"Because this is the first time my aunt is asking me so insistently about my hangouts. Although we don't live together anymore, we have a very close relationship, and when I need to leave my apartment for a journey, I always ask her to take care of the mail, so she knows exactly when I'm away. This was the first time she called me to know where I've been and with whom or what I've done in Paris. I'm wondering whether the police have been questioning my mother about me too?" She glanced around the room, as if she were waiting for something to happen, perhaps the police would suddenly burst into her home to bring her to jail.

The possibility wasn't so remote, and she knew the risks involved in planning the murder of two people. Eventually nobody could connect her to the murder of Igor. *Also, before accusing me of his assassination there must be a corpse, rather than a missing person who is accused of having killed a rival in love.*

Despite the difficulty to be connected to any of the deaths, her soul wasn't at ease. She needed to make sure she would never be suspected either by disappearing, perhaps with a counterfeited passport to another country.

Luciano remained listening to her silence as if he could hear her thoughts and doubts. "Everything will be fine— I promise," he whispered, closing his eyes.

Without replying, she nodded, "Perhaps we should go to sleep. Tomorrow we both need to get back to work."

"Yes, probably it's better for me to quit the University and focus only on leading the firm; there are so many things to learn about it, and I can't pretend to focus and succeed on both tasks. Maybe one day, I'll be able to resume my studies, but for now I need to concentrate only on one task and leave this terrible tragedy behind me. Don't forget I love you," he said, feeling his heartbeat thumping in his chest.

"I love you too. Have a good night," she replied, ending the conversation. Once again, she scanned the room with her eyes, and the feeling of hopelessness grabbed her soul.

Clenching her fists, she gathered all her strength. "It's not over yet. I can't let myself go and get caught off-guard."

CHAPTER 22

Maurizio was driving to the Police Department. He knew he was late, the traffic on the Tiburtine was slower than ever, and with clenched teeth he reached his frustration level to the fact that yet, he couldn't find a new apartment where to move with the family. He didn't have much time to dedicate to the task, and he felt grateful to Anna for not having asked anything about it.

"I need to get rid of this route, one way or another," he hissed as his car slowly proceeded toward the exit where he would have the chance to speed up. The ringing of his phone chimed in his ear through the loudspeakers. Without the need to check who was calling he replied, confident that Chief Commissioner Angelini was wondering where he might have been.

"Scala," he answered with a slightly upset tone.

"Detective Scala, are you upset about my call or anything in general?" The voice of Chief

Commissioner Angelini reached him like a cold shower.

"Sir, I'm in the worst traffic jam on the Tiburtine. Nothing personal, but I know I'm late and there's nothing I can do about it." Maurizio shook his head, still keeping his eyes on the road.

"I feel for you, but I didn't call you simply to remind you that you're late, rather I wanted to inform you about the status of your request to obtain a warrant for Irina Leonova to have the chance to interrogate her. Being the suspect is also an Italian citizen and residing in a European Country should make the task easier and smooth, and a request has been forwarded to the Magistrature." He smirked, imagining Maurizio cursing in the middle of the traffic jam. Everybody who has been living in Rome or visiting long enough to be stuck in the Tiburtine, knows the challenges of having to drive it every day during the peak hours in the morning and afternoon.

"Great news! Thank you. I will get the team together to brainstorm all the clues and evidence we have so far. Then I will be able to generate a report for you this evening, or whenever I reach the precinct," he sighed hopelessly aware of the fact that there wasn't any certainty on when he would have been able to get out of the Tiburtine.

Ending the conversation, he thought about it, starting to create a list of things to be done. Certainly, having Irina back in Italy for interrogation would have been a step ahead in the investigation. He was certain she must have had at least an idea about the location of her father's whereabouts.

I think she was aware since the beginning of his plan to kill Mr. Calvani. The question is whether she is an accomplice, a person who tried to dissuade him, or she was completely ignorant of the fact, and his father left home with an excuse the night of the murder, he reasoned within himself. *There must be something that can give an answer to these questions besides questioning her personally. I need to go through all the DNA traces with Leonardo, and that's exactly what I'm going to do as soon as I get there—if ever I manage to do so.*

It took almost another hour to get to the precinct when Maurizio stormed in, looking like a mad dog, as Leonardo would have described him, when he completely lost his temper.

Leonardo was on his way to the common room to get another coffee when his eyes crossed Maurizio's. They both remained frozen for a moment, engaging in a staredown, their eyes like gunslingers in western movies.

Leonardo opened his mouth, ready to mock his high school friend.

"Don't even think about it!" Maurizio yelled, his voice resounding through the alleys. His finger pointing at Leonardo as if holding a gun.

Releasing a chuckle, Leonardo raised his hands, "Don't shoot! I give up."

"We need to talk, and I need all the brainpower available. I'll come with you to get some coffee, and then we'll gather Officers Silvani and Milani to my room." Maurizio cut it short. The first thing he needed was a coffee to collect his thoughts and forget about the traffic jam. He was confident that staying until late, as he predicted, would have allowed him to skip the worst of the peak hours on his way home.

As they all were gathered to Maurizio's office, he gave a good look at each of them. "We have to take stock of the situation. First of all, we have forwarded the request to the magistrature for an international warrant arrest of Irina Leonova. We have to expect that they will ask for more evidence of her involvement, and this is what we need to do now." He turned to address Senior officer Milani. "What is the news of the officers who are following Luciano Calvani and Madlen Fazekas?"

Opening a folder, she brought from her desk, she cleared her voice. "Concerning the moves of Ms. Fazekas, there hadn't been anything out of normal. She went on with her life like you would expect. She has tried to get her job back at the club, even if no more as a stripper. She hasn't received or made any suspicious calls, so we can certainly continue following her, but I doubt she's involved in the murder. The reason why we might want to do so is her connection with her daughter." She turned to officer Silvani, who had the report of the officers who were keeping an eye on Luciano.

"Instead," Officer Silvani continued, talking with a lower tone of voice. "Mr. Calvani received a few phone calls from Ms. Leonova. All of them took place during the night, which is something that raises many questions. He's working and waking up early every morning, so I would expect him to go to sleep early and keep the phone calls for the late afternoon. Yet, they call each other in the middle of the night. Of course, there isn't any rule that forbids calling at that time, but I personally don't get the reason. According to the recording and transcript of the chats they had, it sounded like they knew they might have been heard."

"Hmm..." Maurizio muttered, biting his lower lip. "Was there any possibility that the officers had been spotted?"

Shaking his head, Officer Silvani was convinced this wasn't the reason for their hesitating chats. "What I know is that her aunt started questioning her about her journeys, and she got wary. I believe this rarely happens, so she probably expects to be invited to present herself here to answer a few questions. Moreover, it was obvious she'd been in Italy entering in a way to elude the border control. The reason why she did so, isn't clear but strange enough to bring her in, if not on the crime scene, quite close to it."

Maurizio remained silent for a moment to elaborate in his mind that information. Then raising his glance, he turned to Leonardo, who had been silent the entire time, almost holding his breath listening to what the other officers had to say. "What about the forensic report? You said once that there was something strange on the DNA traces detected on the murder weapon. Can you tell us anything new that came to your mind, or that came out from further testing?"

Bringing his knuckles against his mouth, Leonardo furrowed his brows, creasing his forehead. "I still find it a bit strange. The touch DNA is indeed different for each human being, and someone might not leave any trace when they touch a certain surface. Some individuals consistently do not leave sufficient traces for a complete DNA profile, making them impossible to trace only on the basis of touch DNA. We are talking about a man who wasn't alien to criminality. He knows perfectly well that DNA is the best way to nail a person to the crime scene." He stood up and walked to Maurizio's desk, where he could find some napkins. He wiped his hands and placed the napkins on the table. "If we're going to examine these, we would find Maurizio's touch DNA, too—just traces, but you get the message."

Drawing a long, deep breath, Leonardo returned to sit at the table. "There are a few points that don't make any sense here: The first, is why didn't he use latex gloves? Whether or not these wouldn't have stopped to imprint some traces, they wouldn't have left any fingerprints, which were there. Secondly is the amount of touch DNA material. If you hold a pistol for a few minutes, you might or might not leave any viable trace. Yet, if you are in an emotional state, like the one of a man who's going to murder a love rival, your hands are certainly sweating, and you're leaving more of a residue than you'd ever wish to. The third point is why in this world would you keep the murder weapon at home without making sure every trace is wiped away? It might belong to a serial killer's profile who wishes to be caught—not an occasional assassin. Then there's the presence of her daughter..." Leonardo shook his head.

"So, she was there by chance?" Maurizio added.

"Sir, I don't believe it was a coincidence that she was there visiting him." Senior officer Milani intervened.

"Neither do I, but I need more proof, and I need to have her here before accusing her formally of the murder, or the participation in the murder of Claudio Calvani." Maurizio grabbed a pen from the table. "Meantime, Igor Leonov has disappeared from the face of the earth, as none of the border police in neighboring countries had recorded him. He's searched internationally, but so far nothing, and I'm not expecting to see him any time soon." He dropped the pen on the table with an angry grin, twisting his face.

"What could be the reason for the girl to kill or to take part in the murder of her mother's boyfriend, who's also her boyfriend's father? She cannot have such a strong bond with her father to agree and make two dear ones suffer." Officer Silvani mumbled, lowering his head.

"Never underestimate the reason of a psychopath," Maurizio lectured. "Besides, let's assume ad absurdum that she is the killer. This would have brought her to enter the Italian territory eluding the border control. She also would have needed a scapegoat, and who would have been better than her father? A man who had all the reasons to get rid of Mr. Calvani. She knows the place where his victim lives and has access to it, being the girlfriend of his son." He stood from his chair and started to pace the room. "She had all the accessibilities to get to know the garage area, and that there would be a maintenance gap, where the cameras weren't on. She had the spare keys to the garage, so Luciano didn't have to go downstairs and open it for her when she arrived in the garage area.

"Still ad absurdum, let's consider she had this plan since before engaging in the relationship with Luciano, and got access inside the apartment of his victim. She knew many things, because her mother would have talked to her about this man, and perhaps her father would have added other details to the picture..."

"But, then where's the father? Where's Igor Leonov?" Officer Silvani asked. "What would have been the reason for her to kill Mr. Calvani? Jealousy? Was she helping her father in getting revenge?"

"Money!" Leonardo smirked. "Don't forget the life insurance the mother would have gotten, in case of death."

"Her mother— not her!" Officer Silvani grimaced scratching his forehead. "Besides, it seems like she had no idea about the insurance..."

"What if all the three would have come to an agreement to get rid of him and split the money? I don't believe the fact that Madlen wasn't aware of the insurance. If Mr. Calvani trusted so much to stipulate a life insurance, he would have let her know," Senior officer Milani intervened.

A pause of silence allowed them to consider what had been said about the case and about the people involved. Yet, something was missing.

Maurizio was sure the details they were missing were right there in front of their noses teasing them by being so evident nobody could have seen it.

"Let's return to the original ad absurdum assumption," Maurizio turned his glance at Officer

Silvani. "You were asking where Mr. Leonov is, which is indeed a great question, because I believe he was involved in the crime, but as an accomplice. He would have been the man who provided the alibi, the gun and the way out for Irina. What if she also killed him? She could have pretended to sympathize with his cause of jealousy, fueling it to get rid of the man who had been psychologically harassing her mother. She intended to get rid of those who would have harmed the people she cared for. So, in her sick mind Igor was to be eliminated to rescue her mother from a long-time stalker. She killed Mr. Calvani, who constantly ignored the attention Luciano was requesting."

"So, you're saying she was the one who called Mr. Calvani that night forcing him to reach the garage. There, she waited for him and killed him with the pistol of her father," Leonardo suggested, rubbing his chin.

"Precisely," Maurizio turned, pointing a finger against him. "This justifies the presence of the pistol still in the house. She wanted us to find it, so we would have thought the father was the killer."

"That would also explain the weakness of the touch DNA on the pistol. If she cleaned it of all the traces, before making sure he would have touched it, even for a few seconds, the amount of DNA material would be consistent with the small amount we've found..." Leonardo muttered with a lower tone of voice as if talking to himself.

"You know what?" Senior officer Milani rubbed her hands together as a grin brightened her face. "This would also bring to light the strange behavior of the captain of the— what was the name of the ship—right! *The Sea Rider*. They might have had a part in the fleeing and perhaps murder of Igor!"

"Ten points to Milani!" Maurizio cheered. "That's a brilliant observation, but who was the trafficker who smuggled her to the French coast? You know what we can do? We'll bring her here and ask her a few questions about her father. Then, we might bring in the captain and see the reaction of both of them when brought together in the same room. I don't expect a Greek tragedy, but neither a complete indifferent behavior. One of them has to be weaker and crack."

"So, now all that we need is having Irina here," Officer Silvani considered.

"Chief Commissioner Angelini has forwarded a European arrest warrant to the Judiciary; they will start the process immediately. The only thing I'm afraid of is the timeframe. The Hungarian Magistrate will have a time limit of 60 days to get consideration and eventually accept or reject our request," he grinned, glancing at the calendar. "This means that at the latest in June, we will have the chance to have Irina as a guest here. In this case, we need to have all the recordings of her

317

telephone calls, either to Luciano or her mother—at least one of the two. I'm expecting her to get in touch, either for help or for advice."

Turning to Officer Silvani and Senior officer Milani, he continued. "Make sure that the surveillance on these two people is intensified; we don't want to lose one single word between them."

"Yes, sir!" they replied in chorus, before leaving the room together with Romizi.

Alone in the room, silence overwhelmed him. The muffled noise coming from outside his door, the movement on the corridor he could see from the window resembled the memory of a dream, seen through the fog of his own thoughts.

This wasn't the first murder he had to solve in his career; there had been, sadly, many others, which, although they found justice, didn't come back to life. The grief they caused to loved ones wasn't solved with justice, and nothing would have given any sort of comfort.

His mind returned to his family, and particularly to his wife and daughter as he wondered whether something like that could ever happen to him.

I'm sure Mr. Calvani didn't for a second conceive the idea of being murdered; this is not something people figure out as a possibility. Although we all know it might happen, we still discard it when there isn't any reasonable hint of any such possibility.

He grabbed the dossier once again in his hands and visually went through the entire documentation.

He wasn't a politician; he wasn't a magistrate investigating on the high ranks of the organized criminality's business. He was a successful businessman like there are many others. He didn't have enemies, or at least so he thought. An unpredictable enemy like a jealous ex-husband can be very dangerous, but I'm afraid there are far darker details than simply jealousy in this murder.

He smoothed his hair back with his hands, holding his head as if to keep it from exploding. The case could have been almost closed in virtue of the fact that the assassin seemed to be clear.

Igor Leonov killed Claudio Calvani; the motive was jealousy. He wrote on a piece of paper.

"But was this all? We can't say much of anything until Interpol can give us a hint of this man's location," he said aloud, grabbing a pen and spinning it around his finger. "The last location we can pinpoint the man is the Civitavecchia Harbor, where he left the car. There, he was traveling with Irina, but as she reached Paris a few days after, he simply disappeared."

"They both had been smuggled through the borders, and I'm wondering whether it's so and the captain of the *Sea Rider* has something to do with it? Some fishermen had been caught by the coastal guards smuggling goods, overfishing, polluting or other similar crimes. Honestly, I wouldn't be surprised if they were Irina's contact to enter the Italian territory illegally."

He slammed the pen on the table and stood up, losing his temper. He knew there was something right there in front of his eyes. The elephant in the room was laughing at him, and yet, he couldn't see it.

For the umpteenth time, he grabbed the dossier and turned the pages to the forensic report. "Those traces of DNA seem... Hold on!" Struck by an idea, Maurizio dashed outside the room, rushing to the lab at the Forensic Department, where he was sure Leonardo had returned.

"Do we have any previous records about Igor's DNA?" He feverishly panted as he reached him.

"Yes, we do, and that's why we could determine that it was him who was holding the gun— but why?" Leonardo wondered, turning his chair toward Maurizio.

"Were those traces gathered on a crime scene or were samples obtained as a routine when he got imprisoned?"

Leonardo grimaced and stood from the chair. "I believe they were taken as a sample when he was in jail, but I need to check on our archives."

He headed to his desk and reached his computer. "So, let's see what we have here."

"Igor Leonov..." Leonardo muttered as he browsed the archives. "Here, we have only one when he got arrested for drug dealing."

"What about the traces collected on the car steering wheel? You said he was the driver, so there must have also been a record about it," Maurizio's voice flickered as his heart started to race.

Raising a finger mid-air, Leonardo turned to get the phone. "Miro took care of the collecting and reporting of those traces. I'll ask him right away where it is."

That said, he called his colleague, and as he ended the call, he looked to Maurizio, impatiently waiting for any response. "He said he saved the temporary report on another folder. I'm getting it—here it is!" he cheered opening the folder.

Silence fell between them as Leonardo stared at the screen.

"What's there?" Maurizio urged, his hands trembling.

"There are the traces of DNA recovered from the steering wheel, and also those on other parts of the car. Generally, the ones on the outer parts, like the trunk, the doors, and handles, are easily deteriorated, either by the wash, rain or other agents that can weaken with the time said traces."

Leonardo pointed the finger at Maurizio. "Nevertheless, they were still clear."

Maurizio mentally returned to the dossier he was reading, trying to find the missing piece that would have made sense to the big mystery.

Narrowing his eyes, Leonardo kept his gaze on him, trying to figure out his thoughts.

It took at least a few minutes of silence, when suddenly a wide grin opened up on Maurizio's face. "THE ELEPHANT IN THE ROOM!" he yelled.

"What do you mean?" Leonardo asked, taken aback by the sudden reaction of Maurizio.

With a sudden move, Maurizio opened up the dossier of the previous report he carried in his hands. Frantically flipping the pages, he reached the part where the traces were described.

As he reached the point, he slammed the folder on the desk with a loud smack that resounded in the room. "Now explain to me the reason why the traces of DNA in the car were clear and, in the pistol where you also confirmed they should have been evident were, instead, weak!"

Leonardo tensed his shoulders, trying to find a plausible reason for the differences in traces. *Indeed, considering the emotional state, his hands would have probably sweated, and it would make sense to have more DNA material on the pistol, rather than in any of the parts of the car, particularly on the outside frame, where it's easier to have them weakened. Yet, they were clearly stronger there.* He didn't dare make any suggestion to Maurizio, knowing him, and recognizing the crazed expression in his eyes, he was expecting a solution from his coworker.

"I tell you what it means!" Maurizio thundered. "That man had nothing to do with the murder of Mr. Calvani," he pointed his finger outside the door as if to point in the direction of Igor, to slam it furiously on the desk immediately after.

He searched around in hopes of finding whatever object that could prove his point. His eyes met a cardboard box where a few test tubes destined to be brought to the adjacent room of the laboratory were waiting. He grabbed a couple of latex gloves and unpacked one of the test tubes.

With a swift move he returned to Leonardo and grabbed his hand resting on the mouse and laid it for a few seconds on the test tube immediately after. "Now tell me, where do you think I will find more genetic material— on the mouse or on the test tube?"

He was panting, barely breathing correctly from excitement, and once again didn't let Leonardo speak. "I tell you, where—on the mouse, because you've touched it and actually used it. The test tube was just recently placed in your hands, where some sweat might have still been present and thus your own DNA. My version of the story is this: Irina, killed Mr. Calvani. She needed a scapegoat, and framed her father, who had a perfect motive." He collapsed on the chair, wiping the beads of sweat from his forehead, trying to take deep breaths to help his heartbeat slow down its rapid pace.

Leonardo didn't look convinced, and rubbing his nose, he shook his head. "It doesn't make sense. Why would she kill Mr. Calvani? What would have been her gain in the murder? She hardly knew him." There was something that didn't fit in Leonardo's mind. It was true that the theory would have perfectly fit the difference in DNA material collected. Yet why?

"I don't know. This is something I need to find out, and perhaps given the right pressure, the captain of the *Sea Rider*, might offer us some information about it. In the meantime, I need to have another chat with Senior officer Milani and Officer Silvani about the team following Ms. Fazekas and Mr. Calvani, whether they have some news to share, some strange and suspicious moves or some peculiar telephone call.

Without waiting for any reply from Leonardo, he turned and walked away. Shaking his head, Leonardo watched him leaving, heading to the door; with a light click closed behind Maurizio, keeping all the unanswered questions inside the room for Leonardo to digest. A sense of urgency in finding out what went on that night and the reason for murdering a person like Claudio Calvani grabbed his soul, impeding him to move from his position.

CHAPTER 23

Four months had passed from the crime, and Maurizio was eagerly expecting the answer from the Hungarian Magistrate, hoping it was positive. There was also the wait for any news from Interpol about the location of Igor Leonov, or whatever information that could have given proof of him still being alive.

His impatient temper made him believe that something was slowing the investigation to the point of being unable to make any progress. "I'm wondering whether the communication from the Magistrate arrived directly to Chief Commissioner Angelini and he forgot to mention it to me?" Shaking his head, he knew there was only one way to find out— and that was going to his office.

Cringing at the thought, he armed himself with all the positive thoughts he could gather in his soul and marched toward Angelini's Office.

He knocked on the door, already regretting his decision, recalling his chattering nature.

"Come in..." The usual busy voice of his supervisor replied.

Pursing his lips, he opened the door and dashed in, closing it behind him.

"Good morning, sir..." Maurizio commenced.

"Oh, Detective Scala, I was thinking about you," he cheered, inviting him with a full gesture of his arm to take a seat in front of his desk. "Once you said you have some relatives living in Aosta, haven't you?"

"Y... yes, my grandmother is still living there— she's alone though, and..." Maurizio was dumbfounded at that question.

"Maybe we can help each other. You see, my son is going to study at the University of Aosta, and he's looking for a place to stay, even for a short period until he gets acquainted with the environment and the services. I was wondering whether your grandmother needs a young man to help her out in exchange for a place to stay," he explained with a large smile on his face. "Of course, there aren't any obligations; if she doesn't feel the need to host him, that would be perfectly fine."

Maurizio thought about it for a moment. Recalling his grandmother, Bruna, he'd feel sorry for Angelini's son, as she was the perfect antithesis of the image of a kind and weak old lady. Regardless of the venerable age of 82 years, she could still keep an entire army of wild youths at bay, still being herself the terror of the neighborhood.

A wide grin flashed on Maurizio's face at that thought.

"I don't know...." He glanced back at Angelini. "It's been some time since I've visited her. It's not like we dislike each other, but the distances sometimes become overwhelming."

Angelini pursed his lips, nodding thoughtfully, "I understand, but I would appreciate it if you could ask her."

The tone of his voice turned insistent, and Maurizio understood he didn't have to deal anymore with a kind request—rather it was an order.

Narrowing his eyelids, knowing that perhaps he deserved to get his wish granted, Maurizio smiled. "I will call her this evening, and ask her if she could help your son."

"That's fantastic! I appreciate your help. So how did your holiday go?"

"Sir, I would love to entertain myself in a casual chat, but this wasn't the reason why I came to your office." Maurizio looked at his wristwatch. "Moreover, I have a meeting with my team soon, and I needed to have some information about the arrest warrant you have forwarded to the Magistrate. Do we have any news coming from them?"

With an almost imperceptible pout, Angelini turned to the computer and scrutinized the content of his mailbox. With a nervous movement, he went through the pile of documents he received by post, wondering whether there was something about it, but it got submerged by other equally important notifications.

It took several minutes for him to scan through the bulk of the content, but then, with a sigh he addressed Maurizio. "No, nothing yet arrived, but they still have time, say another month or so to evaluate and either accept or reject our request. I believe it wasn't the only request they need to evade."

"Yes, of course," he said, standing from his chair ready to leave the room. "Well, if any answer comes from them, let me know. I'm eagerly waiting for it. "

"Of course, Scala. I'll let you know as there is any news on the case. I would have loved to tell you more about my son, just to give you the right impression for your grandmother, but if you're busy, your job is far more important. Perhaps we might have a lunch break together," he proposed.

Feeling his stomach churning at that thought, he smiled weakly. "Let's see if I can take a break."

He exited the room and hurried to arrive at his office and put as much distance as possible between him and chief Commissioner Angelini.

His fast pace was interrupted when from the end of the corridor he spotted something he wasn't expecting. Officer Giuliani was walking in his direction, guiding a man he thought he knew.

The man kept his gaze lowered and walked like a person who was sentenced to death. With his arms limp along his body, his steps heavy on the ground. It took a bit to realize who the man was, and when he was close enough, he could finally recognize Aldo, the captain of the Sea Rider.

Far from the sea, he looked deadly pale—ghostly perhaps. "Detective Scala, Mr. Carrisi asked to see you, and I believe it must be important..." She justified the fact of bringing him directly to his office.

"I bet it is," he replied severely. His gaze turned to Aldo, "Mr. Carrisi, although I wasn't expecting you, I was hoping you would have reached out to me. Please follow me as we will talk in privacy in my office."

Aldo didn't say a word. It was like he didn't understand where he was or how he arrived at the Police Department and the reason why he was there.

Maurizio guided him inside the room. Generally, he would have brought him to the room for the interrogations, where there would have been cameras and recording systems. Nevertheless, he needed to understand the reason for his visit, before moving to what he considered 'the next step.'

Giving a fast glance around before closing the door he made sure not to have the attention of the other officers. "Please have a seat," he commenced as he also closed the curtain on the windows on the corridor.

Aldo went to sit down on a chair at the table in the middle of the room; the one used for short meetings with the members of his team. Maurizio lingered, observing him, to make a fast evaluation of the person in front of him. He wasn't the same person; the conflict tearing his soul apart, transpired evidently from the red eyes. Those were the eyes of a man who couldn't sleep anymore, the ones who had experienced something the soul wasn't ready to cope with.

Keeping his gaze steady on Aldo, Maurizio, slowly sat down in front of him. "Mr. Carrisi, what's the reason for your visit? I once gave you my telephone number and I expected you would have called me, before reaching the Police Department."

Twisting his entwined fingers on the table, Aldo drew a long, broken breath, in the attempt to hold back his tears.

"Aren't you going to record this conversation?" he asked in a whisper.

"Are you going to confess something you've done? Do you want to have an attorney present?" Maurizio asked while keeping his eyes on him.

"Yes, I need to confess something, and I don't need an attorney. I trust I am in the right place to turn myself in."

Nodding, Maurizio stood from the chair and looked toward the door. "Then we need to move to another room. Please, follow me."

Silently, with slow movements, Aldo followed Maurizio out of the room, walking the aisles without caring about the curious glances he'd received.

Together they reached the room for the interrogatories, and as Maurizio prepared for the recording, Aldo went to take a seat at the only table in the middle of the room.

As everything was ready, Maurizio turned his eyes back at Aldo, "What do you need to tell me?"

Aldo kept his gaze lowered on his hands on the table. "I killed a man; I killed a man I've never met before, and who hadn't done anything wrong to me. I killed him to save my life, thinking it was worth living. I've been carrying the guilt of murder." His eyes met Maurizio's, toughening his expression. "I was wrong, and my life wasn't worth his death, and I keep seeing his eyes everywhere I go."

Maurizio knew whom he was talking about, but for the sake of the recording and for proof he had to collect, he had to get the full name.

"Who is the man you killed? Do you know his name?"

Nodding, Aldo turned away from Maurizio. "Igor Leonov, Irina's father. I killed Igor Leonov, and God knows I regret it every second of my life."

"Can you give me more details about what happened? How did you get to know him? On which occasion you killed him, and why you said your life was threatened?" He was sure he knew all the answers to those questions and understood— he reached the conclusion of the case. Nevertheless, he had to make sure he wasn't forced into a false confession to protect the real murderer.

"I've known Irina for a couple of years. Fishing is not a profession to get rich with, but it's something I inherited from my father and my grandfather. Sometimes I round my gain by smuggling people through the border between France, Spain or wherever else. There's a man, Alec Beaufort, he's the contact person to transport people in and out of the Italian territorial waters. I always wondered why Irina who's Italian, too needed my services as she could travel between the EU without any restrictions. Yet, it was clear she necessitated to get in and out without the authorities knowing. I got paid well for the service and so I didn't complain about it.

Concerning the rest of the crew, they simply didn't have any say in this. This is my boat— my business, and they are paid to come with me and fish." His voice started to get steadier, as the weight from his soul got lighter and lighter.

"You are aware those charges will..."

"I know, and I don't care. If I need to go to jail, even for the rest of my life, so be it. All I need is to get rid of the weight I'm carrying on my shoulders, and if I have to carry Irina with me, so much for the better," Aldo confessed. "I don't know whether you've met her, but she's the kind of woman a man can't refuse. She has a way to obtain what she wants, either with her beauty or with the threat she can pose to the life of anyone. She doesn't stop for anything, and whatever goal she has in mind, she will be able to reach it, or to make sure someone will do it for her, like in this case."

There was a short pause of silence, but Maurizio waited for Aldo to finish his story. It would have taken time, but he wasn't in a hurry— not that day.

"She knew I was attracted to her since the first day I saw her, and she used it at her advantage. Months ago, she came to me telling she needed a ride back to France. I told her the date when it would have been possible to arrange a way back and secured the price. In that period the coast guard increased the surveillance on the sea, so I had to raise the previously agreed fee. She didn't like the new arrangement, and she said for that price I had to take care of another problem. Her father was coming to travel with her, but his journey had to end in the middle of the sea."

He wiped his face, trying to regain the strength that was abandoning him one more time. "I had no idea how in the world I would have done it. One thing for sure, was that I had to be alone, as I couldn't allow any of my crew to risk their freedom. For the night, I dismissed them all, by pretending to take care of a problem with the engine. Irina and her father arrived in the late evening and we left, knowing that at the established place, Alec would have reached us to get Irina on his boat to the territorial waters of France."

Maurizio wasn't convinced. *A man can certainly kill another one without the need of any help, but when there's also a boat to navigate, a corpse to dispose of, and a place to clean, one man is not enough.* "How did you kill him?"

"I used a harpoon, the same one I use for big fishes, like tunas. I have no idea how I could do something like that, but I did. I think I was desperate, in a trap I put myself into and from which there wasn't an easy way out. When Irina stated that it would have been a pity to have two deaths instead of one, I realized that the man was already dead, one way or another. The only choice I had left was whether to stay alive or join him in his destiny. Fearing she had also taken agreements with Alec, I had no other choice, but to gather all my strength and kill the man." He buried his face within his hands and held his breath to swallow the bitterness and guilt.

"So, you navigated to a specific point..." Maurizio went on, his eyelids semi-closed, forming a small fissure from which he could spy every single movement.

"I stopped the engine and dropped the anchor. Leaving the deck, I grabbed the harpoon and rushed below deck, where Irina and Igor were waiting. Igor was seated with his back to me. I grabbed the chance and attacked him," his voice hesitating.

"A dead man is heavier than a living one. How did you dispose of the corpse— did Irina help you? She doesn't seem to be a strong woman," Maurizio opined.

"I wrapped some weights in a nylon cloth I carried with me for the occasion. I had the time to plan everything out. That's a job one person can take care of. She helped me to get him on my shoulders, I carried him on the upper deck. I can show you the place where he'd been dropped."

Maurizio didn't believe a single word. *Or better, I do believe he killed the man, but he's obviously trying to cover for the other members of the crew. Their silent behavior didn't fit with the one of people who had nothing to do with the murder.*

"Mr. Carrisi, I need to warn you that the truth will come out. I don't know who or how many people you're trying to cover, but certainly you couldn't take care of everything alone in a single night." Maurizio locked his gaze on him. "Nevertheless, we will certainly want to have the exact location where you dropped the corpse. First of all, because he still has a family who might want to give him a proper burial. Secondly, because the forensic team will have to work on him, and trust me, they *will* find out if there was someone else there to help you."

Aldo remained in silence averting his gaze from Maurizio, who was reconsidering the case was far from being concluded. There were still too many players to bring in and perhaps a whole organization to dismantle.

The murder of Claudio Calvani revealed to be only the tip of an iceberg, and to bring everything to light it might have taken more than one Commissario Scala.

That thought almost caused a grin to appear on his face. *One Commissario Scala is more than enough, when it's me.* His expression turned to a serious one.

"Mr. Carrisi, you're under arrest for the murder of Igor Leonov..." he commenced, cuffing Aldo's wrists and guiding him out of the interrogation room.

CHAPTER 24

It took another two weeks to receive the answer of the Magistrate, and luckily, the Hungarian Magistrate had to agree with the request from Italy and have Irina arrested and surrendered to the Italian Police to be interrogated, no more as a witness but as a suspect.

Maurizio was relieved about the chance of finally going deeper, and at least, bringing the end to the case of the murder of Claudio Calvani. The dismantlement of the whole organization of smuggling human beings and illegal goods across the border required the intervention of others law enforcement's departments, *after all that's why we have a border police and finance Police too.*

He was immersed in bureaucratic matters to be evaded for the arrival of Irina to the Precinct, when Senior officer Milani knocked at his door. "Sir, may I disturb you for a moment?"

"I would be relieved if someone could save me from all of this," he replied, stretching his back.

With a smile Senior officer Milani walked to his desk and sat down. "I have the transcription of the recording of the latest call between Luciano Calvani and Irina Leonova," she started to explain placing a dossier on the desk. "It was a bit strange; she didn't connect with her mother almost at all, lately as if she considered it safer to call Luciano."

"What about the topic?" he wondered.

"The tones remained a bit colder than you can expect between a couple who hasn't murdered a couple of people..." her voice hesitated, and she didn't have any intention to give personal impressions about the situation.

"But you think he's also involved and the reason why she didn't call her mother was to avoid the only person who could recognize her state of mind by simply the tone of her voice..." Maurizio concluded. "That's an interesting point and deserves to be analyzed in more detail. You should never be afraid to make your own conclusion; this is how we solve the cases, by placing our suspects at the crime scene and see if they fit," he added, acknowledging the hesitating tone in her voice as she suggested the involvement of Luciano.

"However," he continued leaning on the chair, "we don't have any leads against Mr. Calvani. Having arguments with a father is something that rarely leads to murder. I would like, first of all, to understand what Ms. Leonova will say to justify her actions or whether she'll admit having committed any of the crimes she's accused of."

"When can we expect to have her here?" Senior officer Milani was intrigued by Irina's personality; she had to admit that before having met her, her charisma and ability to get whatever she had in mind was an admirable capability.

"By the end of the week," Maurizio said, turning his head to focus on the computer screen. "This is at least what they promised. Would you like to assist with the interrogation? As you and Officer Silvani are the youngest recruits, this can be a great chance to learn what isn't taught at the Police Academy nor at the University. Recently we had other interrogations, but this is by far a bigger case, from which you might profit."

Her eyes opened up wide, and sparkled with excitement, as a jolt shook her, she stood from her chair. "I would love to! I'm sure Carlo will be excited as I am to know we might be allowed to assist. I'm going to tell him the news."

Leaving the dossier on Maurizio's desk, she left the office, hurrying off in the direction of the room she shared with Officer Silvani.

***

The following Monday, everything was ready for the interrogation, and Irina was escorted to the Police Department. After having been explained her rights, including the one of not answering any questions, Maurizio nodded at both the attorney and the officer who would have verbalized the whole interrogation.

"Ms. Leonova, I believe you have been informed of the reason why you are here today." Maurizio commenced.

With a hermetic expression from which no sort of emotion could have transpired, she replied. "Yes, you think I am the person who has murdered Mr. Calvani, my mother's boyfriend and Igor Leonov, my father." Her eyes steady on Maurizio.

"You're not?" Maurizio challenged, knowing this would have become another long session.

"I'm not."

"Would you then explain why you entered the Italian territory eluding the border control? We could count at least a few occasions when you have used the service of human traffickers to cross the border between France and Italy." Maurizio took a short pause of silence to let the information sink in. "You are an Italian citizen, and there aren't any legal charges against you. Yet, you chose an illegal way to enter the country."

"I didn't want anyone to know that I came here. I knew my father had intended to kill Mr. Calvani, and I stayed at his place, hoping I could make him reason... Obviously, I wasn't able, and he killed him anyway." Her voice was steady, emotionless— cold, likewise her expression as she glanced at Maurizio.

"What happened the night of the murder?"

"I have no idea. What I do know is that we spent the evening together and then I went to sleep. When I saw the news about the murder of Mr. Calvani, I understood it was too late, and I failed in my intent." she replied, averting her eyes from him.

"Why didn't you talk to the police about it?" Maurizio knew he could have smashed her immediately, but he wanted to play a bit before bringing in his secret weapon. He still wished she would have told the truth about her father and the final resting place he was destined to have.

"He was still my father, and I was afraid of him too. I decided to leave the country and stay away from him for the rest of my life," she replied.

"Did you plan to kill your father to revenge for what he did to your mother's boyfriend?" Maurizio pursued, ready to call Aldo and the crew to enter the room. With the help of the captain, they could retrieve Igor's body, which had been brought to the forensic laboratory and examined, before being stored in one of the morgue's freezers.

"I haven't killed anyone," she simply said.

"What is your relationship with Luciano Calvani?" Maurizio wanted to take all the time and gather all the information about the circumstances in the verbal.

"Luciano is my boyfriend," she replied curtly, clearly aware that the least she would have said the better would have been for everyone.

"In what circumstances did you meet each other?"

At his question she knew a simple answer yes or no, wouldn't have been enough. *I need to find a way out,* she thought.

She remained silent for a moment to think about what she could answer, then, when her eyes met Maurizio's, she grinned. "I prefer not to answer this question."

"Why?" Maurizio wondered, almost amused. *It doesn't make any sense— why not? I know the answer, and unless it was a lie, she thinks she doesn't remember correctly, that might give me an advantage.*

"None of your business, detective," her voice resonated in a firm state. Yet, Maurizio felt a cold shiver crawling his spine, raising the hair on his neck.

"You were living with your father for a period, including the night of the murder. You knew he was going to kill Mr. Calvani. You could have called the police or warned your boyfriend. I believe he was devastated by the death of his father."

Shaking her head, she furrowed the brows creasing her forehead. "Do you believe I haven't thought about it? I was sure he wouldn't come to the point of killing the man. I was sure that until I would have stayed with him, he might have not done something stupid that could have brought him to jail, ruining his life, together with the life of many others— myself included."

"So, what happened the night of the murder?" Maurizio wasn't impressed. Of course, she could have at least warned Mr. Calvani. He would have been wise to hire a bodyguard. *Unless it was her who killed the man, framed her father, and organized his murder, forcing Aldo and his crew to take part in the murder and concealing the corpse.*

"I went to sleep, as usual, at ten in the evening. I wasn't supposed to meet with Luciano, as the following day he needed to go to the University so we would have met in the afternoon. The morning after my father was in his regular mood. He behaved like nothing had ever happened, so I couldn't imagine he killed Mr. Calvani," she replied, glancing around at her attorney, who gave a curt nod.

"Hadn't you heard anything? Like, for example, the door opening or closing. Something that woke you up."

"No."

The noise of someone knocking at the door startled the people present in the room. Maurizio glanced around, knowing it was the time to get

Aldo and his crew in the room, to finally shed some light on the case.

"Yes, come in," Maurizio answered.

An officer peeked from the door, and turning his face at his back, he let the guests come in one after the other. The five members of the Sea Rider entered the room, and silence fell like a heavy drape. Regardless of the fact that this meant the end of all the lies, Irina didn't seem to be impressed by their presence.

With a loud click, the door closed behind the last member who entered the room, and none of them said a word. Everyone was holding their breath, waiting for something to happen.

"Ms. Leonova, do you know any of the people who have entered the room?" Maurizio asked with a quiet tone of voice, trying to hide the turmoil and the racing heartbeat in his chest.

Irina didn't reply, meaning that this was a question he had to ask his counterpart. Standing up from his chair, Maurizio approached the five men. "Do any of you, gentlemen, know who this young lady is?"

They all nodded, "Yes, we know her. She is Irina Leonova. She used my boat on several occasions to enter and exit the Italian territory without passing through the border control." Aldo's voice resounded through the walls, loud and clear.

"Can you tell us your name?" Maurizio asked, glancing at Aldo.

"My name is Aldo Carrisi, and I'm the owner and captain of the *Sea Rider.*" His voice was broken as he tried not to look in Irina's direction.

Opening the folder, where all the documentation about the case was, Scala took out a picture of Igor. He showed it around to all the people in the room, and finally to Aldo. "Do you know this man? Have you ever seen him?"

Aldo exhaled, "He is Igor Leonov. He was introduced to us as Ms. Leonova's father. He is the man she asked us to murder. She made it clear to me that in case I refused to help, she would have killed us both, so it wasn't the time for any brave choice to be made— it was him or both of us. I cowardly chose him, and I regret that decision every second of my life."

Glancing at the same officer who brought the five men in, Maurizio said, "You can bring them back, I guess we have heard enough."

As the crew left the room, Maurizio returned to sit at the table in front of Irina. Her head lowered, regretting not having killed them all.

"Ms. Leonova, do you have anything to say?" Maurizio spelled out his words slowly, hoping she would have finally started to tell the truth.

There was a long pause of silence. Maurizio knew she was trying to fabricate another lie, he had experience with murderers; he knew they always had a good reason to justify their actions. The longer the interval between his questions and her answers was, the more he felt she was confirming his suspects, and she was the one who organized the murder of the two men. *I can understand the reason why you killed your father; he would have been an uncomfortable obstacle to your theory by which he was the assassin. But why in this world would you want to kill Mr. Calvani, a man you hardly knew?*

She shot him a serious glare. "My father was a horrible person; he ruined the life of my mother with his obsessive jealousy. He stalked her and threatened her, even after they divorced," she commenced. "I could tolerate that, but how could I stand the fact that he killed the father of my boyfriend and the man with whom my mother finally found happiness?"

No, you don't impress me, Maurizio thought. "Murdering a man, regardless of what he did is not allowed by the law. For this reason, you're under arrest with the charges of first-degree murder, corpse concealment and illegal immigration. This is validation for the murder of Igor Leonov and Claudio Calvani."

A jolt shook her body. "I haven't killed Mr. Calvani!"

For the first time, her voice trembled in the realization that in case she would have been considered guilty, she could have faced lifetime imprisonment. *That wasn't the way it was planned!*

"Then, I suggest you start telling the truth because nobody is saving you from jail. At this point, you can make your situation lighter by cooperating with us." Maurizio started to feel his blood boiling in his veins and tried everything in his power to keep his temper at bay.

He got as close as he could to her face, "This is going to bring you in jail for at least fifty years, or you can have a lighter sentence based on your cooperation, and if it's true and you haven't killed Mr. Calvani, maybe you might get only fifteen years."

The scent of his aftershave reached her nostrils. She opened her mouth as if she were going to speak, but closed it immediately after, biting her lower lip to avoid saying something she would have regretted.

I need to talk with Luciano, she thought.

He was the only one who could have helped her. First, providing her the best attorney money could buy, and then with a solution to get out of that situation.

Narrowing her eyes, she glared at Maurizio, but said nothing.

"Take her away!" Maurizio ordered, opening the door of the room.

With long strides he reached his room and collapsed on the chair behind his desk. "She killed them both; eventually the reason why she framed and killed her father was indeed the resentment for the pain he caused to her mother. I bet, it hadn't been easy to live away from her and being raised by her aunt, yet what the heck did it have to do with Calvani?"

He grabbed his head between his hands and closed his eyes. He remained in the same position for as long as his arms could give out, then falling limp on his lap.

Opening his eyes, he stared at the ceiling, ruminating about the case.

"What if her mother told her about some arguments she had with Mr. Calvani? Could it be so, and she felt the need to protect her even from him? Was that the reason why she contacted his son and pretended to be in love with him?"

He listened to his voice as if it came from somebody else, and like magic, every piece of the puzzle started to take a place in that crazy plan.

"The mantis generally kills the lover. In this case it's the lovers who eventually hurt the mother," he mumbled through tightened teeth. "Could it be that Luciano Calvani might have been in danger? Was there a trap also set for him?"

Without thinking twice, he stood from his chair and paced out of the room, heading to his parking place. He had to talk with Madlen one more time. First, because he had to inform her about the death of her ex-husband if she hadn't been informed. Secondly, he needed to tell her about the imprisonment of her daughter.

CHAPTER 25

It was around four o'clock in the afternoon. Madlen was returning home from shopping, when she noticed the police car outside her building. Although there wasn't any reason, she could figure out for them to be there, she was sure it was connected to the murder of Claudio. She hurried her steps to the entrance, literally stumbling into Maurizio.

"Detective!" she exclaimed uncertainly.

"I'm terribly sorry, Ms. Fazekas, I didn't want to alarm you. I needed to see you and have a chat; can we go up to your apartment?"

"Of course. Is there any news about the murder?" She opened the door of the building, heading to the elevators.

"Yes, and I'm afraid I have some bad news to tell you unless the media has found a way to release the latest piece."

"I haven't heard anything at this point, and I hope no charges have been raised against me," a nervous giggle escaped her mouth. A couple of months before, Scala reassured her she wasn't considered a suspect anymore, but having him again right at her door, made her as jumpy as a cat on a hot tin roof.

"No, nothing against you. That was the reason why we released the funds from the insurance company," he clarified as they reached the apartment.

She allowed him to come inside and carefully closed the door behind her.

Reaching the living room, Maurizio recognized the familiar place where he'd stepped inside a few times in the past. He turned around to glance at her and drew in a deep breath.

The reason for his visit, although it wasn't to arrest her, wasn't pleasant either, and he had to find the right words to tell her.

"It's better if you'll take a seat. I'm afraid you will need it," Maurizio suggested.

"Detective, now you're scaring me!" her brows furrowed as she sat down on the couch.

"We've arrested your daughter, Irina, for the murder of Claudio Calvani and Igor Leonov. Although she denied the first murder, she had to confess to the second one, as other witnesses provided unquestionable proof of her involvement. I'm afraid that considering all the accusations from the double homicide for futile reasons, the concealment of a corpse, illegal immigration, she might face long time imprisonment." He sat down, speaking with a calm tone of voice, feeling the pain she must be feeling, understanding her daughter was an assassin.

Madlen remained silent for a moment; tears choked her breath, and she felt as if she was going to faint. "That... No!" Covering her face with her hands, both to avoid looking at Maurizio's face for the shame and to hide the pain her expression would have shown. Her heart shattered. Her daughter, the one she considered the most precious gift of life ever allowed her, killed the man who gave her back hope for her future. Even though she was bitter with Igor for the pain he'd inflicted in her life, she would have never wished him dead. The only thing she wanted was to be left alone, and with Claudio around, Igor, too, reached an agreement with his own jealousy.

It had been months since the last time he acted like a jealous boyfriend, and she was sure he started to go on with his life. The death of Claudio caused an endless sense of pain in her heart, but more painful was to know that the one who did this to her was her own daughter.

Maurizio remained silent, sharing her pain. He thought about his own daughter, Giovanna, and wondered whether there could ever have been the chance that she would have ruined her life with a similar crime.

Certainly, Madlen couldn't expect something like that could have happened to her. She would have thought Igor was the one who killed her boyfriend, and he might have had a real reason to do so, but what could have been Irina's reason for it? Why her father and Claudio? Maurizio thought as a lump formed in his throat.

Slowly he raised a hand to Madlen's shoulder. "I'm truly sorry. I wish it wasn't me who had to deliver such terrible news."

She went on sobbing for a few minutes before she could find the strength to raise her head back to Maurizio. "I tried my best; I sent her away from Italy because I didn't want her to be bullied at school for being the daughter of a stripper. I wanted her to grow up in a normal family environment, and my sister was able to offer that." She searched her purse for a tissue to dry her tears. "I did everything I could, detective. Igor was a terrible husband, but he also had been present in her life, like a father should. Irina didn't have any reason to kill him nor Claudio."

"The only person who can answer those questions is Irina herself," Maurizio whined. "I also have a daughter, and I would be devastated if something like that would happen in my family. I know nobody is safe from errors and troubles. I want you to know I feel your pain, and I'm sorry."

A weak smile appeared on Madlen's face. "Thank you, detective. I appreciate your sympathy, and the fact that you haven't judged me for my life choices. I don't know whether it's also my fault; I wanted to give her what I thought was best."

Shaking his head, Maurizio stood from the couch. "It's not your fault; as parents we can simply do our best, hoping it's going to be enough. We can't see the future, unfortunately, so we can't be sure we're preparing our children for a life in a world that's constantly changing. We've learned to live it at our time, and what was twenty years ago, is no more the same nowadays, nor will it be in another twenty years. I hope you will take the chance and talk to her and try to understand her reason and perhaps find a way to forgive her and be at her side."

"I will talk to her, but though I can forgive her, I will never forget, because she took away from me the only chance to be happy. She hurt me, when all I offered her was love." Averting her gaze from Maurizio, she swallowed the tears that returned one more time as she wiped the wet pools from her eyes. "I need to be alone..."

Without saying another word, Maurizio turned and walked out of the apartment. He was heartbroken; that was one of the things he hated about his job.

Wiping the tears from his eyes, he glanced at the sky, with a nod, he strolled back to his car, ready to return to the Department and prepare all the reports ready for archiving the case.

"The judge will decide whether the case is closed. As for us, we don't have any reason to pursue the investigation further. We have a culprit, we have the proof, and for the motives we will need to wait until the final sentence... maybe," he said, entering his car.

***

The trial went on for another three months, and the result, as everyone was expecting, was that the court considered Irina guilty for both murders.

The outcome of the psychiatric examination confirmed that the reason for the murder of her father was connected to a type of obsessive desire to protect her mother and to avoid having her hurt anymore. According to the psychiatrist, her possible reason to murder also Claudio was to avoid her mother another disappointment. He believed she elevated herself to the position of being her mother's guardian, who should have protected her from the abuses of men, which she learned not to trust. Her relationship with Luciano was probably aimed to use him to reach Mr. Calvani and get access to the garage area, obtain information restricted to the inhabitants of the building, like the time of the maintenance of the camera system. In this optic, Luciano was a victim of her clever plan.

Despite the efforts of the attorney to mitigate the sentence, Irina was finally sentenced to thirty-five years. The sentence wasn't mild for the crew of the Sea Rider either, although it was the captain who was condemned more severely with a twenty-five-year sentence.

"So, it seems like we've reached the end of this case," Leonardo glanced at Maurizio, who thoughtfully, in the common room, was immersed in his own thoughts.

Startling at his comment, Maurizio raised his gaze at Leonardo, almost surprised to find him close to him. "Uh... well, yes— I guess this is the case..."

"You don't sound convinced. I think there's no doubt on the reasons for Irina to kill Mr. Calvani and her father. She made a few rookie mistakes, but I have to admit the two murders were carefully planned out." He walked to the vending machine.

"That's exactly what makes me suspicious, you know?" Maurizio followed Leonardo with the tail of his eyes, as if to see something through the darkness of the beverage. "This is something that requires a couple of masterminds, not just one."

"And as she admitted, her father helped her in the planning and execution of the first murder..."

Raising a hand to interrupt what Leonardo was saying, Maurizio moved a couple of steps toward him. "Igor Leonov was a consumed criminal. If he were the one to help his daughter kill Mr. Calvani, there wouldn't have been flaws, but this wasn't the case."

"You are forgetting Mr. Calvani's murder was carried out professionally; the problem arose when she decided to get rid of an uncomfortable witness. Leaving other witnesses alive... I don't know. Maybe I should let this be, as the case is closed, at least considering the evidence we've gathered and the final sentencing of the judge."

"We don't have any clues to lead us to other responsible accomplices. You can't chase ghosts, and there are other cases that need your attention, *Commissario.*" Leonardo chuckled.

"You're right, and as a celebration for the conclusion of this case, since it's almost time for lunch, I'll drive to my favorite kiosk and get me the best Porchetta sandwich they can prepare. I know a place that won't fail my trust." A wide smile brightened Maurizio's face. He gulped the rest of his coffee, and with a wave of his hand, he left the room.

Going to get the first Porchetta sandwich after a long investigation was almost a ritual, and he preferred not to have any company. He glanced at his belly, which had already begun to growl.

As it always happened, he noticed the weight he'd lost during the course of the investigation. He wasn't able to keep a steady diet, whenever he could indulge in the sin of gluttony, he would have, knowing for sure that the next complex case would have brought his weight under the suggested values for a man of his age and body structure.

***

As everything returned to the normal routine and the cases seemed to get of easier solution than the murder of Mr. Calvani, the year reached its end, and with it, everybody at the police department hoped that criminality would for once take a break and let all enjoy the incoming holiday season.

Of course, that was only an illusion, and everyone knew crime doesn't take any breaks. In Maurizio's memory there hadn't been a holiday period, whether Easter, Summer, Christmas, or anything else, when crimes halted for a moment. Those were perhaps the times when they took advantage of the loosened surveillance to strike.

It was a chilly day in early December, and Maurizio was trying to get the grip with the office work that had been left aside before the end of the year. The lights were enough to illuminate the rooms and the corridors, but the thick stormy cover of clouds made the day seem darker.

Looking up from his computer, he grimaced as his eyes met the dark sky outside the window. He stretched his body, releasing a loud yawn, and walked to the window to have a better idea about the weather waiting for him outside.

"It seems like the sky wants to fall, and this means only one thing— the traffic on the

358

Tiburtine will be completely insane this evening," he whined, knowing there wasn't any other option.

He recalled his promise to take care of finding a new apartment to move to, and so far, he was either too busy with the case, or there weren't enough offers for their budget. "There must be a way to get rid of that cursed road," he growled as his mood darkened.

The knocking on his door returned him to reality, and he turned to see who was the visitor, from the window wall.

Noticing Senior officer Milani, he smiled, "Come in."

"I was wondering whether you heard about the news," she commenced introducing the reason for her visit.

"Depends on the news."

"The news from the prison. Irina Leonova killed herself," her voice got lower as she spoke as if her name was no more supposed to be mentioned. "She left a message stating that she wasn't going to stay in jail for most of her life, and that was the only way she could think about being free again."

Maurizio lowered his gaze and furrowed his brows; he couldn't say he wasn't expecting something similar.

Suicide was something fairly common between the inmates, particularly when talking about those who were condemned to a long sentence or were unfairly accused. She admitted the murder of her father and the use of illegal channels to reach Italy. Yet, she pleaded not guilty when they talked about the murder of Claudio Calvani.

Whether it was indeed her father the one who killed him or someone else, it was clear her involvement in that murder too. Therefore, talking about being judged unfairly couldn't apply in her case.

"That's very sad, although I can say I don't understand her act. Many inmates find a new way of life in prison, and use the time to rebuild something, even if it's destined to remain within the walls of the penitentiary; they most often prefer to use their time in a more constructive way, either by studying and getting a degree or thinking about their life and give it a new purpose..." He raised his right hand back on his neck and massaged it.

"Indeed," Senior officer Milani replied sadly. "Although she was a murderer, she could have still given a purpose to her life. Of course, by the time she would have gotten out of prison, she would have been a middle-aged woman... Perhaps she feared she'd lost everything, including the mother she tried to protect. We will never know her reason. I'm wondering whether she got heartbroken by the fact that Luciano didn't remain by her side— who knows?"

"Did she mentioned the fact that he left her?" Maurizio wondered as that could have been the most feasible reason for Irina to decide to end her fight.

"No, this was my personal guess," she replied. "I didn't know her, and I would never condone what she'd done. Murder is something that belongs exclusively to extreme cases of self-defense, not a way to do justice on your own."

"This is the reason why we are here," Maurizio pointed out thoughtfully, wondering whether there were more reasons behind her suicide.

"Do you believe she had other reasons to commit suicide?" asked Senior officer Milani.

"I'm simply guessing too. However, I didn't have the impression she was the kind of person who would have given up without a fight. I thought she would have worked on the way to get a reduced sentence. Working on the defense, she might have gotten out earlier, obtaining partial freedom. There would have been so many chances for her to have the sentence converted into a milder one... I don't understand."

Senior officer Milani inhaled deeply as an uncomfortable feeling grabbed her soul. "Well, that was all I came here for, I thought you wanted to know..."

"Yes, thank you. I guess it's something we all need to think about and digest it. Suicide is the last thing you want to happen in prison. This means the case will forever be closed. She was probably the only one to know the truth about the murder of Claudio Calvani. Whether she kept secrecy to protect someone or to try for a milder sentence, the truth followed her to the grave, and if it's so and one of the murderers is still alive and free, we need to hope this was the last crime." Maurizio shook his head, pursing his lips.

"All the clues lead to her and her father. I think she acted with his help, who hosted her in his house. It isn't credible that one of them could act without the other knowing. Probably her whole plan was to get rid of Mr. Calvani as a possible threat to her mother's happiness. Perhaps she knew about the life insurance and might have talked to her daughter, never believing she would have actually killed him."

A smile relieved Maurizio's face. "Well, that's a reasonable conclusion, and that's the same one the judges reached after having examined the proof and listening to the witnesses. So, case closed?"

"Case closed, Detective Scala," she replied as she walked toward the exit.

"Yes," he said with a long exhale. "Case closed."

EPILOGUE

It was the day before Christmas Eve. Maurizio was able to leave work earlier and on his way home, his attention was averted to a specific car parked outside the cemetery. There weren't many people who owned a black Lamborghini in Rome, and even without checking the plate number, he was sure the owner was none other than Luciano Calvani.

Turning the car in the direction of the cemetery, he parked beside Luciano's car, admiring it for a moment, wondering how it would have been to have no financial problems and be able to afford such luxury.

With a slight shake of his head, he walked inside, knowing perfectly well where to find Luciano—that being at the grave of his father.

Silently, Maurizio strolled through the alleys between the graves until he spotted the figure of Luciano, staring at his father's tombstone.

Without saying a word, he stopped a few steps away, waiting for him to be ready to leave shortly after offering his condolences once again and perhaps wishing him a serene Christmas period.

"Good afternoon, Detective Scala," he greeted without averting his glance from the image on the grave of his father.

"Good afternoon, Mr. Calvani. I was passing by, and I couldn't avoid noticing your car in the parking lot, so I thought I could come to give you my best wishes for this period. I understand it must be hard..." Maurizio almost felt his intrusion inappropriate, but that might have been the only chance he had to greet him.

"I thought it would have been easier. I was sure I wouldn't have missed him as much as I am right now; after all, he never cared about my mother or me." His voice flickered. "We were nothing more than commodities, something vital for his social status. As a successful businessman, it was necessary for him to have a family. Although, my mother had an influence in the growing of the business, and received her recognition, I was never something he wanted."

Maurizio remained silent at that confession. *Money won't grant happiness,* he thought. He had the impression of having arrived at the right time, and Luciano had to take out all his bitterness.

"You see," Luciano turned his teary eyes at Maurizio, "he was the person I admired the most, everything I did was to gain his approval, to feel worthy of his name and attention. Yet, every time

364

it was a flame that consumed itself too fast. There was always something better to take care of. One day it could be his job, then it could be his friends, or again he might have been too tired. I was never a priority.

"But I couldn't hate him. I wish I could... Then one day, my mother found out about the girl he was cheating on her with. There hadn't been a big drama, she collected her things, called her attorney, and left. She had suggested that I go and live with her, if I wanted, but I still wanted to grab that chance of living with him and try gathering his attention."

As tears started to stream from his eyes, Luciano required some time to gather some strength and to get a grip on his emotions.

"I hoped we could still have more time together if we were living together. I desperately needed him, and he never seemed to understand that. He thought it was enough to suffice his lack of love with money." He slowly shook his head, as he lowered his glance down to his feet. "All his free time was dedicated to his new girlfriend. One day, almost by chance I met Irina at the University. I had no idea who she was, but we both felt attracted to each other, perhaps because we both were missing a family. We found in each other company the missing part of our lives, which gave a sense to them both. Her father was an abusive husband who couldn't do anything better than stalk and threaten her mother. My father didn't consider me... We were alike... I miss her, too."

"I'm sorry, it must have been a double shock for you to understand she preferred to die, rather than to wait for her release, which would have happened eventually," Maurizio replied, having the clear impression there was something hidden in his story. He didn't dare to spell it out, but he was sure Luciano was going to answer his final doubts.

Searching his pockets, Luciano slipped a handkerchief and wiped the tears from his eyes. "Yes, I can guess what you thought, and you're completely correct; we planned a way to get rid of those people who would have kept hurting us for the rest of our lives—; our fathers. We weren't supposed to suffer for their sins, and if you're wondering why I haven't thought about killing Irina's mother is because it wasn't her fault the reason why my father ignored me. If it wasn't her, it would have been someone else, or something else. Irina could provide the weapon for the murder and the easiest scapegoat; then we would have been free from them, and we could have lived our lives together in peace. Her mistake was that of trusting other people to eliminate her father."

"So, it was you who killed your father?" Maurizio couldn't say he was surprised. There had always been that little voice in the back of his head telling him that Irina was just one of the players in the murder. What surprised him the most was that there weren't any clues leading to Luciano's involvement— no proofs, no DNA traces, no fingerprints, nothing. Claudio Calvani's murder was almost to be considered the perfect crime, and what churned his stomach was that without a single proof or clue, as Luciano also had an alibi on his side, he couldn't arrest him. With a grimace, he narrowed his eyes.

"Don't take it so badly, detective. You did a great job, and I think I owed you this information, even if it's destined to remain only between us. You can't arrest me without any solid proof. Moreover, I can assure you there won't be any other murders coming from these hands," he raised his palms upward. "It still hurts, and I won't stop regretting it for a single second in my life."

It was true, he had no grounds to arrest him; it would be his word against that of Luciano, and it wasn't enough to reopen a case accusing a person who wasn't possible to locate at the crime scene. His expression toughened, trying to keep the beast that wanted to kill that young criminal right in front of the grave of the father he'd murdered.

Luciano glanced at his wristwatch, "I need to hurry, I'm leaving the country. I can't risk you will find any sort of clues to frame me. Besides, I need a change in the air and think about the way I'll rebuild my life." He turned his shoulder at

Maurizio, "See you in 25 years, detective, and perhaps I will also tell you how I did it."

Maurizio watched him walk away. "See you when the crime will fall into prescription... some son of a bitch!"

He turned to look at the picture of Claudio on the headstone. "You weren't a perfect father, but who is? The only hope is that he will find his karma, and maybe justice can still reach him even at the end of the world... who knows? I also have a daughter, and I know your struggles with raising a child, taking care of business, and trying to enjoy your time in this life. I will try to learn a lesson out of this story, so at least I won't risk being killed by a neglected daughter."

Shivering at a gust of wind that suddenly blew in, Maurizio plunged his hands in his pockets and walked to his car. That was the beginning of his holiday and the end of the year— the year of the Mantis.

THE END...

I hope you enjoyed following the investigation of Commissario Scala. The next appointment with another thrilling mystery is scheduled for **08.30.2021.**

In the next book, a serial killer is threatening the life of people who devoted their lives to charity causes. Yet, according to the messages left, there are dark secrets hidden in the past of those people. But what is the red wire connecting the victims to each other and to the serial killer, who signs his message as 'The Shadows'?

Stay tuned by following me on:
Facebook:
https://www.facebook.com/PJ.Mann.paperpenandinkwell
Twitter: https://twitter.com/PjMann2016
Website: https://pjmannauthor.com

ABOUT THE AUTHOR

Paula J. Mann lives a double life. She is a geologist by day and a novelist by night. She's best known for writing psychological thrillers and dramas, like her debut novel 'A Tale of a Rough Diamond.'

She also writes historical fiction, like Aquila et Noctua, and paranormal suspense like 'Thou Shalt Never Tell.'

Traveling is another passion, and she shares her experiences on her blog together with whatever topic raises her attention:
http://paperpenandinkwell.blogspot.com.

Made in the USA
Middletown, DE
21 May 2022

66040574R00224